The Essay

A Novel

Robin Yocum

Arcade Publishing • New

Dedication for Ronald E. Yocum 1934–2008.
The best man I've ever known

First paperback edition 2016

Arcade Publishing books may be purchased in bulk at special discounts
for sales promotion, corporate gifts, fund-raising, or educational purposes.
Special editions can also be created to specifications. For details, contact the
Special Sales Department, Arcade Publishing, 307 West 36th Street, 11th
Floor, New York, NY 10018 or arcade@skyhorsepublishing.com.

Arcade Publishing® is a registered trademark of Skyhorse Publishing,
Inc.®, a Delaware corporation.

Visit our website at www.arcadepub.com.

10 9 8 7 6 5 4 3 2

Library of Congress Cataloging-in-Publication Data is available on file.

ISBN: 978-1-62872-717-3
Ebook ISBN: 978-1-61145-849-7

Printed in the United States of America

Acknowledgments

A few weeks before my dad died, my mother read the first draft of this novel to him in the hospital. It was the first time in weeks that he wasn't focused on his illness, and I was glad he was able to hear this story. He was a great influence in my life, and I miss him every day. Dad taught me there is no disgrace in failure, and a bloody nose is rarely fatal. And, more important, when you are the recipient of a non-fatal bloody nose, wipe it off and get back in the game. These are pretty simple rules to live by, and they are invaluable if you want to be a writer.

I am extremely fortunate to have Colleen Mohyde in my corner. She is a tremendous agent and a tireless worker on my behalf.

My editor, Lilly Golden, makes the editing process remarkably easy. She is gifted with a keen eye and a light touch, which any writer would appreciate.

I have long relied on the artist skills of Jeff Vanik, the owner of Vanik Design, and I tip my hat for his great work on the cover of this book.

Prologue

Sandor Kardos has spent eighty-one of his ninety-three years on this earth working in a coal mine. His arthritic fingers have gnarled together in a single mass, twisting around one another like a young girl's braids. They have no singular dexterity, and he uses the mass and his thumb to pinch items like lobster claws. "I ain't playin' the piano anymore, that's for sure," he tells me, laughing at his own joke until he falls into a coughing fit that turns his face purple.

He pronounces it "pi-anna," and later concedes he had never played at all. He was simply going for the laugh. The cough is the result of smoking two packs of cigarettes a day for the past eight decades—one million one hundred sixty-eight thousand cigarettes. "It's not a habit; it's a choice," he says. Either way, his voice resonates like the grinding gears of a winch. "The doctor's always on my ass to give 'em up. He says my lungs look like two dead crows. What the hell? If that's the case, sounds like the damage is done. I'm ninety-three. Something's gotta kill me."

Despite his arthritis, Sandor is surprisingly deft with his crustaceous hands. Clutching a fresh pack of smokes in his left hand, he uses the elongated thumbnail of the right and the few snagged teeth remaining in his head to open the pack and work a cigarette between his lips. With the thumb on his left hand, he spins the wheel of a Zippo and lights the smoke. After a deep drag, he presses a palm to his chin, pinches the butt, and pulls it away from his mouth.

By his own admission, Sandor smokes too much, drinks too much, and given the opportunity, he would screw too much. "The problem is, I've outlived all my prospects," he says.

His grandson, Greg, the loud one who has an opinion on every-thing, has just finished loading a dump truck full of coal and overhears his grandfather's comments. "How about the widow Birnbaum?" he offers. "She was trying to jump your old bones for a while."

Greg has a knack for getting under Sandor's aging skin. There's a lot of good-natured ribbing that goes on at the mine, but Sandor thinks his grandson is a wise guy and, worse, lazy, because he drives the truck and refuses to go into the mine where the heavy lifting is done. "She's probably closer to your age than mine," Sandor says. "Why don't you go service her?"

"Not me, pops. I'm a married man."

Sandor grins. The boy has left himself wide open and Sandor counterpunches. "That didn't seem to be a concern when you were traipsing all over Vinton County with that slut Gloria Stephens." This stops Greg in his tracks. The blood drains from his face, and then reappears in brilliant bursts of crimson on his cheeks and neck. His ears look like they will explode. "You didn't know I knew that, huh?"

Sandor shows his teeth in a victory smile as Greg scurries into the cab, but before he can fire up the engine Sandor continues, "If the old man knows, it's not much of a secret, is it? Your wife prob'ly knows, too."

"You wouldn't know it now," Sandor says, "but in the old days, when the coal mines and gas wells and timber mills were booming, McArthur was a jumpin' place. On Saturday nights, the ladies would come up from Portsmouth, if you know what I mean?" He winks. "For two dollars, you could get yourself a belly full of beer and go into the back room with one of the gals—made for a nice night." He squints. "What's a prostitute cost these days?"

"I don't partake," I say, "but I'd wager that it's more than two dollars."

"Yeah, prob'ly so. The price of everything's gone up."

It was a cool Friday in June when we visited the Kardos & Sons Mining Company, a deep shaft operation in Wilkesville Township in the southern part of hardscrabble Vinton County, Ohio.

Sandor Kardos tells me he was not much more than a baby when his parents left the northern Hungarian city of Gyor for southeastern Ohio. His earliest memory is of swaying in a canvas hammock in the steerage compartment of an ocean liner heading to America. As he tells me the story, he claims the swill and fetid human tang of the ship's bowels still permeates his nostrils. He was just twelve when his father Janos took him to the coal mine. He says he can hardly remember a day of his life when he wasn't at the mine. At twenty-two, he bought property and started his own mining company.

The company has ten employees—all Kardos males: Sandor, his two remaining sons, Lester and Pete, five grandsons and two great grandsons. (A ceiling collapse in Kardos Mine No. 3 claimed the life of Sandor's youngest son Benjamin in 1952. "I told that boy a hundred times to shore up the roof with pillars before he ran his bolts," Sandor says. "But, he didn't want to listen. He was a hard-head, that one, and it killed him. A coal mine ain't no place for creativity.")

Coal mining is brutal work, but the Kardos males, save for Greg, don't complain. They know they're fortunate to have the work. It's their heritage, but it is also a dying industry. They aren't rich, but, by Vinton County standards, they're doing quite well. They sell coal to locals, who still use it to heat, and supply Appalachian industries that still have coal-fired furnaces. Unlike many of their contemporaries, they don't drive to Columbus on trash night to scrounge for scrap metal or items to put in the perpetual yard sales along Route 50.

Sandor no longer works inside the mine. His leathery lungs and arthritis have restricted his duties to manning the traction line that hauls the coal cars to the surface of the slope mine. While technology has changed mining operations nearly everywhere else, the Kardos & Sons Mining Company hasn't changed much since he opened his first mine in 1931. The exception is the traction line, which is operated by a gasoline generator that replaced mules for hauling the coal cars out of the mine. "Too damn temperamental," Sandor says of the mules. "And the sonsofabitches will eat you out of house and home."

I like Sandor Kardos. He is the very reason why I'm in the newspaper business. I love capturing snapshots of individuals who have carved a life for themselves from the hardscrabble. And really, who doesn't want to be like Sandor Kardos? He's happy with his life, spry, still excited to get out of bed in the morning, enjoys a nip of whiskey, and at ninety-three years old is still thinking of ways to get laid.

Fritz Avery walks out of the mine at about three, two cameras and a bag of photo equipment draped over his shoulders. He is covered with a thin film of coal dust, and dirty rivulets of sweat streak the sides of his face. He is puffing for air.

As a news photographer, Fritz Avery has few peers. He works hard and consistently gets *the* shot when covering a story. In newsroom parlance, *the* shot is the poignant instant in time when human emotion and drama collide with the real world. It is the instant that a mother collapses in the courtroom after her only son is given the death penalty. The moment a Marine snaps off a salute after handing a veiled widow a folded American flag. Or the jubilant leap of a high school basketball player as a last-second shot hits nothing but net. Fritz has an incredible knack for capturing those scenes.

His considerable photographic talents aside, I can hardly stand to be around him. I like Fritz just fine, but he wears me out.

He talks incessantly, blathering in a high-pitched, squeaky voice that makes listening to him the equivalent of chewing on aluminum foil. He is a notorious gossip and can talk for hours on end. You don't really have conversations with Fritz, you just listen and nod. Reporters at the *Daily Herald* have been known to fake illnesses to avoid prolonged assignments with him. When Harold Brown, one of my colleagues on the *Daily Herald's* projects desk, learned that I was going on a week-long assignment with Fritz, he asked, "Who did you piss off?"

Fritz and I are nearing the end of our week-long sojourn into the hills of the tri-state area of northern Kentucky, southern Ohio, and western West Virginia, working on a series of stories on Appalachia's dying coal mine industry, capturing in words and images those who spend their lives underground. Mining is hard, dirty work, and many live near the poverty level. Still, they singularly pray for a day when the country will again need their coal and men can return to the mines en masse. The Kardos & Sons Mining Company is one of the few bright spots of the week.

Later that afternoon, Fritz and I are on our way to the hotel in Chillicothe when we crest the knoll on County Road 12 just outside of Zaleski where the remnants of the Teays Valley Mining Company town are splayed on the hillside to our right. Most of the wood-frame houses are bleached out and abandoned, but dogs and kids run amid a few where front doors stand ajar and gray smoke curls out of the chimneys.

"Christ Almighty, can you image living in a hellhole like this?" Fritz asks.

I stare at the sad enclave, not answering until it is well in our rearview mirror. "Actually, Fritz, it's not too hard for me."

"What's that mean?"

"I grew up in Vinton County."

"Are you kidding me?"

It's a delicious little nugget for Fritz. It isn't gossip, per se, but it is inside information. He has a glimpse into my past, a little tidbit he can drop during his next gossip session back in the photo department.

I nod and point to a rusty white and black street sign peppered with buckshot. "I grew up right there, on Red Dog Road."

Fritz hits the brakes as we are flying past the dirt and pea gravel lane. We are the only car on County Road 12, so he puts it in reverse and turns onto Red Dog Road. "I can't believe this is where you grew up. Why didn't you tell me?"

I shrug. "I just did."

We drive up the road a quarter-mile to where a two-story home clings to a hillside of foxtail and milkweed. Many of the asphalt shingles that had previously covered the walls of the house had rotted off or blown away, creating a gray and black checkerboard effect. I point again. "There's the old homestead." Across from the house stands the gob pile, a man-made mountain of red dog, the sulfur-laced red ash that remained after the mining companies burned their coal dumps. A short distance up the road, just beyond the next crest, is a reclaimed dump generously called the Turkey Ridge Wildlife and Nature Preserve. In my childhood, killing rats at the dump made for a fun afternoon.

Fritz parks the car at the bottom of a steep, rutted incline that would be accessible only with a four-wheel drive vehicle. "Want to take a hike up and check it out?" I ask.

Silly question. He won't pass up the opportunity for anything.

We climb the hill, following the path between sticker bushes that hook our pants and rip away. Fritz is out of breath halfway up the hill. He points to a snake sunning itself on a rock. "What kind of snake is that?"

"A milk snake."

"Are they poisonous?"

"Extremely," I say.

He hurries up the path, occasionally glancing back at the harmless reptile.

The house appears to be slipping off its foundation and the front porch sags under its own weight. The front door has been torn off its hinges, and every window is busted. It's been years since anyone lived here. We walk through the downstairs, the floorboards groaning under our weight, glass crunching under our shoes. A soiled mattress is on the living room floor amid empty beer cans, reefer nubs, and spent condoms. Fritz snaps photos along the way.

When we return outside, he says, "It must have been a lot different when you were living here."

It seems like another lifetime ago, but the memory is clear. "No, Fritz, not really." I look around. The garage has burned down and the storage shed has collapsed upon itself. "Come on, let's get back to the hotel and get something to eat."

Six weeks later I had completed the series of stories. I was in the photo department with Fritz and our editor, Art Goodrich, reviewing a selection of Fritz's photographs that were to run with the stories.

"Did he tell you he grew up in that part of Ohio?" Fritz asked Art.

"That's not germane to the story," I said.

"It might be," Art said. "I didn't know you were from southern Ohio. How come I didn't know that?"

"That's what I asked him when he told me," Fritz said, anxious to let Art know that he had inside information. "We'd been roaming around those damn hills for an entire week before he said anything about it. He showed me the house where he grew up. It was this little thing stuck back on a dirt road in the middle of godforsaken nowhere."

Art Goodrich and I had worked together at the *Daily Herald* for more than ten years. He had been a reporter on the political desk before his meteoric rise to editor of the paper. We'd always gotten along, but aside from playing on the newsroom softball team together, we'd never had a particularly close relationship. "Come over to my office when you're done," he said.

It was after 5 PM when I walked into Goodrich's office. He popped up from behind his desk and said, "Let's go grab a beer." It wasn't a request. We walked across K Street to the Longhorn Bar & Grill and took seats at the corner of the mahogany bar.

"Do you know what stuck with me about your series of articles?" he asked. I shook my head. "It was the fact that no one ever seems to leave that region. No matter how bad things get, no matter how long they've been out of work, people just stay put. That one family has three or four generations of men working alongside each other in the mine and not a one of them has any desire to leave."

"People get comfortable with what they know, I guess." I sipped at a beer. "You live in this little cocoon and you're not really aware of what's going on outside of southern Ohio. Most of them were content to work in the coal mines like their dad and grandfathers."

"Was your dad a coal miner?"

"No. He worked in a sawmill mostly. Timber was a pretty big industry."

"How come you didn't end up there?"

"I got lucky, I guess."

"What's that mean—you got lucky? I don't think that someone who grows up in abject poverty and ends up on the projects desk of the Washington *Daily Herald* is just lucky." I smiled and shrugged. "How does a kid from southern Ohio end up a writer and not a coal miner?"

"I don't know, Art."

"Of course you know. You were there. I want to know how you got from there to here. I want to hear your story."

"That would take a while."

He signaled for another round of beers and asked for two menus. We ordered steaks and I told Art Goodrich how I had escaped the hollows of southern Ohio and ended up on the special projects team at the *Daily Herald*. When I had finished, the grease on our steak plates had congealed and he was downing the last of his carrot cake. "That's a great yarn," he said. "You should put that down on paper. In fact . . ."

He pulled his cell phone from the inside pocket of his suit coat and pounded out a sequence on the keypad. Art's brother-in-law was an editor with a New York publishing house, and within a month I was offered a contract to write my story. Art suggested I take a sabbatical to write it, but I declined. It was, after all, my story, and I didn't need to do a lot of research.

My story is not unusual. People escape poverty every day. We live in a country where freedom makes that possible. What makes my story different is the fact that I didn't do it alone. I was fortunate enough to have met someone who had both faith in me and the patience to show me I needn't be constrained by my environment or my surroundings. I was shown a path that I could not have discovered alone. And for that, I am forever grateful.

Chapter One

It was never easy being the class dirty neck, the derisive term used for those of us unfortunate enough to have grown up along Red Dog Road, a dead-end strip of gravel and mud buried deep in the bowels of Appalachian Ohio. I accepted my social status early in life. After all, it doesn't take long for a kid to realize that he's the outcast. A few days in school are all it takes, really. The exclusion is obvious and painful.

My classmates didn't accept my offers to come over and play. Parents ordered their kids inside whenever I showed up in their yard. I was never invited to birthday parties or sleepovers. When party invitations were passed out in class, I pretended not to notice, or care, when the little white envelopes were placed on desks all around mine. Usually, my classmates were considerate enough to at least pretend that I didn't exist. The exception was Margaret Burrell, an invidious little brat with an untamed mane of black hair that hung around her head like a hoop skirt, a pronounced underbite, and a lisp, who in the second grade waved a handful of invitations in front of my face and said, "I'm having a theventh birthday party, Jimmy Lee, and we're gonna have ithe cream, and cake, and gameths, and pony rideths, and *you* . . . ain't . . . invited." She shoved her nose in the air, spun on a heel, and strode off, confident in her superiority. It was not unusual treatment. When I was paired with someone for a science project or square dancing in gym class, they would shy away, trying to create distance between us, as though the mere touch of my skin might cause the onset of poverty and body odor.

In our society, you can no longer ostracize the black kid, or the fat kid, or the mentally retarded kid, but in Vinton County, it is still perfectly acceptable to ostracize the ones who are poor, white, and dirty. That was me. Like my brothers, who walked out of Red Dog Hollow before me, I quietly accepted my role as class dirty neck with no small amount of anger and frustration.

When you are the outcast—white trash—your mistakes are more pronounced and open to ridicule. Or, worse—laughter. Such was the case with the erection I threw every morning in Miss Singletary's first-period, junior English class.

This cyclical eruption was purely the product of adolescent, hormonal rampages that I was no more able to control than man can control the tides. I would think about dinosaurs or football, envision myself as a tortured prisoner of war, or review multiplication tables in my head. Nothing worked. Every day, precisely at eight forty-five, exploding like a damn party favor in my shorts, I sprouted a pulsating erection that stretched the crotch of my denims and left me mortified.

Across the aisle, Lindsey Morgan would stare at my lap with rapt attention, as though it were the season finale of her favorite television show. If I looked her way, she would avert her eyes and choke back laugher. Occasionally, if my erection was especially pronounced, she would tap the shoulder of Abigail Winsetter, who would pretend to drop a pencil to steal a glance at my crotch before bursting into uncontrollable giggles.

"Something you would like to share with the rest of the class, Miss Winsetter?" Miss Singletary would ask on each such occasion.

"No, ma'am, sorry," she would eke out, her face turning crimson and the vein in her temple pulsing like a freeway warning light as she vainly fought off the laughter.

I failed two six-week periods of junior English primarily because it is impossible for a seventeen-year-old to focus during such eruptions. When the bell rang at nine-thirty, I would get up holding a notebook over the protrusion and make three quick laps up the stairs, through the second-floor corridor, and back down, working off the erection before American history.

I knew, of course, that Lindsey was telling all her friends about my problem and they were having a grand laugh at my expense. It was just one more thing that Lindsey and her clique of uppity friends had to laugh about. Even by the modest standards of Vinton County, Lindsey's family had money. She also had friends and nice clothes, a smooth complexion, and straight teeth. My family had no money, and I had none of the accoutrements. This made me a pariah in her eyes. It wasn't that Lindsey was openly mean to me. It was simply the way she looked at me, as though my presence in her world was merely for her amusement.

Lindsey's father owned the Vinton Timber Company, a sawmill where my dad worked as a chain offbearer. By all accounts, Mr. Morgan was a benevolent man and a good employer. My dad was a perpetually unhappy soul with the disposition of a chained dog, and there wasn't much about life that suited him, particularly his job at the sawmill and Mr. Morgan. During his many drunken tirades at the Double Eagle Bar—a redneck place where the toilets never worked and pool cues were more often used as weapons than instruments of sport—my dad called Mr. Morgan everything but a white man and told anyone who would listen that Mr. Morgan locked the door to his office every afternoon and got head from his secretary, a plump divorcee named Nettie McCoy, who had hair the color of a pumpkin and a mole the size of a dime above one corner of her mouth. I don't know if the story was true or not, but I desperately wanted to repeat it to Lindsey just to see her get hurt, but I never did.

My name is James Leland Hickam, and I was born with a surname that was synonymous with trouble throughout southeastern Ohio. I hail from a heathen mix of thieves, moonshiners, drunkards, and general antisocials that for decades have clung to both the hardscrabble hills and the iron bars of every jail cell in the region. My ancestors came to this country from Wales in the 1880s and into Ohio from Kentucky just after the turn of the century. I am not privy to why they emigrated from England or migrated from Kentucky, but given the particular pride Hickam males take in their ornery nature, I can only imagine that my kin crossed the Atlantic Ocean and the Ohio River just slightly ahead of angry, torch-carrying mobs.

My namesake and grandfather was an expert car thief and career moonshiner who died in prison when I was in elementary school and of whom I have only a faint memory. He had a thicket of gray chest hair that sprouted over the top of his T-shirt, walked on the cuffs of his pants, and smelled of liquor and dirt and testosterone. Years before my birth, he lost an eye in a still explosion and wore a black patch over the empty socket. When my mother wasn't around, he would flip the patch upward and treat me to a peek at the void, which was rank and dark and sunken, rimmed with a yellow, pustulant discharge that both repulsed and intrigued me to where I never passed up the opportunity to look.

I was barely six years old the day the sheriff's deputies and agents from the state department of liquor control led my grandfather away in handcuffs. He had spent the morning at his still, which was tucked into a ravine and hidden deep in the woods behind our home. I was playing in a dirt patch near the porch when I heard the clinking of glass and looked up to see him walking out of the tree line pushing an old wheelbarrow that he had lined with a quilt and loaded full of

chemicals into our wells. Before he went off to prison, Edgel took great sport in going out to the dump to shoot rats with Dad's .22-caliber rifle, usually to the great annoyance of Chic McDonald, who scavenged the dump for scrap metal and still-good items that he could drag back to his perpetual yard sale.

The houses that lined Red Dog Road were paint-starved and frail, looking as though a strong wind would splinter them across the hillside. More often than not, the roofs were corrugated steel and turned into sieves during a heavy rain. Wringer washers stood by the front doors, outhouses were not uncommon, and running water came from wells laden with iron oxide that stained sinks and tubs and toilet bowls a bright orange. Children, barefoot and dirty, played with mangy dogs in dusty yards strewn with trash and rusting cars.

Beauty was rarely a part of my youth. The exception was the visits to my grandfather Joachim's farm in Scioto County. Papaw Joachim died when I was in the fourth grade, and when he was breathing, like almost everyone else in Appalachian Ohio, he didn't get along with my father, so my trips to the farm were few. But the beauty remains engrained in my memory. It was a magnificent piece of land that ran from a bluff nearly to the Ohio River, where the morning fog rolled off the shoals and snaked around the tobacco plants on its uphill creep toward the white farmhouse, which stood in stark contrast to the dense green of its surroundings. The Silver Queen corn he raised was so nourished by the unctuous soil that it towered along his lane and created a cavern of green that by the end of July could only be penetrated by the noonday sun. The stone outcroppings in the pasture above his home stretched into a plateau lush with trees and full of deer and rabbits. It was like much of southern Ohio in its beauty. There was, of course, the exception to this natural splendor, such as the godforsaken stretch of Vinton County land on which we lived.

Our house was built into a steep, rutted slope on the tallest hill lining Red Dog Road on land so rocky and thin with soil that honey locust trees and foxtails struggled for footing, and copperheads sunned themselves on the exposed stone. The hills were once like those in Scioto County, lush with dense groves of oak, shagbark hickory, buckeye, eastern cottonwood, black walnut, and beech trees. But in the 1920s, the hills along Red Dog Road were timbered out, the tree trunks cut to ground level. The erosion that followed swept away the topsoil and left precipitous, moonscape slopes of rock and clay. The sun baked the surface and created dust as fine as talcum powder that swirled in the slightest breeze, often creating mini twisters that skittered over the rocks and covered your teeth and nostrils with a fine, brown film.

A quarter mile beneath our house stretched the abandoned Hudson Mining Company's No. 2 mine. It had been more than three decades since the mine closed, yet its spiderweb of shafts continued to collapse upon themselves with such force that our windows and water pipes rattled with each implosion. The natural resources above and below the ground had been stripped away, and it was unsuitable for farming. It was worthless, and thus the only property my family could afford. In 1961, my dad paid twenty-three hundred dollars for the dilapidated mining company house—a two-story, brown, asphalt-shingled home with a metal roof and a slight list to the west. The window trim and porch were painted an industrial gray, which blistered and shed with each passing summer until it had the parched feel of driftwood. The wooden gutters were full of dirt and maple saplings sprouted from them each spring, sometimes growing nearly a foot high before performing a death bow when the gutter could no long support the roots.

The only access to our house was a dirt drive gouged by years of runoffs that made a treacherous descent from below our front porch to Red Dog Road. The rusting corpses of every two hundred dollar car my dad had bought in the previous fourteen years lined the drive; saplings and thistles pushed up through engine blocks, and vacated trunks provided refuge for families of raccoons and possums. Each year, the junkyard grew and the drive became steeper and more dangerous as the spring rains washed away another layer of clay, pushing stones and mud flows across Red Dog Road and into the Salt Lick Creek.

Across Red Dog Road from our house was the man-made mountain of red dog—a "gob pile," in miner parlance—from which our road got its name. For dozens of years, before going out of business in the early sixties, the Hudson Mining Company dumped its red dog on the marshy plains that served as the headwaters of Salt Lick Creek. Long before I was born, Salt Lick Creek was a cool, clear-running stream that made a shaded trek through a canopy of poplars, oaks, and weeping willows. Trout and crawfish and freshwater clams thrived in waters that traversed eastern Vinton and Athens counties, emptying into the Hocking River two miles north of its confluence with the Ohio. The gob piles were full of sulfuric acid and eroded iron. As rainwater seeped through the red dog, it collected its contents and carried them to the Salt Lick Creek, turning the pristine stream into an ecological nightmare. The runoff from the mountain of red dog caused the stream's waters to run orange, killing off the fish and plants. The massive roots of the willows drank in the poison and slumped into the waters. The mudflats and stones and tree trunks near the waters all became stained in dirty, muted orange. As a young boy, I watched dump trucks haul loads of smoldering ash up the hill. When they dumped the still-hot loads, plumes of white smoke seeped out of the hill, giving it the ominous look of a volcano primed to erupt. Even so, local boys still took sheets of cardboard or food trays and slid down its slopes of red dog like volcanic bobsledders, sucking red dust into their lungs and leaving their teeth covered with a powdery, red scum.

On a cold February afternoon—I couldn't have been older than ten—I was playing on the banks of Salt Lick Creek, when I looked down to find a maple leaf lying in the shallows of the stream. All around me were the colors of dead winter—browns and grays and shades of straw. Yet the leaf was a bold russet, a reddish-brown that should have fallen from an October sky, not the limbs of February. I reached into the frigid water and grabbed the leaf by the stem. It extended in front of me as rigid as a frying pan, fossilized by a patina of iron oxide from the contaminated water.

The massive hill of red dog was the source of a derisive nickname for the rednecks who lived in view of the giant red dog pile on the poorest road in the poorest county in the poorest part of the state. We were known as "doggers," and people around Vinton County used the term "dogger" with the same ease and contempt that the word "nigger" rolled off my dad's tongue. Oddly, those of us who lived in penury and filth around the giant mound of ash took particular pride in the "dogger" designation.

Although I looked like my mother, there was no mistaking me for anything but a Hickam, and that was poison in Vinton County. It wasn't unusual for me to overhear someone say, "That's one of Nick Hickam's boys—the youngest one, I think. They're all trouble." In the privacy of their home or in hushed tones when they saw me on the street, parents would say, "Don't let me catch you hanging around with that Hickam boy." Even when adults whispered, I knew what they were saying; I could read it in their eyes and in the sideways glances they gave me. I never stole anything in my life, but if a classmate lost a dollar, I was the first one to get pulled into the hall and accused of stealing it. Teachers would make me turn my pockets inside out, then go through my gym bag and tear everything out of my locker.

I was "one of them Hickams" from the day I entered the first grade. On days that it rained, Mrs. MacIntyre would keep us inside for recess and play a game called "Seven-Up." Seven kids would line up in the front of the room and the rest of us would put our heads on our desks and hide our eyes in the creases of our elbows. If you got tapped on the head, you raised your hand. When the seven tappers had returned to the front of the room, you would try to guess which one had tapped you. If you guessed right, you got to change places with them. During one such game, I had not gotten to play once. As recess was nearly over, Mrs. MacIntyre said, "We have to let everyone play; next time, someone needs to tap Jimmy Lee."

Margaret Burrell blurted out, "My momma said not to touch him on the head because all them Hickams has lice."

Mrs. MacIntyre looked at Margaret and then at me with a wide-eyed, slack-jawed look of astonishment, as though Margaret had just busted loose with a barrage of profanity that would make a millwright blush. I didn't even know what lice were, but I knew by the look on Mrs. MacIntyre's face that it was bad and I started crying. She told us to get out our coloring books as she was dragging Margaret into the hall by her collar. I could see her shaking a finger in Margaret's face and they both came back into the room all red-faced; Margaret was sniffling and teary-eyed.

That night, I asked my mom, "What's lice?"

"Little bugs that dirty people get in their hair," she said. I frowned, pondering her answer. "Why do you want to know, Jimmy Lee?"

"Margaret Burrell's mom said I have lice. She said all us Hickams have lice and that's why Margaret's not allowed to pick me during Seven-Up."

My mom picked through my hair, inspecting for the bugs, and said, "Some people's ignorant, Jimmy Lee. Don't pay them no mind." The next day, as soon as she left her shift at the truck stop, Mom drove down to school to get the story directly from Mrs. MacIntyre, then she paid a visit to Mrs. Burrell, who stammered around and said she had no idea where Margaret had heard of such a thing and it certainly wasn't from her, then she quickly shut and locked the door.

The next time we played Seven-Up, the rules changed and you no longer tapped your classmates on the head. Rather, you tapped them on the back or shoulder. Mrs. MacIntyre changed the rules, I guess, so even us dirty necks could play.

I won't lie. Being treated like an outcast makes you angry and bitter and itchy for a fight. It gnaws at your gut and makes your face hot, not the pink tinge of embarrassment, but the scorching, crimson burn of ridicule and exile. I was a raw-boned kid, hardened by years of fighting with other boys on Red Dog Road and taking regular beatings with a strap from the old man. It wasn't unusual for me to have belt bruises crisscrossing my ass and upper legs. Sometimes I deserved it, but there were a good number of times when I was just a target. Girls like Lindsey Morgan had fun at my expense, but I didn't get much grief from the boys because I wouldn't hesitate to bust their heads.

Early in my freshman year, Danny Clinton thought he would get some laughs in the locker room by taking a tongue depressor of orange muscle balm and trying to swipe my asshole while my head was under the shower. I twitched as soon as I felt it and he left a streak of orange along the side of my crack. He laughed and pointed until he saw my fist driving toward the middle of his face. The cartilage in his nose sounded like a dry twig snapping and the punch sent him sailing on his back across the shower room floor, water flying away from his shoulders like the wake of a speedboat. I broke his nose and split his lip, and he ran bawling from the shower, blood gushing from his face.

Our principal, Theodore Speer, a tired little man with sad eyes who hitched his slacks up just below his nipples and earned the nickname "Teddy High Pockets," summoned me to his office the next morning. He sat there for a long time massaging his temples, his eyes pinched shut, before he asked, "Are you going to give me problems, too, Jimmy Lee?"

I knew what he meant. My older brothers had been nothing but trouble at school before Edgel got expelled after being accused of stealing from a teacher's purse and Virgil dropped out to join the carnival, neither of them finishing their sophomore years. "No, sir. I don't go looking for trouble, but I don't take to people messin' with me. Danny was trying to put hot stuff up my butt to get a laugh at my expense, and I won't have any of that."

"I certainly see your point, Jimmy Lee, but you nearly put him in the hospital. He's got a broken nose, it took more than twenty stitches to close up his lip, and he's got a lump on the back of his head the size of a baseball where he hit the shower floor. I just can't have students assaulting other students."

"But he started it," I countered.

"The punishment didn't fit the crime."

That was easy for Principal Speer to say, I thought, because it wasn't his rear end getting the furnace treatment. In reality, he was saying that Danny Clinton's dad was vice president of the school board, and my dad was a split-tooth drunk from Red Dog Road. Danny got off with a warning to knock off the horseplay, and I got hung with a three-day suspension, but it was the first and last time anyone at East Vinton High School ever messed with me.

That was the difference between being the kid that everyone picks on and the one no one wants to be around. I didn't get picked on because most of the kids were afraid of me, and if they weren't before the Danny Clinton incident, they were afterward. Sometimes, I think it's worse to be the kid who gets ostracized. I would walk down the hall and I wondered if I were invisible or a ghost. Other kids were talking, flirting, horsing around. It seemed like no one even saw me. It's tough not having any friends. It makes you not want to go to school.

The thing that most of my classmates never knew was that I was pretty smart. I liked to read and write, and math came easy to me. But I didn't get good grades because I didn't try, and I didn't try because I didn't see any margin in it. And, since I was a Hickam, the teachers never had any expectations that I would excel. I thought my life's course had been predetermined. Someday I would be working at the sawmill with the old man or at the carnival with Virgil or sitting in prison with Edgel. There weren't many opportunities for Hickams, so why bother with schoolwork?

I might have finished my sophomore year, but I doubt I would have gone to school much longer if it hadn't been for football. During gym class the second week of school my sophomore year, we were playing flag football. Petey Kessler, who was the starting halfback on the varsity, ran around left end and was heading for a touchdown except I ran him down from across the field. Coach Battershell, who was the gym teacher, put down his newspaper and watched me play for the rest of the period. After class, he pulled me aside and asked, "Young man, how come you didn't try out for the football team?"

I shrugged. "I don't know. I've never played sports."

"There's a first time for everything, you know? You've got good speed. You could help us out."

To be on the football team you had to buy your own shoes, mouth guard, and game socks. I didn't have that kind of money. "I can't afford it."

"I'll find you a pair of shoes. You stick it out and I'll pay for the mouth guard and socks."

"Okay," I said.

After school, I reported to the locker room and the student manager fixed me up with gear and a practice uniform. The restriction of the shoulder pads and helmet felt funny. The helmet had a face mask with a protective bar running down the middle and I couldn't not focus on it, causing me to see double. "You'll get used to it in a couple of days," the equipment manager said.

I ran out to the field where the team was doing stretching exercises. "What are you doing here?" Danny Clinton sneered.

"I'm gonna play. Coach Battershell asked me to come out for the team."

He snorted. "This'll be fun."

I wore black dress socks to my first practice and put my thigh pads in upside down. I stumbled through the grass drills, and the first pass that was thrown to me during individual linebacker drills went through my hands, hit me square in the face mask, and shot fifteen feet in the air. This all drew a lot of snickers. I was pretty raw, never having played any sport before, but I was fast, strong, liked to hit people, and soon learned that I had a knack for football. Also, it provided me a way to take out my frustrations. Not only did you not get in trouble for smacking around people like Danny Clinton, but coaches and teammates patted you on the back and said things like "nice job" and "great hit."

Coach Kyle Battershell had been a star quarterback for the Ohio University Bobcats and his name was legendary in southeastern Ohio. He had been an assistant coach at Marietta High for a couple of years before coming to Vinton East before the previous season. It was big news in Vinton County when he took over our pitiful football program. East Vinton hadn't had a winning season in my lifetime, but Coach Battershell was not accustomed to losing and while he was pretty easygoing as a gym and health teacher, he didn't put up with any nonsense on the football field. I liked that because it meant we were all treated equal, and it didn't matter if you lived on Red Dog Road or your dad was the vice president of the school board—the best players got on the field.

Each day after practice, Coach Battershell took a few minutes to work with me and told me not to worry about never having played before. "You'll pick it up," he assured me. He said I was a natural-born linebacker and gave me a playbook with defensive schemes. During gym class, while the rest of the kids were playing games, he would take me off to the side and drill me on my footwork and how to read a quarterback's eyes. By the end of my second week on the team, I was the starting outside linebacker on the varsity. This steamed a lot of kids who had been playing for years, but I was better than they were. For the first time in my life, I was someone other than "one of them Hickams." I still didn't have a lot of friends, but the guys seemed glad to have me on the team. Parents nodded at me after games and said, "Nice game, Jimmy Lee," which was a far sight better than, "Did you steal that, Jimmy Lee?"

I was named honorable mention all-league and earned a varsity letter. We had a banquet at the end of the season and I was presented with my letter and a certificate, and for two days I just stared at that award. My mom got me a varsity jacket for Christmas—a navy jacket with gray leather sleeves and the words EAST VINTON ELKS on the back—and sewed the gray chenille letter, an interlocked EV, to the left breast. Dad said it was a damn waste of money, but I had never been so proud of anything in my life. I was a varsity letterman and it made me someone. It made me want to stay in school. My grades got better and I went out for the track team in the spring and earned another letter as a sprinter, anchoring the 440-yard relay team that won the districts.

My junior year was even better. I was first-team all-league and all-district, third-team All-Ohio, and enjoying the recognition that accompanied my achievements on the football field. Coach Battershell stressed the importance of keeping my grades up as he expected some college coaches would be interested in me if I had a solid senior year. "You mean I could get a college scholarship?" I asked.

He nodded. "Possibly, but you've got to keep the grades up."

The very thought boggled my mind—a son of Nick Hickam earning a college scholarship.

By the end of my junior year, I was carrying a B average in most classes except English, where my morning erections were contributing to a downward spiral that was bringing me perilously close to failing for the year. At the end of English class on Friday, two weeks before the end of the school year, Miss Singletary handed out our homework assignment and as she slipped behind her desk said, without making eye contact, "Jimmy Lee, I would like to speak with you after class, please."

"But I have American History," I said, not so much worried about missing class as I was losing the time I needed to dispose of the expansion in my jeans.

She looked up, her brows arched. "I'll write you an excuse."

When the bell rang, I stayed in my seat, second from the back in the third row. When the classroom had cleared, Miss Singletary said, "You can come up here and sit, Jimmy Lee."

"If it's all the same to you, Miss Singletary, I'm pretty comfortable right here."

She frowned, but picked up her grade book and sat in the chair of the desk in front of me, maneuvering around to face me. "We have a big problem, Jimmy Lee," she said. "You are about to fail my class. I've been looking at the grades and right now you have a fifty-two average for the last grading period—an F. If you get an F, you fail for the year. If you somehow manage to get a D, and that doesn't seem likely, you would pass by the slimmest of margins. Frankly, Jimmy Lee, I don't see any way you can even salvage a D at this late stage."

It had been years since I cried, but I had tears in my eyes. "I can get a D, Miss Singletary," I said. "I've got two weeks until the final. I'll pull it up."

"Even if you did get a D, I'm not sure it would be in your best interests to tackle senior English without a better foundation. I think you need to repeat junior English." She pulled out her grade book. "You failed more in-class quizzes and assignments than anyone in the class. In six grading periods you have two C's, a D and two F's. And, frankly, the D was a gift. You're struggling, Jimmy Lee."

"If I don't pass, I won't be eligible for football in the fall."

"I understand that, but there are things in life more important than football."

"Not in my life, Miss Singletary. Football is just about the only thing I have going for me. It's the only thing that makes people look at me like I'm somebody. Before I started playing football, I was just another Hickam. I might as well have been invisible in this school. You went to school with my brother, Edgel. You know what I'm up against. The only reason I get any acceptance is because of football."

I blinked away a tear. She took a deep breath and tapped the eraser of her pencil on the grade book. "What happens . . ." Her voice trailed off as she seemed to struggle for the right words. "What happens if you manage to get a D, but get into senior English and fall even further behind? Then what?"

"I won't fall behind. Just give me a chance. I don't want any gifts. I'll work hard, I swear. I'll get the D. I'll do better in senior English, I promise. I'll work a lot harder, you'll see. I had some distractions this year. I'm not stupid, Miss Singletary."

"I don't believe you're stupid, Jimmy Lee. I think you're very capable when you put your mind to it. But, for whatever reason, you just didn't put forth much effort this year."

"I have a good reason."

"Care to share that with me?"

I shook my head. "No, ma'am, not really. But if you give me a chance, I promise you won't regret it. I won't let you down."

Chapter Two

We visited my brother in prison every other Sunday.

He was an inmate at the state penitentiary in Mansfield, a hundred forty-two miles and a three-and-a-half hour drive from our house. It was an arduous ride, during which my dad cursed the ignorance of other drivers and chain-smoked, filling the interior of our car with plumes of blue haze and bluer language.

About six months after Edgel was sentenced to Mansfield, Mom wrote a letter to the Ohio Department of Corrections and Rehabilitation requesting that he be moved to a prison closer to home to make it more convenient for our visits. "If you could move him to the prison in Lucasville, that would be nice as it is only about fifty miles from our house." In response, she received a curtly worded letter stating that the state couldn't honor such requests, which came as a surprise to no one but Mom.

On the first Sunday of my summer vacation before my senior year, Mom made a breakfast of biscuit gravy and fried eggs, after which I put on a clean shirt and sat on a front porch swing that was sun-bleached gray and suspended from exposed joists with a rusty chain. I put my feet on the porch railing and slowly rocked, listening to the chain squeak and the house groan with each push, enjoying a moment of solitude before we began the journey north to the Mansfield State Reformatory.

My father was next to appear on the porch. He shot a brief glance my way, his eyes unable to conceal the indifference he felt toward me, and did not speak. The moisture of his bath remained on his body; his forehead was slick and his shirt clung to his chest and back in damp pools. The old man was still hard and muscular, and the half-football bulge just above his belt was solid to the touch. He stood at the edge of the porch for a minute as he fished a cigarette from the pack in his breast pocket, slipped it between his lips, and began patting his pockets to locate his lighter. Once the torch had been found, he lowered himself down on the top step to fire up his smoke. A high-pitched whine escaped from deep in his body as he inhaled hard on the first draw, then allowed the exhaust to slowly escape from his mouth, sending up tendrils of white smoke that danced in front of his face. Streaks of gray were starting to show at the old man's temples and the white scars of a hundred fights flickered like bits of neon on his tanned face. He smelled of Marlboros and the hair cream that glistened on the back of his pockmarked neck. While he sat and smoked, Dad pulled and twisted the metal wristband of the watch that hung loose around his left wrist. He twisted the watchband whenever he got nervous or anxious, and the trips to the prison always caused him angst. He didn't like the visits, and I don't think he liked Edgel. I grew up never understanding the underlying reason for the dislike, but I assumed it was simply the result of two hotheads living under the same roof.

Mom was last out the door with a bag of cookies and treats for Edgel, which were packed up in a shopping bag that dangled from her right wrist. In her right hand were the house keys. She pulled the knob with her left hand, snugging the door tight against the jamb, then locked the deadbolt with the key in her right. I continued to rock and Mom stood quietly until Dad flicked the burning butt of his Marlboro into the yard, the tacit signal that he was ready to go.

On this Sunday, the first in June, he pitched his cigarette when he saw the rattletrap, red pickup truck begin its ascent from Red Dog Road, groaning and throwing stones as it strained against the steep drive. It was my brother Virgil, who had called collect the previous night to say he was coming home for the day. Virgil had worked through the night tearing down a carnival in Parkersburg, West Virginia, and had a day off before heading to a festival in Huntington.

I had never gotten along with Virgil. The truth is, I couldn't stand to be around him. He was very much like my dad, bitter and always angry at the world, and as a brother seven years his junior, I had proved to be the perfect punching bag on which he vented his myriad of frustrations. From what I could tell, Virgil had never made a single mistake in his life. To listen to him talk, you would have thought the entire world was involved in a sinister, conspiratorial plot to make his life a living hell. Virgil had always been my dad's favorite. He and Virgil got along, in part, because they seemed to share a soured outlook on life and a mutual lust for alcohol and fighting. Dad couldn't control Edgel and thought I was a momma's boy because I didn't like to go looking for a fight.

Virgil took the backseat behind my dad and immediately bummed a cigarette and the old man's lighter. The car's undercarriage scraped on the gravel as it dropped onto Red Dog Road, and Virgil settled back in his seat, his elbow resting on the knee of his filthy jeans. His sinewy forearms and hands were black with grease that was ground deep into the pores and lines of his hands. Beneath the grime on his right forearm, I could see the faint outline of where Virgil had tattooed himself with a needle and ink and had given himself blood poisoning when he was fifteen; the tattoo was of a misshapen skull and crossbones and the words, BORN TO DIE, which

Virgil always said was his motto. His fingernails were caked with dirt and grease, and a rim of shiny black oil ran around the cuticles, outlining the tiny bit of visible pink beneath the nail. When he saw me staring at his hands, he asked, "What are you lookin' at, junior?"

"Nothing."

He held up his hands and twisted them so I could see every line of filth. In his heavy, southern Ohio twang, Virgil said, "Them's the hands of a working man, but you wouldn't know nothin' 'bout that, would ya?"

"Yes, I would. I've got a job this summer."

He smiled and chuckled. "Really? Doing what?"

"Mr. Monihan hired me up at the truck stop. The county's making him clean up all the truck tires he's been rolling down over the hill all those years. Must be twenty years' worth—a couple thousand of them by now, I bet, and he's going to pay me ten cents for every one I haul up and stack."

He dragged on his cigarette. "When you decide to trade in that snatch and get yourself a dick and balls, let me know and I'll get you a real job." He blew smoke in my face. "That's pussy work."

"No it's not."

"It ain't a man's work."

"Well, at least I'm no carnival jockey who looks like he hasn't had a bath in a month."

Virgil's eyes turned to slits and the skin drew back around his mouth. "You best shut your mouth, boy, or I'll bust your head, and don't think I won't."

"Shut the hell up, both of yuns," my dad yelled. "Jesus Christ, it's like havin' a couple of goddamn six-year-olds in the car."

I fought back a grin. I was now twice the size of Virgil and the days when he could whip me were long over, and he knew it. Of course, the threat of a good beating never stopped a Hickam from diving into a fight.

Virgil took a long drag on his cigarette, this time blowing the smoke out the window. "And to think I was going to get you a job on the carnival this summer," he said. "That ain't happenin' now, that's for damn sure."

"He couldn't go anyways," Mom interjected. "He's got football practice starting in July."

"Football," Virgil said, like he had a mouth full of curdled milk. "That don't put no money in your damn pocket."

"Coach Battershell said if I keep improving and keep my grades up I might get a scholarship to play in college."

"Yeah, that'll be the day that *you* go to college. Barber college, maybe." Virgil and my dad both laughed aloud. I expected resentment from Virgil as it seemed to be his lot in life to assemble and disassemble Tilt-A-Whirls, but it was hurtful to hear my dad laugh. I don't think Nick Hickam ever wanted any of his sons to make more of their lives than he had made of his, and he was secretly glad that my brothers were failures. The fact that they had no more education than he had, and one was an inmate and the other a carnie, allowed Dad to maintain his stature within the family.

We arrived at the reformatory at one-thirty and walked into the large lobby where we had to sign in. Construction on the prison began in 1886 and it looked like a European castle with its ornate architecture and stone walls. Stepping into the building gave me chills as I joined the pathetic lot of human flotsam, black and white, that wandered through the lobby, waiting to be called behind the bars for their visit. Visitation was strictly on the terms of the State of Ohio. The slightest infraction of the state's rules would keep you from the visitation room. Even the angriest of men, like my dad and brother, understood this and kept their tempers and mouths in check.

I don't have much of a memory of Edgel before he went to prison. After he dropped out of high school, he worked odd jobs and was rarely around the house. Edgel and our father had such a tense relationship that I think he found it easier to sleep in his car or at the home of a friend rather than stay at our house. The summer before I entered the sixth grade, I was in the front yard hitting stones with a broom handle when Sheriff McCollough pulled up in his cruiser. He got out of the car before the dust had settled around the tires. He was a big man with shoulders that strained the fabric of his white shirt and hands that could hide a softball. A toothpick was tucked into the corner of his mouth. He nodded and said, "Howdy, buster. Your brother hereabouts?"

"Which un?"

"Edgel."

"Uh-huh. He's out back in the shed with my pa."

He winked and headed around the house. As soon as he had disappeared beyond the porch, I dropped the broom handle and ran around the other side of the house, creeping up to the back of the old shed with the gambrel roof where I knew there was a gap in the old plank sheeting.

The sheriff didn't announce himself but just walked right into the shed and said, "Whoa, would you look at that, an Oldsmobile Rocket 88. Ain't that somethin' to behold?" Sheriff McCollough put a massive hand on each fender and leaned down into the hood of the car my dad and Edgel were working on. "Remember that old slogan, Nick? 'Make a date with a Rocket 88.' Yes sir, they sure don't make 'em like this anymore, do they?" Neither my dad nor Edgel responded. Hickam men had enough experience with the law to know that the sheriff never paid them a social call. The sheriff watched them work for a minute, then said, "Edgel, the Radebaugh place over on Township Road 22 got burglarized and torched the other night. You wouldn't happen to know anything about that, would you?"

"No, sir. Why would I?"

"I talked to a couple of people who said they saw someone sitting in a car at the school bus turnaround just west of the Radebaugh place last Tuesday, the same night it burned." Sheriff McCollough stepped back to the open shed door, rubbed his chin and squinted hard at the Olds. "In fact, I believe it could have been this very car. The witnesses said it was a 1950s Oldsmobile, maybe a Rocket 88 coupe, white over orange, maybe red, with lots of primer spots. And this car right here is an Olds, Rocket 88 coupe, white over orange with lots of primer spots. What year is this car, Edgel?"

"It's a . . ." my dad started.

"Is your name Edgel?" the sheriff's tone was suddenly harsh as he cut off my dad. He arched his brows at my brother.

"It's a fifty-five," Edgel said.

"Well, see, there we go. This car matches the one that was seen down by the Radebaugh place the night it burned. And since this is your car, and there aren't many like it around these parts, I'm going to go out on a limb and say it was you sitting in it that night. What do you think, partner?"

"You accusing me of something, sheriff?"

Sheriff McCollough slowly shook his head. "No, Edgel. I'm just wondering if you could help me out. I thought maybe you saw something, since you were sitting out there near the place."

"I never said I was out there."

"No, you didn't. So, where were you last Tuesday?"

"I don't remember, right off."

The sheriff's face grew cold and he chomped on his toothpick. "You don't remember? Well, son, you better start thinking real hard."

"You got no right to talk to him like that," my dad said.

Sheriff McCollough never took his eyes off of Edgel. "It's been a while since I gave you a good beatin', Nick. Open your mouth again and I'll be obliged to bring the score up to date." He grabbed the shoulder of Edgel's T-shirt and pulled him out from under the hood.

"I think that was you out there, Edgel. Since last April there've been five houses burglarized and torched in Vinton County." He held up a big hand, his thick fingers spread wide. "Five of 'em. I'm an elected official, Edgel. The people of this county elected me to enforce the law and protect them and their property. And now those same people are real upset that I haven't caught the piece of shit that's doing this. I don't like it when voters get upset, 'cause that means I have to work a lot harder to keep my job. Now, if you know anything about this, Edgel, you better come clean. A little guy like you would have a tough go of it in prison. You better keep that in mind." He released the grip on Edgel's shirt and walked out. I scampered back around the house and was again hitting stones by the time the sheriff appeared around the corner. "You get yourself an earful back there, buster?" he asked. He stared at me until I nodded. "Keep your nose clean, you hear?"

"Yes, sir."

All that summer I'd heard people talking about the rash of burglaries and arson fires. Not until Sheriff McCollough drove on to our property had I even considered that it could have been Edgel. But it made sense. He didn't work, yet always seemed to have cash. According to the newspaper, the burglar had been stealing coins and jewelry and items that could be easily fenced. The arson fires, it was assumed, were an attempt to destroy any physical evidence.

At dinner a week after the sheriff's visit, Edgel slid a black, cloth-covered box across the kitchen table at my mother. "What's this?" she asked.

"It's a present."

She put her fingertips to her breast, smiled, and opened the box. Resting atop a patch of cotton was a gold chain, from which hung a sparkling pink sapphire the size of a nickel.

"Oh my." My mother rolled the box in her hands, watching the light dance off the stone. "Oh, it's beautiful, Edgel, but where'd you get the money for this?"

"Why are you worrying about that? I just picked it up some-where."

"Where?"

My dad was looking at the gem in disbelief. "Yeah, Edgel, where did you get that?" he asked.

"What difference does that make? It's a gift for Mom."

"Alice Radebaugh had one just like this," Mom said. "She used to wear it to work. She had matching earrings."

Mrs. Radebaugh was a widow who worked the cash register at the truck stop with Mom. "Alice Radebaugh doesn't have one like this, 'cause this one's yours," Edgel said.

Mom sat motionless as Edgel took the necklace from her hands and walked behind her.

"Her husband bought it for her on their twenty-fifth wedding anniversary," said Mom, still not moving. "Alice said he saved for a year to buy it, and she was so upset when it got stolen." As Edgel clasped the chain behind her neck, Mom looked as though the hangman were tightening a noose. Dad's eyes darted back and forth from the necklace to Edgel, who just grinned at my dad with his bulbous lips.

When Mom got up to clean the dishes she said, "It's lovely, Edgel. But I'm going to take it off so I don't get anything on it." I watched her drop it in her apron pocket and she never wore it again.

After dinner, my dad and Edgel got into a terrible fight out behind the shed. My dad grabbed a sun-dried two-by-four and busted Edgel over the head and shoulders. Given my dad's penchant for trouble, I found it a little unusual that he would get upset with Edgel for stealing the widow Radebaugh's necklace, but there was no predicting the irrational behavior of Nick Hickam.

Late that summer, Edgel got drunk at the Antler Room Bar in McArthur and ran the Rocket 88 into a ditch off of London-Athens Road. Edgel was arrested for drunken driving and the car was impounded. When Sheriff McCollough searched it, he pulled out the backseat and found matches, a can of jellied fire starter, two pry bars, and a pair of pink sapphire earrings, which Mrs. Radebaugh identified as the ones stolen from her house. Edgel went to prison and the burglaries and arsons stopped.

A buzz-cut guard with a square jaw and lazy eye came out from behind the nearest barred door and said, "Hickam." Although we knew the drill, we listened intently as he explained the rules of the visitation room before leading us through the door, which was electronically opened by a guard seated in a nearby room with a two-way mirror. The visitation room was pale blue and the size of a high school basketball court. Square tables were lined up in neat rows across the concrete floor. On a catwalk ringing the room, humorless, armed guards marched their paces, eyes darting for the first signs of trouble.

A haze of cigarette smoke hung over the room. No one smiled, inmates and their wives argued in hushed tones, and at least once every visit my mother remarked, "It smells so angry in here."

Edgel was already seated at a table in the middle of the room. He was only five-foot-five and a hundred thirty-five pounds, and the prison-issue clothes he wore—a denim shirt and blue slacks—were always too baggy and made him appear comically small. As we approached, Edgel glanced up but gave no sign of recognition as he rolled the tip of a cigarette in the aluminum ashtray, sharpening the point of the burning ember.

Sometimes, I wondered why we bothered to visit with Edgel. One visit was the same as the next. As we took our chairs and crowded in around the table, Edgel just sat there, playing with his cigarette and picking at his cuticles, head down, hands in plain view as required, and saying little.

"Are they treating you right, sweetheart?" my mom asked.

"It's prison, Mama. They don't treat nobody right."

"Them guards give you a hard way to go?" my dad asked.

He shrugged. "I don't give 'em any reason to bother me. You mind your own business and toe the line, they leave you alone. Besides, it ain't the guards you got to be watching out for."

"What happened to your eye?" Mom asked, nodding toward the pad of faded purple that stretched beneath Edgel's right eye.

"Nothin'. Bumped it on my bunk is all."

It was another lie, but my mother knew better than to press the issue. At least twice before, she and dad had pressed Edgel for answers to questions that he didn't want to answer. Each time he simply stood up and said, "I'll see you all in a couple of weeks," and went back to his cell. Frankly, I don't think Edgel cared if we visited or not. But that was Edgel. He didn't care much about anything. Of Edgel, my dad liked to say, "He's a thief and he's crazy, and that's a bad combination." Even by the questionable standards of the Hickams, there was just something wrong with the way Edgel was wired. Frankly, the more I heard my dad talk and the more I witnessed Edgel's morose, sullen moods, the more I believed that prison might be the ideal place for him.

From the time I could remember, Edgel was always stealing—from Mom, Dad, teachers, anyone. He didn't care if he got caught. He stole my dad's wallet one time and went out for the weekend. By the time he came dragging in Sunday night, my dad had had about forty-eight hours to build up a good froth and he took to beating Edgel with a belt. He folded the leather strap in half, wrapping the ends around his hand, and he hit him everywhere—on the arms, back, legs, ass, neck. The old man beat him until he was exhausted—red-faced, bending at the waist, and sucking for air. Edgel had welts swelling up everywhere and thin lines of blood seeping through his T-shirt in the back, but he never showed any sign that it hurt. I swear he didn't feel pain like a normal human being. He had these soft, heavy lips that always seemed pinched up in a perpetual smirk. The more my dad saw that he wasn't hurting Edgel and that he seemed to be grinning, the madder the old man got and the harder he swung, but Edgel just took it.

When Dad stopped to catch his breath, Edgel pulled the old man's empty wallet from his hip pocket and dropped it on the living room floor, then went to his room while my dad hunched in the middle of the living room, hands on his knees, struggling for a breath of air. My mom walked in from the kitchen and asked, "Was it necessary to beat him like that?"

Between wheezy breaths my dad said, "He's . . . a thievin' . . . son of a bitch."

"Yes, he is," my mother said in a calm voice. "And just who, Nick Hickam, do you s'pose he larnt that from?"

The old man spun on his heel and hit my mother full in the jaw. The blow was so hard that she left her feet, landing hard on her shoulders just before her head snapped back and thudded against the floor. It took her several minutes to roll over and get on all fours. When she was finally able to stand, she had tears streaming down her cheeks and a thin line of blood extending from the corner of her mouth. "You're quite the man, aren't you, Nick?" she asked.

Edgel stopped talking and stared down at his shoes while a prison guard made a slow pass by our table. When the guard cleared earshot, Edgel took a draw on his cigarette and looked at me. "You playin' football this year?"

"For sure. It's my senior year. I think I've got a good chance to be named the defensive captain."

"That's good. Keep busy and stay out of here. This is no place to be."

"I know."

"Maybe if you keep working hard, you'll get yourself a college scholarship."

I smiled and looked at my dad and Virgil. "The coach says I might if I keep working hard. I'm hopin'."

"Maybe I'll get to see you play." Edgel pinched his cigarette between his lips, squinting as smoke rolled into his eyes, reached into his breast pocket and produced a letter that he handed to my mother. "It's from my attorney. I go before the parole board in October. He said because I haven't had any recent infractions in prison, and because the place is overcrowded, I've got a good chance to get out on parole."

"Oh, Edgel, that would be wonderful," my mother said, tears starting to roll down both cheeks. She read the letter for a moment and said, as though Edgel had just been awarded the Congressional Medal of Honor, "It says here that you've been a model prisoner."

"Yeah, ain't that somethin' to be proud of? I'll be sure to put that on my next job application."

"This is such wonderful news."

Virgil said, "Maybe when you get out, I'll talk to Mr. Barker, who owns the carnival. His son, Bart—me and him's real tight—and I'll bet I can get you a job with the carnival."

Edgel looked at him and shrugged. "We'll see, Virg."

I could have told Virgil right then and there that Edgel Hickam was never going to work as a carnie, but I kept my mouth shut.

"When in October does the parole board meet?" my dad asked.

Edgel shrugged. "I don't know. All the letter says is October."

That was four months away and ample time for a Hickam male to get in plenty of trouble. "Oh Edgel, please promise me you won't get any infractions between now and then," my mom said.

"Yeah, okay, Mom. I'll try not to run into any more bunk beds."

Chapter Three

Polio Baughman was my best friend, though it was a position he held by default.

I met Polio when we were both six years old and waiting for the bus to take us to school for the first day of first grade. The Baughmans had just moved to a small one-story shanty on Red Dog Road and I was surprised to see this new kid standing at the bus stop. He was a skinny, malnourished little guy who smelled like a musty basement. He had a crop of unruly blond hair, untied shoes, and a perpetual line of snot running from his nose to his mouth. His real name was Kirby, but as a young boy he was so thin and bony that the kids gave him the nickname of Polio, which, like so many unfortunate nicknames, stuck. By junior high, even the teachers called him Polio.

Polio and I were the only two doggers in the first-grade class at Zaleski Elementary School. Thus, we rode the bus together, sat beside each other in the slow reading group and, since the other kids had been forewarned to keep their distance from us doggers, pretended to be army commandos together during recess. Red Dog Road was segregated from the rest of Vinton County by prejudice, barren hills, and miles of bad country lanes. Consequently, Polio was my only friend. He spent countless hours at my house, coughing,

swiping his snotty nose with his forearm, and looking for something
to cram into his pocket.

Polio didn't have another friend in the world, yet he would steal
from me at every opportunity. If there were a few pennies on my
dresser when he got to the house, they would be gone when he left.
Over the years I trudged over to Polio's house to retrieve money,
toys, the pocketknife my grandfather Joachim had given me, and three
arrowheads that I had found on the ridge behind our house. Twice, I
had to grind his face in the dirt and threaten him with a beating if he
didn't return stolen toys, but mostly he just gave them up.

"Why do you steal like that?" I asked him once.

"'Cause you got stuff and I don't," he responded.

"But that doesn't make it right, Polio. You don't steal, especially
from your friends. My brother Edgel's like that, always stealin', and
he's in prison now."

Polio just shrugged.

Like most doggers, Polio was a survivor. He was the middle one
of five kids, and even by the standards of Red Dog Road, they were
poor. They had running water, but no indoor toilets. Polio did his
business in a fetid outhouse that was the only thing on Red Dog
Road that smelled worse than the dump, or he simply unhitched his
pants and pissed in the yard. His father was a silent, grease-stained
man who had chewing tobacco stains caked to the corners of his
mouth and a growth on the top of his forehead the size of a lemon.
He worked in the junkyard outside of Zaleski. Every day, Polio's
mother wore the same faded blue, sleeveless housecoat that revealed
a mass of gray armpit hair.

I understood this and that is why I tolerated Polio's thievery.
He was the only kid my age within miles and the only one whose
parents didn't mind having a Hickam in their yard. My Grandpa
Joachim had an old billy goat on his farm that would butt you the
second you turned your back on him. You had to be careful and you

couldn't take your eye off him. Dealing with Polio was no different from dealing with that old billy goat. If I was careless enough to leave something where Polio could get his hands on it, shame on me, because I knew he would steal it. It's just what he did.

Mr. Monihan sent word home with my mother that the hillside cleanup had to be a two-person job. I protested this, having no desire to share my ten-cents-a-tire commission. "Jimmy Lee, have you seen how many tires have been dumped over that hillside?" she asked.

"No, ma'am."

"Well, there's a slew of 'em, and they're truck tires, which are a lot bigger than car tires. You'll be glad for the help when you see 'em all."

"Who does he have to help me?"

"He said for you to find someone."

Polio Baughman was the obvious choice. Like me, Polio was hungry for money and this was an opportunity to make more than he had ever seen—or stolen—in his life. I walked over to his house and asked him if he wanted to help me remove the tires. "What's it pay?" he asked.

"A dime a tire."

"That ain't much."

I took a breath and rolled my eyes. "It's more than you're making now, isn't it? I don't see people lining up on Red Dog Road to offer you work, Polio."

"Okay, what time?"

"Be at my house no later than five forty-five."

When we reported to work with my mother at 6 AM on the Wednesday after our visit to see Edgel, I realized how right Mr. Monihan had been. The truck stop garage backed up to the crest of a hill. For two decades or thereabouts, mechanics stood inside the garage and rolled tires out the bay door and across a small patch of asphalt, where they would bounce once on the lip of the hill before disappearing over the hillside, bowling over saplings and landing somewhere between the asphalt and the nameless ditch four hundred feet below.

"You can't hardly see any grass for all the tires," Polio said as we surveyed the hillside.

"That's a lot of money there," I said.

"That's a lot of work, Jimmy Lee," Polio said.

"Have you got better plans for the summer?" I asked.

"No, I was just sayin', it's a lot of work."

"I can find someone else to help me if you're not interested."

"I'm interested," he whined. "I'm here, ain't I?"

I needed to set Polio straight from the start as I knew he would try to find a way to do as little work as possible. Mr. Monihan had backed a topless semi rig to the edge of the parking lot, between the garage and the diner, down an asphalt slope from the top of the hill. We created a system by which we rolled the tires across the parking lot and up a makeshift ramp that we made with scavenged two-by-eights and into the back of the trailer. This was a nice system until the top ridge of tires was gone and we had to climb down the hill and haul them back up. This was dirty, brutal work. The tires were nearly all half full with putrid water that slopped all over me. Many had to be untangled from weeds and vines and I had poison ivy the whole damn summer. By August, my forearms were all scarred up from digging at the blisters. I could hoist a tire over each shoulder and carry them to the top of the hill, although I frequently slipped in the grass and weeds we had tromped flat. Polio could only carry one tire at a time and it was a struggle for him to drag it to the top of the hill, leaving me with the lion's share of the work. I also learned that black rat snakes loved hiding in the caverns created by the spent tires. We spooked dozens of snakes, and they spooked us an equal number of times.

Mr. Monihan paid us at the end of every day. I counted the tires and reported to his office at two every afternoon when my mother was getting off work. He paid me cash and I split it with Polio. It was all done on the honor system, which seemed ludicrous to Polio. At the end of the first day on the job, he said, "Why don't you add about ten extra tires to the total every day? Not so much that he would suspect anything, but that would fetch an extra two-fifty a week for us, and he'd never know."

I poked him in the chest with an index finger and said, "We ain't cheating him because I want to keep this job, Polio, that's why. If I catch you trying to pull some shit and it costs me this job, I swear to Christ I'll break your fingers."

"I was just sayin' . . ."

"I know what you were saying, Polio, and if I catch you cheating Mr. Monihan I'll beat your ass. We clear?"

He just shrugged and muttered a weak, "yeah." It was incomprehensible to Polio that I wouldn't cheat Mr. Monihan for a few extra dimes when it would have been so easy.

I don't know what Mr. Monihan was doing with the tires. Every morning the semi would be backed up to the edge of the parking lot, empty. I assumed that another hollow somewhere in Vinton County was filling up with used truck tires, but that wasn't my concern.

In mid-July, Coach Battershell stopped by the house to find out why I hadn't been to any of the summer weightlifting sessions for the football team. He took one look at my arms and shoulders, thick and cut from hefting truck tires up the side of the hill, and said, "Never mind. Whatever you're doing, just keep it up."

One afternoon toward the end of the month, while we were riding home, Polio leaned up from the backseat and asked, "Jimmy Lee, what are you going to buy with your money?"

"I don't know. Nothing right now. I'm going to save it until there's something I need, probably."

He laughed. "No, seriously, what are you going to buy?"

"I'm saving it, Polio."

He looked at me like I had a horn growing out of my forehead. The concept of saving was foreign to Polio. The summer following the first grade, after discovering that pop bottles had a two-cent deposit, Polio and I spent the entire summer combing the banks and waters of Salt Lick Creek and the ditches along every road within walking distance for our quarry. When we each had an armful, we made the perilous quarter-mile hike down the berm of County Road 12 to Pearl's Grocery, a little country store built so close to the road that you had to check for oncoming traffic before you left the bottom step. I am sure that Mrs. Consitine tired of seeing us drag those scummy bottles to the store, but she would patiently split our reward on the counter. My money always went directly into my pocket; Polio always bought candy, soda pop, or toy balsa wood gliders.

"What are you spending your money on?" I asked.

"I'm going to buy me a motorcycle."

"You've saved enough to buy a motorcycle?"

"Uh-huh. Junior Kelso is going to sell me his old Yamaha for a hundred and fifty dollars. It needs a little work, but I'm gonna fix it up so I can ride it to school instead of taking the bus."

The Kelsos lived in a silver house trailer on Buckingham Ridge. Their front yard was always adorned with two or three used cars that Angus Kelso had for sale. He was a shyster who, despite his moaning and groaning, never got the short end of a deal. One of the rusting hulks in our front yard—a 1962 Pontiac Grand Prix—was bought from Angus. My dad cackled for three days about how he had pulled one over on Angus. Then, on the fourth day, the transmission went out. My dad and Virgil dropped the transmission and found it full of sawdust, an old mechanic's trick to make a manual transmission run smooth just long enough for the check to clear the bank. The next time Angus walked into the Double Eagle Bar, my dad smacked him in the side of the head with a Rolling Rock bottle.

His son Junior had learned at the foot of the master, so I could only imagine that the motorcycle he was offering Polio needed more than a little work, or Junior wouldn't be letting it go for one fifty. The motorcycle, I knew, would end up just another rusting lawn ornament in the Baughmans' yard, but it was useless to try to talk sense to Polio. In his mind, he was already feeling the wind in his face as he cruised to school on Junior Kelso's Yamaha.

The final tire was hauled from the bottom of the hillside the last week of July. In all, we ridded the hillside of 6,720 tires and we each made three hundred and thirty-six dollars for the summer. In my world, it was a fortune. I found a canvas bank envelope in the basement and used it as my cache. Each day, I would come home and add that day's take to the envelope, recounting every dime and writing the total on a slip of paper before hiding it in my closet behind a stack of fishing magazines.

The first week of August, I began two-a-day football practices, and Polio bought Junior Kelso's Yamaha. The second week of August, as I returned from the afternoon practice, Polio was struggling to push the Yamaha up Red Dog Road, the back tire frozen and dragging in the gravel. I stood at the bottom of our drive, my duffel bag tossed over my shoulder, and watched as black oil the consistency of honey dripped from the engine, leaving a dotted trail in the dust. "What happened?" I asked.

"What the fuck does it look like?" Polio sneered. "The piece-of-shit engine froze up."

He trudged past, straining, and I watched until he slammed it into his yard. It never moved from that spot.

Chapter Four

I became a Bull Elk that fall.

The Bull Elk Club was the physical education class at East Vinton that was the high school equivalent of boot camp. Coach Battershell was the instructor and while the other physical education classes were playing badminton or soccer, we were running two miles with thirty-pound sandbags on our shoulders, flipping tractor tires the length of a football field and back, performing forty-five minutes of nonstop calisthenics, jumping rope until our calves knotted up, running outside when it was snowing and twenty degrees, or any number of other torturous exercises designed to make us the toughest, most physically fit students in the high school. It was worth a half credit, the same as the class that played badminton, but those who successfully passed the class received a Bull Elk Club T-shirt and certificate at the end of the year. Most of the boys who signed up for the class did it as a test of their testosterone. I was comfortable with my testosterone levels, but signed up for the Bull Elk Club because it was scheduled for first period and the rigors of the class assured me that I wouldn't be bothered by the daily embarrassment I had endured in English class the previous year.

The football team started the season 2-0, and, as sad as this sounds, it was East Vinton's best start in two decades. I had been named captain of the defense by a vote of the team. It was the greatest honor of my life. The other honors I had earned had been voted on by my coaches or sportswriters who didn't know me. Being named captain, however, was a position of leadership bestowed upon me by my teammates. I wore a C on my jersey and would get a gold captain's bar for my varsity letter at the end of the season.

I was a starting outside linebacker and having a great year. I loved being on the football team. It gave me a sense of accomplishment that no one could take away from me because of my last name. After three years, I was finally accepted by the other members of the team. It was the first time in my life that I didn't feel like a total outsider. As I became more confident in my position, I began taking charge of the defense and noticed that teammates who for years had looked at me with disdain were now looking to me for leadership. Before the game against Upper Meigs High, the football boosters club hosted a spaghetti dinner for us and I overheard one of them say, "He's a Hickam, but he's a damn good football player." I had to smile. It was, I suppose, as close to a compliment as any Hickam had received in recent years.

When I was about seven, Polio Baughman and I were across the road by the mountain of red dog taunting a neighborhood mutt named Primo. When we pulled Primo's tail, he would twist his head and snap, a low, guttural growl rolling into a high-pitched bark as he lunged for the offender's hand. This was great fun until I miscalculated Primo's quickness, or teased him once too often, because a few minutes into the game he turned and sank his teeth deep into my forearm. It was my fault, but I was never comfortable around dogs after that, no matter how friendly they appeared to be. And dogs sensed my fear.

That's the way many of my teammates and their parents felt about me as a member of the football team. They thought I had made a remarkable turnaround. They liked having me on the team, but they still were uneasy around me. They didn't trust me. I was still Nick Hickam's kid, and it didn't seem that I would overcome that burden in one lifetime. Football had enabled me to earn a degree of respect, but no real friends. This was not something I found particularly upsetting, but simply reality. I was, after all, the interloper. They had been friends for years while I was an outsider. They joked with each other, but were uncomfortable joking too much around me. Perhaps they retained vivid memories of Danny Clinton sliding across the shower with blood spilling from his face. While I had earned their respect, I was still the cur that might lash out at any moment.

My eligibility for the football team had remained intact by virtue of the fact that Miss Singletary had given me a D for the final six weeks of my junior year. She allowed me to hand in extra credit and I knuckled down the last two weeks of the grading period. Two days before the end of the year, she again asked me to stay after class. Her cheeks were already glowing red when she handed me an extra credit book report I had written on *A Connecticut Yankee in King Arthur's Court* by Mark Twain and said, "I can't begin to tell you how much this aggravates me, Jimmy Lee. That's one of the best book reports I've ever read, which proves to me that you can do the work when you put your mind to it." She glared at me in a way that made my knees feel a little weak. "I ought to fail your lazy butt because you've had the potential to do well, but chose not to use it. However, against my better judgment, I'm going to pass you on to senior English. I know how important football is to you, and, believe me, that is the only reason I'm going to give you the D." She put an index finger near my nose, her brows furrowing into one continuous, knotted line across her forehead, and said, "But so help me, Jimmy Lee Hickam, this is your last break. If I don't see more effort out of you next year, I'll make you wish you were sharing a cell with your brother Edgel. Do you understand me?"

I was so relieved I had to fight off a grin. "I understand. I'll do better. You have my word."

She drew a deep breath and pointed toward the door with a thumb.

I knew little of the Alpha & Omega Literary Society or the Ohio High School Essay Competition until the second Monday of my senior year when Miss Singletary passed out flyers in class announcing the annual writing contest. The Alpha & Omega Literary Society sponsored the Vinton County competition. The best essayist at each school would be selected to compete against winners from the other schools in the county. The winner of the county competition would earn a thousand-dollar scholarship and their essay would be put on display at the Ohio State Fair the following summer.

Miss Singletary explained the rules of the competition, but not once did she make eye contact with me. She was speaking primarily to a group of girls who sat in a cluster of chairs that surrounded the teacher's desk in the front of the room. I liked Miss Singletary, but she seemed to favor the girls in our class, as if anyone with a penis was incapable of understanding English or would have no interest in the essay competition. And frankly, as a group, we did very little to disprove that theory. My football teammates were either reading magazines or whispering among themselves. I took a few notes. The competition was mandatory for Miss Singletary's senior English students and she would grade all entries for twenty percent of our grades for the six-week period. The competition would be held the following Monday morning in the school cafeteria. The topic was: A place and time that I wish I could revisit.

The words were no sooner out of her mouth when I knew the place I wanted to revisit. I had thought about it often.

I never thought writing was that difficult. Like so many aspects of my education, I never put any real effort into writing because I saw no future in it. But, despite the fact that the rest of my family seemed to shun outside intellectual stimulation, I had become a reader. In our house there was a staticky AM radio in the kitchen, no books or newspapers except for the supermarket tabloids my mother brought home from the truck stop, and rarely a television. Occasionally, Mom would buy a used black-and-white TV from the appliance store in Chillicothe or find a bargain at a flea market, but generally they didn't last long. If the tubes didn't burn out, my Dad found their screens wanting targets for beer bottles during his drunken tirades, and after a few such incidents, Mom just quit buying them.

I was not immediately drawn to reading in my first years of school. I was always relegated to the slower reading groups, not for a lack of ability, but for the fact that I refused to read aloud. I was terrified of making a mistake and subjecting myself to even more derision, so when called upon, I would shake my head and sit with my shoulders hunched forward, staring down at my desk.

The summer following my fifth-grade year, I climbed into the attic for the first time in my life. In my younger years, Edgel and Virgil had told me that human-sized bats lived there and swooped into the upstairs hallway at night in search of food, particularly tasty second graders. I peed my bed on several occasions because I was afraid to walk down the hall to the bathroom. By the time I was twelve I was relatively sure that bats didn't grow to the size of humans. Still, before entering the attic, I slowly cracked the trapdoor in the ceiling and scanned the rafters, just to be on the safe side.

It was not unlike any other attic—dark, dusty, and stifling hot. I retrieved the flashlight from my hip pocket and shined it around the attic, which was cluttered with old newspapers, a mound of clothing peppered with mouse turds, an open and empty suitcase, a broken kitchen chair, a stack of shingles, and a petrified carcass of either a rat or a squirrel. I explored for a while, looking for nothing in particular but hoping to discover some long-forgotten treasure, when I opened a cardboard box resting atop an old steamer trunk. It was full of books—the Hardy Boys, Nancy Drew, and the Bobbsey Twins—apparently left behind by the previous owners of our house.

I brushed the dust off the top book and with my flashlight began reading about the adventures of teenage detectives Frank and Joe Hardy and *The Mystery of Cabin Island*. I read until the beam of my flashlight began to fade, by which time I was two chapters into the mystery. I went outside, climbed into the crook of a low-hanging apple tree limb and read without interruption until I had finished the book in the late afternoon. There was barely enough time to get back into the attic and exchange the book for another Hardy Boys mystery before my father got home from the sawmill.

From my father's perspective, reading was just one more indication that I was an unfit Hickam male. He never once told me not to read, but there was something about the sight of me sitting with a book on my lap that rankled the old man. On one of the few occasions that he caught me reading that summer, he said, "Hey, prissy boy, got nothin' better to do but sit around with your nose in a book? Let's go outside. I'll find something for you to do." I spent the rest of the day picking up stones around the house and piling them behind the shed.

It didn't stop me. The day I discovered those books in the attic was the day I discovered freedom. I kept the cache to myself, reading the books in the solitude of my room or in the apple tree when my dad wasn't around. By the end of the summer, I had read each book twice.

The following summer, I was slinging skippers across Salt Lick Creek when an old school bus that had been painted lime green and had steel plates welded over most of the windows rolled up Red Dog Road. It stopped near our drive and the man behind the wheel motioned me over to the open door. He had a brush cut of white hair, black horn-rims, and an easy smile. Leaning forward with his arms crossed atop the steering wheel, he asked, "Do you want to get some books?"

I frowned and peeked inside. The seats had been taken out of the bus and replaced with shelves, which held hundreds of books.

"What is this thing?" I asked.

"Why, it's a bookmobile. It's a library on wheels. Haven't you ever seen one?"

I shook my head. "No, sir. Never in my life."

"Well, do you want some books?"

"I don't know," I said, unsure of the proper answer.

"Can you read?"

"Sure I can read."

"Do you have a library card?"

Again, I shook my head. I didn't. There was a library in McArthur, but I had never set foot inside. "No, sir."

"Do you want one?"

"How much does it cost?"

He held my gaze for a moment, and then I saw the familiar look of pity in his eyes. "Not a dime, son." He turned off the engine and spun sideways in his seat. "If you get a library card, I can let you borrow some books to read." He affixed a sheet of paper to a clipboard and handed it down to me. A piece of string was tied to the steel clasp on the clipboard and taped to a pen, which I used to fill out my name and address.

He nodded and filled out a blue, cardboard library card, handed it to me and said, "Okay, James L. Hickam, pick yourself out some books." I wandered up and down the aisle several times without so much as touching a book, almost paralyzed with fear of the opportunity before me. "You can take four. I'll be back about this time next week. When you bring those back, you can get four more." I looked, but didn't touch, and couldn't make a decision. "What are you interested in?"

I shrugged. "I don't know."

"You're not much for talkin', are you James L. Hickam?" He walked back and pulled a book with a red cover from the shelf. "Do you like pirates?"

"Sure." Polio and I played pirates in the big oak tree across the creek.

"*Treasure Island*," he said, handing me the book. "There are lots of pirates in that one. Here's *Peter Pan,* there's a nasty bit of a pirate in that one, too." He pulled out two other books, the titles of which have since escaped my memory. I thanked the old man and scampered back up the hill.

We walk through many doors in our lifetime. It is the accumulation of these seemingly minor passages that shape our lives. Most often, it is years after we pass over a threshold before we realize the significance of the moment.

That was not the case with the books I read that summer. I remember distinctly sitting in the crook of the apple tree and realizing the impact they were having on my life. It was as though a seal around my brain had been broken and my imagination was finally free to roam. I enjoyed the Hardy Boys and Nancy Drew, but the books I read from the bookmobile enabled me to create in my mind's eye a world beyond Red Dog Road. I began traveling the world and beyond with Mark Twain, Jules Verne, Jack London, Stephen Crane, Arthur Conan Doyle, and Herman Melville. Our high school had a library and I checked out books regularly, often forsaking my texts and schoolwork for the fiction of John Steinbeck or Ernest Hemingway.

I did not associate reading with education. I associated it with escape, if only temporarily, from the dust and despair of Red Dog Road. Over the years, I envisioned worlds beyond the one in which I lived, though my imagination was not great enough to fathom an escape.

I certainly had no intention of winning the essay contest. I was sure that some of the smarter girls with their flowery prose and excessive use of adjectives would win. That was fine. I didn't make the decision to put effort into the essay because I thought I had a chance to win the competition. That wasn't the least bit important to me. Rather, it was important that I demonstrate to Miss Singletary that she had made the right move by allowing me to advance to senior English.

After dinner that night, I went out back to the shed where Edgel's Rocket 88 rested under a tarp covered with dust and pigeon droppings. The last of the evening sun had disappeared beyond the mountain of red dog, but the stark boards of the shed radiated the heat of the afternoon. I squatted down on a cement block and leaned against the shed, closing my eyes to the last of the orange rays. My mind's eye took over and slowly, I began to focus on a time and place years past. At first, I was surrounded in a muted gray fog. Then, like a gentle breeze forming up behind me, the fog began to part and I could see the water. It was greenish-brown and still, and then the tip of the canoe cut through the river, pushing a tiny wake toward the shore. At the helm of the tiny outboard that was clamped to the side of the canoe was a young boy in a faded, hand-me-down T-shirt and dirty canvas sneakers with holes in the toes. There was a red cooler, sandwiches, bass in the snags, and a pie-faced man with sunburned cheeks and an affable grin. The images continued to grow. There were footfalls in the shoals and the eruption of the sandy bottom where crayfish darted as the craft scraped on its way to deep water. Snappers sunned themselves on outcroppings and dragonflies danced inches above the water's surface, taunting the bass below.

Occasionally, I would open my eyes a sliver to jot down ideas in my notebook, small phrases that I wanted to retain. For the next week, I kept the notebook in hand, recording ideas as they crossed my mind. As the story began to take shape, I found it difficult not to think about the essay. By the following Monday, the day of the competition, I had practically memorized all that I wanted to write.

As we entered the cafeteria, we were each handed a blue notebook into which we would record our essay. A round little woman from the Alpha & Omega Literary Society explained that the completed essays would be sent to the English Department at Ohio University for judging. The judges would select the top three essays.

A portable chalkboard was dragged to one end of the cafeteria where Miss Singletary wrote, "A Place and Time That I Wish I Could Revisit."

Miss Singletary said, "No talking. There are to be no other papers on your table. Spelling counts, but you may use your dictionary. You have until the end of third period to complete your essay. You may begin."

Chapter Five

I had not openly expressed affection for a girl since the Rebecca McGonagle debacle in the fifth grade. Or, as I referred to it in later years, the St. Valentine's Day Massacre. After that particular incident, girls were off-limits to me as a possible repeat of that humiliation was more than I could bear.

Rebecca McGonagle had a cute, round face, a slight overbite, and wore her hair in an auburn braid that swung like the rhythmic movement on a grandfather clock when she walked. Her voice was soft and lilting, and she spoke as though she were always short of breath. Rebecca's desk in Mrs. McKinstry's fifth-grade class was diagonally in front of me, so I could catch glimpses of her without fear of being caught. I would often daydream that we were married and living in the shed out back of the house, which I had, with my own hands, converted into a dream home where we ate popcorn, drank sodas, and cuddled under a quilt while watching television.

I was so enamored with Rebecca that I made her a special Valentine's Day card out of construction paper, a paper doily that I found in a buffet drawer, and a candy heart that had I LOVE YOU printed on it. I folded a piece of red construction paper in half, pasted the doily to the front of the card, added a heart of pink construction paper, and then pasted the candy heart in the middle of the one made of paper. Inside I wrote:

Dear Rebecca:

I like you. A lot. Will you be my girlfriend?

Signed,

Jimmy Lee Hickam.

The card was too big for any of the envelopes we had around the house so I used red foil Christmas wrapping paper to make a special envelope. At our class Valentine's Day party, I watched as Rebecca emptied her Valentines on her desk. Mixed in with the small, store-bought Valentines was my oversized envelope. I struggled to keep a smile from consuming my face as I watched her separate my envelope from the also-rans. She shook her head and shrugged as the girls around her desk asked who it was from and urged her to open the envelope.

She smiled as she gently pried open the foil while the other girls gathered around. When she opened the card and the others saw it was signed, "Jimmy Lee Hickam," they sang like a perfect chorus, "eeeew," then began laughing. They sang:

Rebecca and Jimmy, sitting in a tree, K-I-S-S-I-N-G;

First comes love, then comes marriage, and then comes Rebecca with a baby carriage.

As the girls continued to laugh, Rebecca burst into tears and ran from the room. Mrs. McKinstry sent two of the girls to the restroom to check on Rebecca and then inspected the card. She stared hard at me and sneered, "You shouldn't embarrass people like that, Mr. Hickam."

I had never meant for anyone but Rebecca to see the card, but it got passed around the room so that everyone had a chance to laugh at Jimmy Lee. They were unmerciful in their teasing of Rebecca and I felt bad for having put her through the ordeal. Subsequently, I stopped daydreaming of the two of us living happily together and eating popcorn in the shed.

After that day, I did not give girls much consideration. The change in this policy was initiated two weeks into my senior year when, as we were walking off the football field after practice, Hugh Figurski asked me if I was going to the homecoming dance. "Probably not," I said.

He frowned. "Why not? It's your senior year. You have to go to the dance."

To that point, I hadn't given it a second's thought. Social events had never been part of my life. It was bad enough getting shunned at school. The last thing I wanted to do was provide an additional venue for abuse. But since I was the captain and one of the stars of the football team, I convinced myself that that would make me more appealing.

I had decided to ask Ruth Ann Shellabarger to the homecoming dance. Ruth Ann was a sweet girl with a cute bob haircut and big brown eyes. She smiled a lot, seemed to laugh easily, and said hi when we passed in the hall. She wasn't part of the snobby clique of Lindsey Morgan, Abigail Winsetter, and Rebecca McGonagle, so I thought I had a legitimate shot.

On the Monday before the dance, the entire school had gathered in the auditorium for the announcement of the Alpha & Omega awards. I was seated in the middle of the auditorium; Ruth Ann was sitting two rows down and to my right, unaware that she was the object of my intentions. I stared at her, making sure I averted my eyes when she turned her head to talk to Melinda Jameson.

As my mind focused on the loveliness that was Ruth Ann Shellabarger, Ernestine Wadell, the president of the Vinton County Chapter of the Alpha & Omega Literary Society, was introduced by Principal Speer. Mrs. Wadell was a little butterball of a woman who wore bright orange makeup that stained the lapels of her blouse. She was up on her tiptoes to see over the lectern as she began a painful history of the Alpha & Omega Literary Society.

I wonder if I can summon up the courage to ask Ruth Ann to the dance? What if she says no? That's a definite possibility, but I won't know unless I ask her.

"Winning third place in the Alpha & Omega essay contest at East Vinton High School is Ida Mae Belair." Ida Mae was a classmate of mine, though I hadn't heard her say two words the entire time we had been in school together. She was gangly with blackheads peppering her cheeks and heavy glasses that sat unevenly across her nose. She wore dresses without belts and ankle socks. Ida Mae walked across the stage to accept her bronze medal, and walked back to her seat without once smiling or lifting her head.

If I ask Ruth Ann to the dance while I'm at school, I risk a repeat of the St. Valentine's Day Massacre. Maybe I'll call her at home. Yeah, that's what I'll do. That way, if she says no it will be less humiliating because I will be able to quickly hang up. Then I will pray to Jesus and all the known saints that she doesn't tell anyone that I asked.

Mrs. Wadell said, "Our second-place winner is Catherine Johanessen." She was a senior and destined to be the class valedictorian. She also was the daughter of the freshman and sophomore English and literature teacher. Second place apparently wasn't to Catherine's liking because she frowned all the way to the stage and back.

If she says yes, how will I get her to the dance? Crap. Dad's car looks like a rolling landfill, it's covered with rust, smells like stale beer, and needs a new muffler. I'd be embarrassed to show up in that.

"This year's first-place winner of the Alpha & Omega Essay Contest wrote a simply marvelous memoir."

Maybe I can get Lenny Ianarino to double-date with me. He's taking Truddie Walkup to the dance. I'll bet he'll let me double up with him. Of course, you have got to ask Ruth Ann first, chickenshit.

"The judges from Ohio University said this was one of the finest essays they had ever seen submitted."

Christ Almighty, I don't even know how to dance. That's a problem. God, what if I start to dance with her and get a hard-on?

"One judge wrote of this essay, 'This writing displays a maturity and depth seldom seen in a high school student.'"

I've got money saved. I could afford to take her to dinner up in Chillicothe and buy one of those mums that people always have on their coats at homecoming. That would be a nice touch. Yes, a mum, I definitely will have to buy one of those.

"It gives me great pleasure to present the gold medal to this year's winner of the Alpha & Omega Literary Society essay contest . . ."

I'll still be nervous, even on the phone. What if I get all tongue-tied and I can't talk? Oh, that would be great. I'll write myself out a script. That's it. I'll have it all written out in front of me and I'll practice before I call.

"Mr. James L. Hickam."

I'll do it, by God. I'll summon up the nerve and call Ruth Ann Shellabarger and ask her to the homecoming dance.

It became apparent that the auditorium had gone silent, like a church during the stretch of time when the preacher says, "let us pray," and the actual prayer begins. I'm certain that I heard my name, but it seemed so out of context that it didn't register. However, as I looked around, trying to process the events of the past few seconds, I noticed that everyone was staring at me. It was not unlike having the teacher call on you in the middle of a daydream. After several seconds, Kip Fillinger, our offensive center, smacked me on the back and said, "That's you, numb nuts."

I jerked upright and after a few more seconds stood to slide my way to the aisle and walk to the stage. There was a smattering of applause and a few audible gasps, and a female voice—I think it was Catherine Johanessen, but I never found out for sure—said, "I absolutely *cannot* believe this." Miss Singletary was the lone teacher to stand, and she applauded with great enthusiasm. The principal and the other teachers stared in slack-jawed amazement. Members of the football team began pounding on the armrests and chanting, "Jim-my Lee. Jim-my Lee. Jim-my Lee."

Mrs. Wadell draped the gold medal over my head, shook my hand, then put her arm around my waist and pulled me closer to the lectern. "As is tradition, the winner will read the winning essay."

I pulled back a step, "Ma'am?"

"You have to read your essay, Mr. Hickam." She handed me my blue notebook. "You should be very proud to do so. It is very good."

My heart was about to beat out of my chest. I can't recall ever being as nervous as when I stepped up to begin reading. Principal Speer stood and stared down the football players until they quieted and settled back in their seats. I flattened out the first page of the notebook, cleared my throat a few times, and began.

I would like to revisit a muddy stretch of the Scioto River where the oak trees bend in from the banks and meld together high over the water, and the river's surface is dappled with thin shafts of sunlight that somehow penetrate the dense canopy. Bass leap where fallen trees crowd the shallows, snappers sun themselves on the exposed rocks, and the air is heavy with the stagnant scent of slow-moving water.

When I last visited this place, I was only nine years old and yet, the soft, slow voice of my Uncle Boots remains clear in my mind.

"Are you sure you can handle that, padnah?" he asked as I struggled with my end of the canoe.

"Uh-huh," I strained.

With one of his thick hands, he grabbed his end and tried to conceal a grin as he watched me strain to hold my end as I backed toward the river. "Set 'er down right at the edge of the water."

We unloaded his pickup truck in the shadow of Mount Logan, along a wide bend in the Scioto River south of Chillicothe. To that point, it was the biggest day of my life. I had never been on a boat of any kind. I had been fishing a few times with my dad and brothers, but those were usually beer-shortened events that ended with my dad cursing at the fish and the river and his tackle box, and we always went home without a catch. Uncle Boots was my mom's brother-in-law. He was a soft-spoken, pie-faced North Carolinian who had that summer retired after twenty years in the U.S. Army. His real name was Beaumont, and he and my Aunt Stephanie had moved back to Ohio so Uncle Boots could take over the family farm in Scioto County. He had grown up fishing the rivers and streams of North Carolina and had moved north with his canoe, which had a small outboard motor rigged to the side. When he stopped by the house the night before to ask if I wanted to go fishing, I couldn't believe my luck.

Once he had unloaded the fishing tackle and his cooler, he instructed me to get into the canoe. He put one foot in the canoe, the other on the bank, and gave us a quick push. We scraped bottom, then headed toward the middle of the river. It was the most incredible sensation to be gliding over the water, the tiny waves slapping at the side of the canoe. I held tight to the sides, mesmerized by the passing water.

With one quick pull of the starter cord, he fired up the outboard motor. He adjusted the idle, then looked at me and asked, "Want to drive 'er?"

Oh, how I wanted to drive, but I was paralyzed with fear. "No," I said. He frowned. "Why not?"

"I don't know how."

"It ain't rocket science." He reached out for my hand and guided me to the seat next to the motor. "Grab the handle. You twist that to give it gas. You turn the handle the opposite way you want the canoe to go. Think you can handle it?" I gave him a little frown, and he laughed. "Okay, padnah, it's all yours. Keep it in the middle of the river and stay away from the snags."

Slowly, I twisted the throttle and the canoe seemed to lurch out of the water. I made a big circle in the river and we headed upstream. I couldn't stop smiling. It was the most grown-up thing I had ever done in my life. Uncle Boots watched for a few minutes until he was sure I had it under control, then he began arranging the fishing poles. After a while, he winked and said, "You're doing a fine job there, padnah."

Two miles upstream he pointed to the little kill switch and said, "Hold that down a second." I did and the river became eerily quiet. "We're going to drift fish," he said. "We'll cast toward the snags where the bass are hiding. That sound good to you?"

"Sure."

He reached into the bait bucket and produced a minnow. "Watch close," he said. "If you're going to fish, you've got to bait your own hook." He held up the hook. "You see the barb on the end of this hook? If you get that caught in your finger, the fishing's over because I'll have to take you to the emergency room so they can cut it out. That sound like fun?"

"No, it doesn't."

"Good, because it isn't." He winked. "Trust me." He held the minnow between his index finger and thumb and slickly slipped the hook under its chin and through both lips. "You see how I did that?" he asked. I nodded. "You hook them through the lips so they try to swim off the hook and attract the bass."

He showed me how to cast and we began to fish, slowly drifting back down the Scioto River. Uncle Boots occasionally took a paddle and gave a couple of strokes to keep us on track. "Check your bait," he said after a while. It was gone. "Get you a new minnow and hook 'er up."

I fished the bait bucket with my fingers until I trapped my unfortunate lure. As I tried to maneuver it between my fingers, it wiggled and I instinctively released my grip. The sliver of silver hit the bottom of the canoe and flopped around on the hot aluminum.

I could feel the look of panic consuming my face and I found it difficult to keep my lower lip from quivering. It was the kind of youthful infraction that would have sent my dad into a screaming rage. As I waited for Uncle Boots to explode in anger, he calmly reached down, scooped up the minnow and put it back in my hand. "Try it again," he said calmly.

We had a wonderful time. We talked in whispers, drank Coca-Colas, ate ham salad sandwiches and potato chips that my Aunt Stephanie had packed, and got sunburned. After we had been on the river a few hours without a bite,

Uncle Boots handed me his pole and said, "Here, you try my pole. Maybe that'll change our luck."

No sooner had he handed me the pole than I felt a violent tug. "I've got one."

Maybe he'd already caught the bass and set the hook before he handed me the pole, but the next few moments replaced driving the canoe as the biggest thrill of my life. I reeled the largemouth bass close to the canoe and he netted it.

"You caught a monster."

It was nineteen inches long and weighed better than four pounds. We caught a few smaller fish before calling it a day, and I was their guest for a fish fry dinner that night. Before we cleaned the fish, Aunt Stephanie took a photo of Uncle Boots and me with my trophy.

As I look back, it was perhaps the best day of my life. I had a great day with a man I admired. He seemed to enjoy being out on the river with me, teaching me to fish and talking to me as though I was significant. For the first time in my life, I realized that a man doesn't need to yell to be heard. A man doesn't have to throw a punch to make a point. And a man who is comfortable in his own skin doesn't need to constantly prove his worth to the world.

We went fishing four more times that summer. Each time he let me steer the canoe upstream. We caught bass, joked, and ate ham salad sandwiches from the cooler.

Uncle Boots died the following spring. He was tilling a hillside stretch of their farm when the tractor rolled over and he was crushed.

Aunt Stephanie had the photo of the two of us and my bass framed; it's on the wall beside my bed. I think of Uncle Boots often and wish the two of us could have one more sunny Saturday together, sipping Coca-Colas and drift fishing down the Scioto.

Chapter Six

When I got home that night, my brother Edgel was drunk and slouched in a chair at the kitchen table.

As I had trudged up the rutted drive from Red Dog Road after football practice, I knew something was going on. Halfway up the drive, I could hear men laughing in our kitchen. This was peculiar as humor was not commonplace in the home of Nick Hickam. As I climbed the steps to the back porch, the heat and smells of the kitchen wafted out the back door, a twisted aroma of cooking meat, biscuits, and cigarette smoke.

Through the screen door, I could see the Farnsworth twins—a pair of hard-working, hard-drinking boys who ran the auto salvage yard on Taylor-Blair Road—sitting at the table on either side of my dad. Mark had no teeth, the result of poor hygiene and too many bar fights, and his lips surrounded the lip of a beer bottle like a baby nursing at its mother's breast. Luke had his teeth, but the scarred face of a lost battle with acne. He was a terrible stutterer and didn't say much. They had killed a case of beer and dozens of cigarette butts had been drowned in the spittle and flat Pabst Blue Ribbon in the bottom of the bottles that covered the kitchen table.

Edgel heard me coming up the back steps and as I reached for the doorknob he said, "Here comes the football star." He was seated at the head of the table, a lopsided, alcohol-induced grin on his face and a cigarette dangling from the middle of his pouty lips. He was wearing blue jeans and a gray, pullover sweatshirt, which fit him much better than the saggy prison garb I was used to seeing him wear. "Hey there, little brother, help yourself to a Pabst."

"He can't have any beer," my mother chimed in. "He's too young and besides, the coach don't allow that."

"One beer isn't going to kill him," Edgel slurred.

"When'd you get home Edgel?" I asked, anxious to change the subject.

He stood up and shook my hand, hugging me tight with his left. "They cut me loose this mornin'. Can you believe that shit?"

My dad seemed more sullen than the others and just sat between the twins, drinking from a bottle.

"He called me at seven o'clock at the truck stop," my mom said. "He said to come and get him, and he'd be standing out front of the prison. I drove up there as fast as I could and sure enough, there he was, sitting on the front steps with his duffel bag."

Edgel looked at me and shrugged. "They got my ass up at five o'clock this morning and told me my time was up and they were letting me go. I think they've run out of room and I was next on the list to be released, so they busted me out a little earlier than expected. Ain't that the shits? I said that was fine with me. The quicker I could get my ass out of there, the better." He snorted into his half-empty beer bottle, creating a humming sound like a riverboat horn. I pulled out a chair next to Edgel and sat down. He reached out and patted me twice on my shoulder. "Damn, my little brother ain't so little any more, is he?"

"Y-y-you should see him p-play f-f-football," Luke said. "H-h-he can knock a g-guy's d-d-dick off."

Edgel nodded. "That a fact?"

I shrugged. "I'm having a pretty good year."

Mom set a plate of ham, boiled potatoes and green beans, and biscuits in front of Edgel. He pushed it toward me. "Let's feed the football player first. He's the one workin' up an appetite. I want to see you play Friday night. Who do you play?"

"Clearcreek Local."

"Look out! Them Clearcreek Local boys are always tough."

"We'll take 'em."

"Atta boy."

Mom took the plate and slid it back in front of Edgel. "You eat that. This is your special dinner for your special day."

"Is that what it takes to get my special dinner—nine years in the joint?"

He snorted a laugh and mom slapped him on the shoulder with the serving spoon. "Hush up and eat."

Edgel sank a fork into a boiled potato and popped the entire, steaming orb into his mouth. As my mother dished out plates of food for the Farnsworth brothers and my dad, I wrapped my hands around the gold medal that was in the pocket of my varsity jacket. She handed me a plate, then fixed one for herself and, after hugging Edgel around the neck and kissing him on top of the head, sat down to his right. I said, "They had this contest at school, an essay contest, and you had to write a paper on a place and time you'd like to visit again." I pulled the medal from my pocket and held it by the lanyard so my mom could see. "And I won first prize out of the entire high school."

"Oh, that is so nice, Jimmy Lee." She turned her head back to Edgel and said, "Are you getting enough, sweetheart? You're so skinny. You need to eat."

My dad had barely looked my way. I slid the medal back into my pocket and started cutting my ham. Edgel slapped at my elbow and wiggled his fingers, indicating he wanted to see the medal. "Lemme see that, junior," he said, a little slur to his words. I retrieved it from the pocket and dropped it into his hand. He frowned as he read the engraved back of the medal. Alpha & Omega Literary Society Essay Contest. First Place. East Vinton High School. James L. Hickam. He looked up at me and said, "Damn, boy, that's fine. You got this for writin'?"

I nodded. "An essay."

"Well, hot damn, that's gotta be the first time in history that a Hickam's ever won an award for writin'." The Farnsworth twins laughed. "And this is first place out of the whole school?" I nodded. He continued to inspect the medal, rubbing a thumb over the gold quill and inkwell relief on the front. "What did you write about?"

"It was about the time Uncle Boots took me fishing in his canoe."

"Where is it? I want to read it."

"Uh, it's still at school. Miss Singletary is grading it for class. I should get it back in a week or so." When I wrote the essay, I had no idea that I would end up reading it in front of the entire school and I had stumbled over the reference to my dad and brothers' drinking and my dad's fits of anger. I would have to rewrite the essay and change those passages before I brought it home.

"Don't forget," Edgel said, pointing at me with his fork. "I want to read that."

"I won't." I thought it odd that my ill-educated, semiliterate brother, who hadn't made it through the tenth grade, actually wanted to read the essay while neither parent expressed any such interest.

"That Miss Singletary you talked about, is that Amanda Singletary?"

"Uh-huh. She said she went to school with you."

"She did. She's as smart as they come, too. You stay close to her. She's solid; she'll do right by you." He looked up and frowned. "Is that other English teacher still there, Gloria Johanessen?"

"Yeah. She teaches ninth- and tenth-grade English. She doesn't like me very much."

Edgel's brows arched. "She was a piece of work, that one. I don't think she cares much for me, either."

Given Edgel's checkered history at East Vinton High School, that didn't surprise me.

After admiring the medal for several minutes, rubbing the surface with the tip of his thumb, Edgel set it on the edge of the table between us and neatly arranged the ribbon under the medal. He tapped the thick nail of his index finger on the table next to the medal and said, "Jimmy Lee, this is important." He used the same digit to point at the varsity letter on my jacket. "That right there, your football award, that's nice, but it ain't important. Okay? But this . . ." He pointed back to the medal. ". . . this is important." He picked up the medal and dangled it six inches in front of my face. "It's important, because it's a ticket. You understand?"

I did. Perfectly.

"A ticket to where?" Dad snorted from the far end of the table.

"A ticket off Red Dog Road," Edgel said.

The Farnsworth brothers extended their arms, toasting me with their Pabst Blue Ribbons, and Luke said, "H-h-hear, hear."

Chapter Seven

Most of the teachers at East Vinton High School thought Miss Singletary had a big chip on her shoulder. As a student at the school, she was quiet and reserved. When she returned to her alma mater as an English teacher, her colleagues and the administration expected her to be the same Amanda Singletary who had spent her free time in the library and was president of the Future Homemakers of America.

Much to their surprise, and in some cases, dismay, a totally different Amanda Singletary emerged from college. The mousy girl who dutifully obeyed all authority figures had turned into an outspoken, opinionated hellcat. Most annoying to her employer was the vociferousness of her belief that the East Vinton Local School District did a poor job of preparing its students for college and a life outside of Vinton County. The school district, she contended, expected too little of its students and set the bar for graduation far too low.

The caste system still lived in the hills of Vinton County. With few exceptions, we understood our predetermined lot in life. If you dared to dream, you dreamt in silence, keeping those fantasies to yourself, lest they die upon the derisive laughter of classmates. There were those few of whom you believed success was a certainty. No one doubted that Roy Otto, our handsome class president, the quarterback, straight-A student, and the lead in the senior musical, *Li'l Abner,* would graduate from college and someday make a million dollars in business. Or that Lindsey Morgan, by virtue of her beauty and money, would someday dance onstage in New York in front of thousands of people. To those select few, success seemed plausible. But those dreams were beyond most of us.

We lived in a community where for years the girls graduated, got married, and got pregnant. The boys, whether or not they bothered to finish school, went to work in the coal mines, timber operations, or paper mills.

The East Vinton Local School District was formed in 1946 with the consolidation of four small, extremely poor school districts— Brown Township, Moonville Local, Wilkesville Village, and Zaleski Village. Together they created East Vinton, a slightly larger, but still extremely poor school district. The former Moonville Local School, a two-story, coal-heated building built in 1903, became East Vinton High School. It was not pretty or sleek, but it was solid, built from sorrel-colored bricks fired on the property. Millions of footfalls had worn trough-like grooves in the gray and white marble steps leading to the two front doors, which were ten feet tall and so heavy that skinny girls needed both hands and a foot brace to pull them open. Students referred to the school as "the sweatshop" because it had no air conditioning, making the late spring and early fall days stifling, and the custodians never managed to regulate the heat pouring out of the coal furnace, causing teachers to open windows in the dead of winter. A few years after the school opened, a new gymnasium and a wing to house the wood and auto body shops were added to the original structure, and the people of eastern Vinton County were content. Education was not seen as a transport to greater opportunities. Rather, it was something endured to meet the requirements of a state mandate. Graduating from East Vinton High School could be assured simply by showing up on a regular basis.

But Miss Singletary wasn't satisfied. At a Parent-Teacher Association meeting her second year at the school, Miss Singletary addressed the crowd and said the school district was doing a poor job of preparing students to meet the challenges of life after graduation. She said, "Parents, you must demand more of the teachers. And teachers, you must demand more of our students. Otherwise, how can we expect them to achieve at their highest levels? The coal mines are closing, we have only a handful of timber mills in operation, and the paper mills are moving to the south. If we don't get these children ready to meet the challenges of the real world, and that means preparing them for college, we are failing them."

Forest Brubaker, the industrial arts and auto body teacher at the school, stood and said, "Miss Singletary, I think your heart is in the right place, but most East Vinton students are not college material. When you suggest that we need to prepare them for college, you're just setting them up for failure."

Red blotches broke out all over Miss Singletary's neck, which her students recognized as Mount Singletary getting ready to blow. "Mr. Brubaker, you should have your teaching certificate revoked for making such an asinine statement," she said to the auditorium full of teachers and parents. "We must demand more, or these kids will all end up in Vinton County, living on welfare."

It was not a popular stance and she had the entire community in an uproar. The *Vinton County Messenger* got wind of her speech and followed up with an article, which brought the school board members and the superintendent to a boil, but she never backed down. She had done her homework and had statistics showing East Vinton's poor drop-out rate and a history of poor performance on the state's standardized tests. For those who did graduate, a ridiculously low percentage went on to college or technical school.

Her English and literature classes were the most difficult in the school. She constantly preached to us the need to strive for excellence. "You are capable of achieving much more than you realize," she was fond of saying. "Geographical location needn't be an impediment to success. Show me that you want to achieve. Prove to me that you want to succeed, and I will walk with you every step of the way."

She was a powerful ally.

"Jimmy Lee, Principal Speer wants to see you in his office right away." Abbie Winsetter was wearing a green jumper and a smug grin when she delivered the summons. The Bull Elk Club had just finished fifty minutes of running and calisthenics; I had sweated through my T-shirt and drops of perspiration were falling in rapid succession from the tip of my nose, forming a small pool on the gym floor. "All right," I said.

"He said right now."

"I heard you, Abbie. I'll be there in a minute."

She stood there for a long moment, squinting and looking as though she had gotten a whiff of something unpleasant, then spun on her heel and left.

Principal Speer had not congratulated me after I had won the Alpha & Omega essay contest the previous day and I tried to convince myself that was the reason for the summons. Perhaps he was going to slap me on the back and give me an "Atta boy, Jimmy Lee, you've made us proud." Of course, I knew better. My name had been Jimmy Lee Hickam long enough to know that a call to the principal's office was never good news.

I swapped out of my gym clothes and, still perspiring, reported to the office. Mrs. Green, the school secretary, opened the door to Principal Speer's office and poked her head inside. This was followed by a few seconds of inaudible conversation, and then she pushed open the door for me to enter. Principal Speer was seated at the end of a mahogany conference table that was gouged and dull with wear. Mrs. Gloria Johanessen, the freshman-sophomore English teacher, and Ernestine Wadell of the Alpha & Omega Literary Society were seated to his right, neither of them making eye contact with me.

"Sit down, Jimmy Lee," Principal Speer said, nodding toward an empty chair to his left, and giving not the first indication that I was there to be congratulated. On the corner of the table near his left hand was the blue notebook that contained my essay. With great deliberateness, he picked up the notebook and held it in front of me like a prosecutor displaying a murder weapon to the jury. "We want to talk to you about your essay."

"Yes, sir. What about it?"

"We have some concerns."

I shrugged. "What kind of concerns?"

He nodded toward Mrs. Johanessen, who passed a manila folder to him. He pulled out a packet of stapled papers that I assumed were my transcripts. "It seems that you barely passed junior English—two C's, two D's, and two F's." He looked at me as if waiting for an explanation.

"Yes, sir," I said, not offering any detail.

"And yet, you created this essay for the contest that is nearly flawless in its grammar and tells a very compelling story." It wasn't a question, so I didn't respond. "Who wrote this?"

"I did."

"Did you have help?"

"Help? What kind of help?"

Mrs. Johanessen asked, "Did someone else write it before the contest so that you could just recopy it?"

Prickly chills ran up my spine and spread into my rib cage. "No."

A faint grin pursed her lips. "You're perspiring a great deal, Jimmy Lee. Are you nervous?"

"No. I just came from gym class."

My answer wasn't important. It was the question she wanted Principal Speer and Mrs. Wadell to remember. *You see he's sweating, don't you? Liars always sweat when they get caught. Look at him. Look at the perspiration streak down his face.* She folded her hands in front of her on the table and said, "Well, Jimmy Lee, doesn't it strike you as a bit odd that someone who could barely pass his junior English class suddenly wins the school's biggest writing contest?"

"Are you accusing me of cheating, Mrs. Johanessen?"

"We just want to know if you had help. That's all."

"Uh-huh, that would be called cheating, wouldn't it? You're accusing me of cheating."

Mrs. Wadell cleared her throat and said, "Mr. Hickam, we just want to make sure that your essay was completely your own. This is a marvelous essay, but it is imperative that it be original work. That is clearly stated in the rules of the competition."

Anger was replacing the timidity with which I had entered the room. I pointed at the booklet and said, "Mrs. Wadell, that is my work. No one else helped me, not one bit."

"Jimmy Lee, are you sure you want to go through with this?" Mrs. Johanessen asked. "The county essay competition is a lot of pressure."

"Pressure doesn't bother me, Mrs. Johanessen. The only thing that bothers me is people thinking I cheated or that I'm not good enough to represent their school just because my last name is Hickam."

"That's not what we meant, Mr. Hickam," Mrs. Wadell said apologetically.

"Maybe that's not what you meant, ma'am, but that's exactly what they meant. Believe me, I've been a Hickam long enough to know what's going on here. Mrs. Johanessen's upset because I won the contest and her daughter won't get to compete in the county competition."

I knew I had stepped over the line with that comment. Mrs. Johanessen said nothing; she just peered at me with a hateful look. When she was angry, Mrs. Johanessen had a habit of squinting her left eye, like a hunter taking bead on a quarry, and her lips drew up in a pucker. At that moment, she was at full squint and pucker. Mrs. Wadell now had beads of sweat appearing on her upper lip and a tiny rivulet rolling down the side of her orange face. After a moment of uncomfortable silence, Principal Speer said, "Given your history of poor performance in the classroom, Jimmy Lee, I'm afraid that in order for you to compete in the county competition you're going to have to prove that this essay is your original work."

"How am I supposed to do that?"

"Before you arrived we agreed that you would have to write a second essay under the observation of Mrs. Johanessen and Mrs. Wadell. If you create an essay of equal quality, we'll accept this as your original work."

"So, you've already decided that I cheated."

"We're just trying to be fair," he said.

"No, you're not. You're just trying take away my award. You would never ask one of the girls to rewrite their essays."

"Both of the other girls passed freshman, sophomore, and junior English with near perfect scores," Mrs. Johanessen said, the faint grin returning to her lips. She produced another blue notebook from the stack of papers in her lap and slid it across the table to me.

Principal Speer said, "We believe this is the only way we can be fair to everyone who ..."

Outside of some out-of-shape linemen struggling through summer conditioning drills, I have never in my life seen a face the shade of maroon as that of Miss Amanda Singletary when at that moment she barged into Principal Speer's office. She pushed the door with the flat of her hand and I thought it was going to come off its hinges. The warning–light red blotches scarred her neck and the muscles reaching down into her clavicle strained like bridge cables. She asked, "What is this all about?" She looked at the adults, leaning forward like a dog at the end of its leash, her knuckles digging into the mahogany table; Mrs. Johanessen and Mrs. Wadell looked at Principal Speer. Mrs. Wadell was now perspiring worse than me.

Before he could speak, I said, "They think I cheated on my essay, and Mr. Speer said I have to write another one before they'll let me compete in the county competition."

Miss Singletary's fisted hands went to her hips and she said, "Absolutely you will not. And, since I oversee the competition, why wasn't I consulted on this?" No one answered. I could see the muscles in Miss Singletary's jaw working beneath the skin. She stared hard at Mrs. Johanessen and said, "Of all the . . ." She stopped, took a breath, and put her hand on my shoulder. "Wait for me out in the attendance office, Jimmy Lee."

I scraped my books off the table and went to the attendance office just outside of the principal's office. It was a futile attempt to shield me from the ensuing conversation; I could hear every word through the closed door. Miss Singletary said, "Mrs. Johanessen, I am outraged that you would attempt to pull a shameless stunt like this. And Mr. Speer, I'm even more outraged that you would sanction it!"

"Miss Singletary, I would strongly suggest that you not forget that I am the principal of this school."

"Then I would strongly suggest that you start acting like it. I am the teacher in charge of this competition, and I will not have my authority or the integrity of the papers submitted called into question."

"This is a very important competition with scholarship money at stake," Mrs. Johanessen said. "We believe that the school might be better represented if . . ."

"If what? If we were represented by someone whose last name isn't Hickam? Let's see, if Jimmy Lee doesn't go, then East Vinton's representative would be the runner-up. Who was that? Oh wait, now I remember, it was your daughter, wasn't it, Mrs. Johanessen?"

Mrs. Wadell attempted to speak, but was cut off by Principal Speer, who said, "We just think it might be better for everyone concerned if someone more appropriate represented our school."

"More appropriate? Did you just say, 'more appropriate?' Of all the unmitigated gall. I don't give a damn what that boy looks like or what his last name is. Jimmy Lee Hickam won that contest, and he won it fair and square."

"I seriously doubt that," Mrs. Johanessen sniffed.

"Do you have proof that he cheated?"

"I have his transcripts from his previous English class and . . ."

"That's not what I asked you."

"No, I don't have *proof*. I don't think proof is required. All one needs to see that Jimmy Lee didn't write this is a little common sense." A faint smile creased Mrs. Johanessen's lips.

There was a moment of silence before Miss Singletary continued, "You better wipe that smirk off your face before I help you."

I wanted to stand up and cheer.

"That will be enough of that kind of talk, Miss Singletary," Principal Speer said.

Mrs. Johanessen said, "His grades were abominable in my freshman and sophomore classes, and I know he struggled last year. In fact, it would appear that his passage to senior English was probably a gift. Then, miraculously, he wins the essay contest with a nearly flawless paper. Does that make any sense to you?"

"A lot of students entering my junior English class struggle, but rather than write them off as idiots, I'm more inclined to believe it was a lack of preparation during their freshman and sophomore years."

The gloves were off. Miss Singletary had lunged for the jugular.

"Again, we don't need this kind of talk," Principal Speer said. "Simply, we're here to discuss the validity of Jimmy Lee's paper and whether he should be the one to represent East Vinton in the county competition."

"Obviously, he should not," Mrs. Johanessen said.

"You're not taking this away from him," Miss Singletary countered. "If you try, I'll go to the superintendent and if that doesn't work, I'll go to the newspapers."

"You are treading on dangerously thin ice," Principal Speer said. "Are you willing to jeopardize your teaching career for this boy?"

"It looks to me like I already have."

The door to Principal Speer's office flew open, and Miss Singletary snatched me by the shoulder of my shirt and said, "Get up. To my room, now!" She pushed me down the hall to the empty classroom. She pointed to the chair just in front of her desk and I sat without comment. She paced the front of the room for several minutes until the heaving in her chest subsided, the pulse in her neck slowed, and the red blotches began to fade. Finally, she said, "Jimmy Lee, I am so very sorry for what just happened. It was inexcusable."

"You didn't have anything to do with it, Miss Singletary."

"What did they say before I got there? Did they accuse you of cheating?"

"Mrs. Johanessen did, more or less. She asked if someone else wrote it for me and I just copied it down in the book. I think she's the one who's making the big stink, and I don't know why. I never gave her a hard way to go."

"It's not about you winning, Jimmy Lee. It's about Catherine *not* winning. If you had come in second, she would never have said a word." She took a cleansing breath and sat down in her chair in front of me. "You showed me last year that you're capable of doing the work. But, Jimmy Lee, I would be lying to you if I said that very thought didn't cross my mind."

"I think you're insulting me, Miss Singletary."

"This has nothing to do with your last name being Hickam. Mrs. Johanessen had a valid point. You virtually crapped out of junior English and then come back after the summer and write this marvelous essay. It sends up a red flag, Jimmy Lee."

"When I put my mind to it, I can be a pretty good writer, Miss Singletary. I read a lot, too."

"With very few exceptions, you've not displayed that in my class."

"Do you want me to write another essay while you sit here and watch me?"

"I certainly do not. I will go to the mat for you, Jimmy Lee. All I want you to do is look me in the eye and tell me that essay was your work." For a long moment, I looked at Miss Singletary and digested her words. Never in my life had a teacher or anyone else shown such faith in me. Never before had anyone agreed to take me at my word. "Jimmy Lee, was that essay your own work?" she repeated.

I focused on her green eyes and said, "Yes, ma'am. Every last word."

When I got to the bus stop the next morning, it was misting and a low fog was rolling down off the giant pile of red dog and across Salt Lick Creek, and the smell of sulfur hung in the air. I could hear the footfalls of Polio Baughman shuffling through the loose gravel before his outline appeared from the fog. He was wearing saggy jeans and a red and black flannel shirt. His hands were buried in his front pockets.

"Hey," I said.

"Hey," he replied.

"What's going on?"

He shook his head. "Nothin'." He paused a moment, looking at the ground and toeing some random designs in the gravel. "I heard you cheated on that writing contest. Is that right?"

"Hell, no, it ain't right. Who told you that?"

He went back to playing with the gravel. "Lots of kids are talking about it. Most everyone thinks you cheated. There's talk that you paid someone over at the college to write that paper for you."

"That's ridiculous. I wrote it. Period. Anyone calls me a cheater better be ready to back it up, and that includes you, Polio."

"I was just telling you what I heard. Catherine Johanessen said you stole the story from a magazine and just copied it. She said she remembers reading it in a magazine and she said she's going to find it and prove you're a cheater."

The low groan of the school bus downshifting as it turned on to Red Dog Road filled the heavy air. It stopped for the Klamecki girls and only the faintest outline of its flashing red lights could be seen.

"Catherine Johanessen's got her panties in a bunch because she finished second. I wrote that essay. I wrote all of it, and I don't appreciate people talking about me behind my back, especially someone who's supposed to be my friend."

"Just seems awful funny that someone who never got any good grades in his life could all of a sudden . . ."

I dropped my books and grabbed Polio by the ears, twisting them toward me until his knees started to buckle. He whimpered and pulled harmlessly at my knotted forearms. "You better look at me, Polio, or I swear I'll twist 'em right off your head." When he finally looked up, I said, "I wrote that paper, every goddamn word, and I better never hear you tell anyone otherwise."

I let go of his ears and scooped up my books before the bus materialized out of the fog. I went to the back of the bus and sat alone.

Chapter Eight

Miss Singletary pulled me out of my eighth-period study hall the next day and walked me back to her classroom. On her desk was a six-inch stack of new, blue notebooks. "I'm going to make this harder than summer football practice, Jimmy Lee," she said.

"Ma'am?"

"Sit down." She pointed to the desk to the left of her own. "I believe you wrote that essay, Jimmy Lee. Unfortunately, I don't think anyone else in the school or the county believes it. And, if I had to bet, there are several people in this school who would like nothing better than for you to fall on your face at the county competition, just to prove they're right and that I'm wrong for standing up for you."

"You think Principal Speer wants me to fail?"

"I'm not mentioning any names, Jimmy Lee. I'm just saying that some people are a little upset that I've taken your side on this."

"I don't think you know how much I appreciate that, Miss Singletary. It's not every day that someone takes an interest in a Hickam. You and Coach Battershell are the only two people in this school that have never treated me like a dogger."

Her cheeks flushed, seemingly embarrassed by the compliment. "Jimmy Lee, we are not going to lose that county competition. We have six weeks to get ready and we're going to practice here every day and you're going to practice at home every night. You are going to be ready and you are going to greatly disappoint all those people who want to see you fail."

She made me smile. "I like your attitude, Miss Singletary. Maybe you should give the pre-game pep talk this week."

"I'll leave the football team to Coach Battershell." She inched her chair up to her desk and in a serious tone said, "But, like Coach Battershell, I don't like losing. And I especially hate losing to a particular teacher, if you know what I mean."

I did.

"This is going to be hard work and I expect you to put as much effort into practicing for the essay contest as you put into football practice. Is that understood?"

Miss Singletary had wavy blonde hair that hung around her shoulders and emerald eyes that danced when she smiled and drew fire when she was angered. There wasn't a boy in the school who wouldn't want a private tutoring session with Miss Singletary, but I knew this would be like boot camp. Still, I grinned and said, "Understood."

"Okay, let's get started. When you thought about writing your story, how did you do it? How did you come up with the ideas and how did you put it all together?"

"I started thinking about what I was going to write the day you told us about the essay. I thought about it until it was like a movie in my brain, and I could see it happening."

"So, you first visualized you and your uncle heading out on the canoe and took it from there?"

"No, not exactly. I took it from the water. I just focused in on one little spot in the river and watched the water."

"You went to the river?"

I squinted at her for a minute to see if she was kidding, which she wasn't. "No, ma'am, it's all in my head. I saw the center of the river—just the water—in my head."

"You remembered what it looked like from that summer?"

"More or less. I know what river water looks like, so I focused in on that. I closed my eyes and tried not to see anything but the water—the dirt floating in it and the ripples. But pretty soon other things start coming into the picture that my brain is creating. I can see fish and water bugs skipping across the surface, dragonflies buzzing around the muddy banks."

"How come I didn't read about the water bugs and dragonflies? That's excellent detail."

"I don't know. If I'd known it was important I would have put it in."

"Okay, go on."

"At first, I'm up close, staring at the water, but the more I stare, the further I get from the water and that's when the other stuff comes into view. Like, when my Uncle Boots and I are unloading the canoe? I'm not seeing that from my perspective as a little kid trying to unload the canoe. Rather, it's like I'm seeing it from a distance, like a third person with a camera, and I'm watching this happen. I'm in the movie, but I'm also the man behind the camera taking a movie of me when I was little."

"Have you always done this?"

"I grew up on Red Dog Road, Miss Singletary. You know what it's like out there. Sometimes, there's not much else to do but daydream."

"So, when you sat down to write your essay, you closed your eyes and started to picture the story in your head?"

"Oh, no, ma'am. I did that a bunch of times before I wrote the essay. I memorized everything I saw. That way, when I went in to write the essay, all I had to do was write down the movie while it replayed in my brain."

"Say that again."

"I just replayed the movie."

"In the county competition, they don't give you the topic in advance. You'll get two hours to write your essay, but you won't know the topic until you get there. How are you going to react to that?"

"I'll have to speed up the movie, I guess."

She smiled and said, "I guess." She handed me the blue notebook on the top of the stack. "Here's what we're going to do. You'll come here every day and we'll write a practice essay. Each night, you'll take home a notebook and an envelope." She plucked a white business envelope from the corner of her desk, slipped it into a notebook and set it on my desk. "When you get home, open the envelope and you'll find a topic on which to write. Time yourself. Don't take any more than thirty minutes from the time you open the envelope. You have to learn to think and write quickly. I like the way you play the movie in your head, but you're not going to have that kind of time at the county competition. Got it?"

I nodded. "Got it."

"Open your notebook. Your topic is, 'If you could meet someone from history, who would it be and why?' You have thirty minutes. Start writing."

Chapter Nine

Edgel came to my football game that Friday night against the Clearcreek Local Stevedores.

He told me that he liked it that people were cheering for me and the way Mr. Evans announced my name over the public address system every time I made a tackle. *On the tackle for the Elks, Jim-my Hick-am.* For those couple of hours, people didn't look at him like the dogger ex-con that he was, but as the big brother of the starting linebacker. He sat in the bleachers next to my mom and just before kickoff, Sheriff McCollough stepped over several rows of bleachers to shake Edgel's hand. "Good to see you, Edgel. You doing well?"

The sight of the sheriff caused Edgel to pucker up and a weak, "Yes, sir," was all he could muster in response.

"That brother of yours is playing some good football for us this year."

Edgel smiled and said, "That's what I hear. He just won him a big writin' contest at the school, too."

The sheriff nodded and winked. As he stepped back down the bleachers he said, "You be good, Edgel."

"You can count on it, Sheriff."

My dad never came to any of my games. He thought playing football was a waste of time. The only bigger waste of time, he said, was sitting in the stands watching football. It was just as well. The few school functions I recall him attending he was drunk and made a spectacle of himself. He showed up at my fourth grade Christmas pageant so hammered that he fell on his face on the front steps of the school. Polio Baughman came running backstage and said, "Your dad's out on the front steps and he's havin' a heart attack or something."

I went running out just in time to see Sheriff McCollough snatching my dad by the collar of his shirt and lifting him to his feet. The front of his shirt was soaked with slush and blood and vomit. He looked toward me without recognition. "Go on back inside, buster," the sheriff told me. "He'll be all right after he sleeps it off." As he led my dad toward the cruiser, I heard him say, "Nick, goddammit, you ought to be ashamed of yourself for embarrassing that boy like that."

My dad responded by sending a laser of yellow vomit on to the sheriff's shoes.

We beat Clearcreek Local 24-6. I had a good game—not great, but good. The highlight of my evening was catching their halfback flaring out of the backfield for a pass. I hit him just as he touched the ball, putting the top of my helmet under his face mask. The crack of my helmet on his chin could be heard throughout the stadium. They helped him off the field and the last time I looked over at their bench, they were waving an ammonia capsule under his nose.

I walked out of the locker room after showering, my hair still damp, my duffel bag slung over one shoulder, and a bruise the size of an egg welting up on my right forearm. The parking lot behind the school was full of parents and siblings and girlfriends, all milling around and awaiting their own Friday night hero to emerge. Edgel was on the far side of the lot, alone, leaning against the fender of the Rocket 88, arms crossed, a cigarette wedged between an index and middle finger.

A few folks patted me on the back and stated their pleasure with my performance that night as I made my way toward Edgel. I was nearly to the edge of the parking lot when Donetta Kammer materialized out of the crowd and stepped between the Rocket and me. "Hi, Jimmy Lee," she said.

"Hey, Donetta."

"That was a great game you played tonight."

"Thanks."

Donetta was a year younger than me, a cheerleader with high cheekbones and long, brown hair. Her father was the county auditor and they lived in a big home on Birnbaum Ridge. She was the kind of girl who I long believed to be out of my league. However, she had been smiling at me in the halls, and when she spoke and smiled at me in the cafeteria, Kip Fillinger nudged me in the ribs and said, "I think she's sweet on you, Jimmy Lee."

She stepped closer and ran her fingertips near the bruise. "You better get that looked at," she said. The light scraping of her nails over my skin and faint smell of jasmine in her hair caused a jump in my loins. "The cheerleaders and some guys from the team are coming over to my house for pizza. Do you want to come?"

Of course, I did, but before I could respond a harsh, "Donetta!" emanated from the darkness. A moment later, her father emerged from between two cars and said, "Get over here," pointing to the ground directly in front of him. He yelled at her in a restrained whisper that turned his face crimson and pointed to the passenger seat of the car. When the door opened and the illumination from the dome light spilled out, Donetta appeared to be in tears. Before driving off, he nodded at me and said, "Nice game, Jimmy Lee. Better get some ice on that arm."

This brought Edgel off the fender of the Rocket, that vein in the side of his neck pulsating. He said, "What kind of horseshit was that?"

"The usual kind," I said. "Just let it go. Where's Mom?"

"Went home to check on the old man," he said. "Want to get something to eat?"

"Sure," I said. Eating out was a treat that I rarely enjoyed.

"Is that burger joint still open in McArthur?"

"Paddy's? Yeah."

He tossed me the keys to the Oldsmobile. "Let's go."

The Rocket 88 had been another of the rusting heaps that littered our property when Edgel took to restoring it the winter before he went to prison. He was good with his hands and had the engine humming in no time. Restoring the body was more tedious work and it was covered with primer and body putty. Once Edgel had the majority of the body work completed and it looked as though the project was going to be successful, my dad inserted himself in the process. He didn't do much work, but was happy to drive the car on his late-night circuit to the local taverns. This caused even more tension between my dad and Edgel. The Rocket was nearly ready for paint when Edgel was arrested. Dad ran it until the first time it wouldn't start, then pushed it into the shed where it remained for the duration of Edgel's prison term. The morning after Edgel got home, he was out in the shed tinkering with the motor. He got a battery and a set of used tires from the Farnsworth twins and had it running again inside of two days.

The 88's 324-cubic-inch V8 engine roared to life as I turned west on Route 50. I drove under a clear September sky and a half moon that climbed in my rearview mirror. Edgel slouched in the passenger seat, his window down and his head resting on the top of the door. His eyes were closed and his head tilted back, as though trying to fill his nostrils with free air, which was dank with the smell of wet leaves that littered the ditch along the road. "You played a good game tonight," he said. "You were bustin' some heads out there."

"I like playing football, Edgel. It makes me feel like . . ."

My words trailed off, but Edgel completed the sentence. "Like a somebody?"

"Uh-huh."

He smiled. "There's nothing wrong with that. It was fun being up in the stands and hearing everyone talkin' good about you."

We drove in silence for a few minutes, the wind rushing through the open windows and the rumble of the engine bouncing off the steep hills that lined the country road. "You glad to be out of there, Edgel?"

He opened his left eye. "Little brother, do you even need to ask me that?"

"Probably not."

"You can't imagine how glad I am to be out. No bars, no walls, no guards, no other prisoners trying to fuck with you every hour of the day and night. I'm never going back, I'll tell you that much."

"What are you going to do about a job?"

"Beats the piss outa me. You know anyone anxious to hire an ex-con?"

I shrugged. "Maybe Mr. Morgan would hire you on down at the sawmill."

"I can't imagine that a man who owns a sawmill would be all excited to hire a guy who was convicted of arson. The Farnsworth twins offered to give me some work driving a flatbed truck, shuttling cars and parts to other junk yards. It's not much, but it's a start."

The Rocket 88 got some stares when I pulled it into the lot at Paddy's. I was wearing my East Vinton varsity jacket and two kids from Wellston looked at me and nodded. They knew who I was and for a moment I savored the attention.

Paddy's Drive-In was a McArthur landmark, famous for maintaining its 1950s-era style with carhops on roller skates, jukebox kiosks in each booth, homemade ice cream, and hamburgers made from beef that was ground on the premises. I loved their double cheeseburgers, which came with a heaping mound of French fries, onion rings, and breaded, deep-fried pickles, which were served in a plastic basket lined with white paper that quickly became a translucent gray with grease. Paddy's had a variety of faithful customers. A coffee klatch of farmers met on Saturday mornings to grumble about one thing or another. Early Sunday afternoons drew the church crowd for lunch. It did a brisk carryout business at lunchtime during the week, and truckers floated in at all hours. But on Friday nights in the fall, Paddy's was a post-football game hangout for kids throughout Vinton County, and a myriad of varsity jackets mingled in relative harmony.

We took a corner booth at Paddy's. "I don't have much money," I told him.

"I got it," he said, scanning the restaurant full of high school kids. "Tonight was homecoming. Isn't there a homecoming dance?"

"It's tomorrow night."

"You goin'?"

I shook my head. "Nah. I'm not much for dancing."

The side of his lip curled. "How come? I figured the star of the football team would have lots of girls after him. That girl back in the parking lot seemed awfully interested."

"She was just being nice. I'm not exactly a ladies' man." I ordered a lemonade and a cheeseburger platter. Edgel did the same. "There was one girl I was thinking about asking, but I didn't get around to it."

"What's that mean? You didn't get around to it?"

"It means I was a chickenshit and didn't ask her."

"Well, that isn't the first time that's ever happened," he said. "Who is she?"

Then, as if on cue, Ruth Ann Shellabarger and two other girls walked through the side door near our booth. I waved and nodded. "Hi, Jimmy Lee. Nice game tonight," Ruth Ann said, smiling, but never breaking stride.

"Thanks." When they were out of earshot, I said, "That was her."

Edgel took note of the trio, flicked his cigarette ashes on the linoleum, and asked, "Which one?"

"The first one, the one who spoke—Ruth Ann Shellabarger."

"She's cute."

"Real cute."

"Doesn't look like she came with a date." He started to push himself out of the booth. "I'll go tell her that you'd like to take her to the dance."

I practically jumped out of the booth, knocking over the ketchup bottle as I reached across the table to grab his forearms. "Noedgelpleasedon't."

He snorted laughter and cigarette smoke came out his nose and mouth. "Relax. I was just funnin' ya."

Edgel thought it was big fun; my heart was thumping against my ribs. I ate my burger and fries quickly so we could leave, just in case he wasn't just "funnin'" me. And, with Edgel, you never knew for sure.

He let me drive the Rocket home. Edgel smoked and watched the road, comfortable with the silence. The eleven-year gap in our ages had left little commonality in our memories. I was still in early elementary school when Edgel dropped out of school and began, as my mother described it, "roaming the countryside." I was only in the third grade when he was arrested for arson. While the collective memories were few, there was one evening in particular that, I was sure, remained etched in both of our minds. "You remember that night?" I asked.

The corners of his mouth curled in a slight grin. He knew exactly which night I was talking about. "It'd be a little hard to forget, don't you think?"

Edgel's nickname in high school had been Slugger. He earned this nickname because it was said that when Edgel Hickam stood naked, it looked like he had a baseball bat hanging between his legs. I became a personal witness to this on a steamy July night the summer before I was to enter second grade.

My mother's Aunt Eunice had died and my parents had driven to Ironton for the weekend, leaving Edgel in charge. That night, he sat me down in front of the television with a bottle of Mountain Dew and a bag of pretzels, and said, "You watch television and don't move your little butt until I get back."

"Where you goin'?"

"That ain't none of your concern. Just do what I told ya." He headed out the back door.

Thirty minutes later, I went to the bathroom and peeked out the back screen door. There was an unfamiliar sedan parked behind the shed. The windows of the car were down and I could hear the muffled groans of what sounded like a woman being attacked. She was moaning and crying out in what seemed to be extreme pain.

I slipped out the door, easing it back into the jamb, and crept alongside the shed, inching through the darkness until I was just outside the open back window of the car. In the backseat, Edgel was naked. I could see the top of Edgel's head and his sweat-streaked back hunched over the woman. He was breathing hard and gasping, and I assumed straining to hurt the woman, whose black hair was tousled, her hands digging into Edgel's back. I watched for several minutes before Edgel must have felt my eyes on him. He looked up, his nostrils flaring, and said, "What the fuck are you doing out here?"

Before I could move the woman beneath him twisted her head back toward me, her face contorted, the moist hair matted to her forehead, and said, "Jesus Christ, what's he doing here?"

I ran. I had no idea what was going on in that car, but I was certain that it was not intended for my eyes. As I pulled open the back door, I heard Edgel say, "Goddammit, you better run." I climbed the stairs on all fours and dove under the covers of my bed, pulling the sheet up over my head in a vain attempt to hide. It was only seconds before I heard the back door slam and stairs creak as Edgel took them two at a time. I curled in a ball and began crying when I heard him enter my room. He stripped off the sheets I was hiding beneath and said, "I thought I told you to stay in the house, goddammit."

I knew what was coming and began crying in anticipation. "No, Edgel, no, no, no."

He snatched me up out of the bed by my nose. I flopped onto the floor, squealing and bawling in anticipation of the punishment I was about to receive. Edgel was barefoot and bare-chested, having only slipped on his jeans before beginning his pursuit. His face boiled with anger as he grabbed my shoulders and pulled me to my feet, digging his fingers into the soft flesh around my collarbones until I thought I would faint from the pain. "What the hell did I tell you? Huh?" he yelled. "Didn't I tell you to stay in the house?"

"I heard that lady cryin' and I thought someone was hurtin' her."

"The only one whose gonna get hurt is you if you ever tell anyone what you saw." He shook me hard. "Say one word and I'll blister your ass raw, you understand me, boy?"

"I don't even know what I saw, Edgel. I won't say anything, ever. I promise. Stop it, you're hurtin' my bones."

"I'm gonna hurt more than your bones if you ever tell anyone. Not Mom or Dad or anyone, got it?"

Tears were streaming down both cheeks. My nose felt like it had been rug-burned from Edgel using it as handle to yank me out of the bed. "I won't, I promise."

Edgel released my collarbones, and then slapped my ears with the flat of his palms, sending echo daggers into my brain. I cried harder. He snatched me up by the waistband of my jeans and threw me onto the bed. "I'm warning you, junior, don't say a word."

I was too upset to sleep. I sat in the corner of the bed, my knees tucked under my chin, my chest heaving, waiting for the tinnitus to exit my ears when Virgil walked in an hour later. He smelled of beer and funk; a middle finger was jammed into the top of a half-empty Pabst Blue Ribbon longneck that dangled at his side, and the corner of his upper lip was curled in a smirk. "Hey, little man, I heard you got your ears boxed tonight for snooping around where you shouldn't been."

I said nothing for a while, waiting until he had quit chuckling. He leaned against his chest of drawers, uncorked his finger from the bottle and drained the contents, his Adam's apple rolling up and down with each gulp. "Virgie, what was he doing to that lady?" I asked.

Virgil set the empty bottle on the top of the chest and made a fist with his right hand, jamming it back and forth like the driver on a steam engine. "He was giving her the high hard one."

"What's that mean?"

"She was riding the bone pony." He thrust his hips forward twice. "You know, giving her the big nasty."

I had no earthly idea what he was talking about. It would be years before I discovered a stack of my dad's skin magazines and began piecing together the puzzle, but on this night, I could do nothing but stare at Virgil in bewilderment. "I don't know what you mean," I confessed.

He gave me a look of disgust, as though he couldn't believe that we were spawned from the same gene pool. "You will someday." As he grabbed the doorknob to leave, he looked back over his shoulder and said, "But in the meantime, you best be quiet. If you tell anyone what you saw, Edgel will cut off your pecker."

It had been more than a decade since that night, but the memory of Edgel's footfalls racing up the stairs still sent chills up my spine. "You wouldn't really have cut off my pecker like Virg said, would you?"

He looked at me sideways and shrugged. "You never know."

As I approached the steep drive leading up to our house, I was careful to run the wheels of the Olds over the humped middle of the road and the berm to avoid scraping the undercarriage. I was focused on this task when Edgel groaned, "Oh, Mother of Christ." I looked in time to see a kitchen chair crash through the dining room window and tumble down the hillside. Two other first-floor windows were broken. White linen curtains dangled through the openings, hung up on the sharp corners of busted glass. The flow of yellow light coming out of the house gave the curtains the illusion of being on fire. My mother was running across the side yard toward our car, crying and frantically waving her arms in the air. "This is great. I see not much has changed around here in the past nine years," Edgel said, flicking an orange-tipped cigarette into the weeds as he pushed open the passenger side door.

"Oh, Edgel, thank God you're home. He's out of control," my mother cried. "He went and lost his job at the sawmill and now he's crazy mad—drunk and crazy mad." My mom had a knot between her left eye and ear; the right side of her face was swollen and red, and a smear of dried blood covered her upper lip.

"Mr. Morgan fired him?" Edgel asked. "He's been at the sawmill for twenty-some years. What happened?"

"I don't know. When I got home he was sitting at the kitchen table with a beer. All I said was that Jimmy Lee played a good game and it was a shame that he missed it. He blew up and threw a beer bottle at me and started screaming." She pointed to the knot on the side of her face. "I've never seen him like this." A frying pan flew out an already broken kitchen window. "He's tearing up the whole house."

I followed Edgel as he deliberately walked across the yard toward the house. He stopped at the bottom of the back stairs and peered inside. The old man was standing in the living room, chest heaving, eyes glazed, hair hanging in his eyes. "Well, lookie who's here—the convict and the football star, or is it the convict and the writer?" He laughed. "Did your mother send you in here to try to calm me down? Good fuckin' luck. Come on in here and I'll take you both out."

"You call me a convict again and we'll see who takes who out," Edgel said, starting up the stairs.

Dad took one step toward the back door, stepped on the leg of his sagging jeans, and tumbled forward, sprawling on the kitchen floor. "Sumbitch," he muttered, trying to push himself up.

Edgel grabbed him under the shoulders and with surprising ease hoisted him upon the only remaining chair in the kitchen. "Dad, you need to settle down. Look what you're doing to the house."

"Fuck it," he slurred. "Who cares?"

"You will when you sober up and have to fix all this stuff. You've already done a couple hundred dollars damage." Dad looked around the kitchen for a few minutes, then waved a hand at the mess. "What happened at the mill? Mom said Mr. Morgan fired you."

"Fuck that, he didn't fire me. I quit."

"You quit your job. Why?"

His head rolled around on his shoulders and he seemed close to passing out. He leaned toward me and said, "Mister football star." His breath was heavy with the stale stench of beer and cigarettes.

Edgel's left hand shot out and grabbed my dad by the chin, twisting his head around. "This ain't about Jimmy Lee. You leave him out of it." My dad made a fist and started to rear back to deliver a blow. "Go ahead. Try to hit me. It'll be the last thing you remember when you wake up Sunday afternoon." My dad relaxed his hand and his shoulders slouched. "Now, why'd you quit?"

"He took me off my job," Dad said.

Dad had been an offbearer at the mill for years. After the logs were cut into planks, they were sent down a conveyor belt where Dad pulled, sorted, and stacked the lumber. It was heavy, but relatively clean work.

"Why'd he take you off the job? You've always done good work for him."

"He called a meeting today and said he was making some changes in work shifts and responsibilities. He posted the new work schedule and said if any of us had any issues, we should come talk to him after the meeting. I checked the work schedule and he had me working in the pit on the midnight shift. I've been there twenty-two years and that's how I get rewarded—greasing machines and shoveling sawdust from midnight to eight in the morning. Nigger work, that's what it is."

"Did you go talk to him?"

"Hell, yes. I went right to his office and asked him, 'What's this shit?' You know what he said? He said, 'I understand you take great pleasure in talkin' about my personal life over at the Double Eagle Bar.'"

"What the hell does that mean?"

"I have no clue. I asked him what the hell that was supposed to mean and all he said was it means I'm working the pit on the midnight shift, that lousy sumbitch."

"You don't know what he was talking about?"

Dad shook his head. "No idea."

It was classic behavior for Dad. It was never his fault. "Maybe he heard you were telling people that he's getting head from his secretary every afternoon," I interjected. "You told Mom and me that a bunch of times."

His eyes turned venomous and the muscles in his jaw tightened. He was getting ready to lash out at me when Edgel said, "So what happened next?"

"I told him he could kiss my rosy red ass. I quit. I told him I wasn't going to eat another of his shit sandwiches, so I knocked all the papers off his desk and left."

Edgel rubbed his face. "You need the work, Dad. Maybe you should talk to Mr. Morgan on Monday and see about getting your job back."

"Fuck him. I'll shovel shit before I go crawlin' back. And I don't need a little peckerhead convict like you telling me how to run my life."

"I told you not to call me that again."

Dad threw a fisted right hand toward Edgel's jaw, but it never came near his mark. Edgel blocked it with his left forearm, then fired a right jab that hit my dad on the bridge of his nose. Dad and the chair went over backwards; his eyes rolled to the back of his head, and he was unconscious before he slammed into the oven door and slid to the floor, drool running over his chin and down his neck.

As we stood amid the trashed kitchen, Mom crept up the back steps and peeked inside. She strained her neck to see around Edgel. "Did he pass out?" she asked.

"More or less," Edgel answered. He motioned me across the room with a nod of his head. "Help me carry him up to bed. Maybe we can talk some sense into him in the morning after he sobers up."

Chapter Ten

"*Jimmy Lee, you smell bad.*"

We had finished our daily writing lesson and Miss Singletary said, "Jimmy Lee, I need to talk to you for a minute." She massaged her temples for a moment, then said, "Jimmy Lee, you . . ." She stared into space for a moment, then said, "Jimmy Lee, I . . ." She squeezed her eyes closed for a moment, then said, "Jimmy Lee, this is difficult . . ."

It was becoming more frustrating for me than her. I said, "Just spit out it, Miss Singletary."

And, she did. "Jimmy Lee, you smell bad."

It was a knife to the heart. They were not the words I wanted to hear from anyone, let alone my favorite teacher.

"What do you mean?"

She swallowed. "Just what I said. You smell bad. You have body odor—very bad body odor. Your clothes are dirty. And, frankly, your breath needs some work, too."

"Christ, are you kidding me?"

"No, I'm not, and this is not an easy thing for me to talk about with you. If you're uncomfortable having this conversation with me, just say so and I'll drop it right now."

I wanted to run and hide, but I said, "No. Go ahead. I want to hear what you have to say."

"You're going to go into that county competition and it's important that you make a good impression. If you win, you're going to have to give a presentation at the Alpha & Omega Literary Society annual banquet. We need to work on your hygiene before you go to the competition. Well, we need to work on it for a number of reasons, but it would be good if we could get things under control before the competition. Has your mother or father ever talked to you about the importance of personal hygiene?"

"You mean like washing and . . ."

"Like soap, shampoo, deodorant, toothpaste? Wearing clean clothes?"

"Not that I can remember."

"I overheard some of the football players talking about you. They said you wear your underwear to school, then to practice, then you wear the same shorts home?"

"Yeah?"

"Well, Jimmy Lee, no wonder you smell bad. You've got to change your sweaty shorts."

"How often?"

Her chin dropped and her eyes widened. "Are you serious?" I could feel tears of humiliation welling up in my eyes. At that moment, all I could think about was that I was glad I hadn't asked Ruth Ann Shellabarger to the homecoming dance. "As often as necessary, Jimmy Lee. At least once a day, twice if you're playing football, three times if you've got gym class." She reached into a bottom drawer and produced a paper bag from the Abel's Drug Store in McArthur. She held up a can of aerosol antiperspirant and deodorant. "Every time you get out of the shower, you use this. Do you know what it's for?"

"I know what deodorant is. We just don't have any at my house. My dad says it's a waste of money."

Her eyes squinted. "It's not a waste of money, Jimmy Lee. Civilized people use deodorant." She shoved the aerosol can back in the bag and produced a bottle of shampoo. "Wash your hair every time you take a shower. Every time! There's soap, toothpaste, a toothbrush, a hair brush, and a tube of face wash. Use them. If you run out and can't afford to buy more, tell me."

"This is pretty embarrassing."

"Don't be embarrassed."

"When someone tells you that you stink, it's embarrassing, Miss Singletary."

"If no one told you, how could you be expected to know?" She folded down the top of the bag and shoved it across the desk to me. "Now, as long as we're on this subject. Let's talk about your clothes. Make sure you change your socks every day. And, you need to get some clothes besides those old T-shirts and blue jeans and work boots."

"Like what?"

She smiled. "Some nice khakis or navy pants and dress shirts. I've got someone who can help us with that. Will your parents buy you some new clothes?"

I shook my head. "No, but I've got some money saved from working at the truck stop this summer. How much will I need?"

"We could probably get you set up for about a hundred dollars."

"That's a lot of money."

"It's an investment in your future. It will make a big difference in how you look at yourself, Jimmy Lee. Now, let's talk about your hair."

"What about my hair?"

"Jimmy Lee, it's a half-inch long all around your head. Where do you get your hair cut?"

"My mom cuts it with a pair of clippers. She's cut it for years. She got upset when I was in the first grade and Margaret Burrell said I had lice."

Miss Singletary rubbed at her eyes and said, "Oh, Jimmy Lee, you poor thing."

"I don't want your pity, Miss Singletary. Just show me how to do things right. I'll listen."

Chapter Eleven

I tried to hurt my opponents.

I particularly liked it when a running back came out of the backfield on a screen or flare pass and had his back to me while he waited for the quarterback to deliver the ball. He would never see me coming. I would run as hard as I could and use my helmet like a battering ram, trying to put my helmet between his shoulder blades or go for a helmet-to-helmet collision just as his hands touched the ball. I wanted to hear the breath rush from his lungs and see the look of fear in his eyes. On more than one occasion, I had given up the chance to intercept the ball in order to put a hard lick on a kid. The crack of the helmets always brought the crowd to its feet. If I could horse collar a running back trying to turn the corner, I would spin him off his feet and try to slam him hard on his shoulder and give him a stinger. Done successfully, this would send a volt of searing pain down his spine and cause his arm and side to go numb. I was good at filling the hole and meeting running backs at the line of scrimmage. As I was making the tackle, I tried to get my helmet under their chin and drive them hard to the ground.

The East Vinton fans loved it. They cheered my name. When Mr. Evans on the public address system announced my name on a tackle, it would echo through the narrow valley that encased our field. Coach Battershell and the assistants would slap my helmet and say, "Hell of a hit, Hickam." I loved the game, and football provided an outlet for my anger, a chance to dish out revenge for years of being scorned. I didn't crave the spotlight; I craved acceptance. Football gave me a degree of acceptance. The booster club president would never invite me to his house or allow me to date his daughter, but he was quick to put a hand on my shoulder after a game and praise my effort. The harder I hit my opponents, the louder they cheered, and the more I liked it.

Miss Singletary's talk about my hygiene left me angry and ashamed. Mostly, it made me feel ignorant and inferior. I was angry with her, with my parents for not having talked to me years ago, but mostly with myself for being just another stupid dogger. At the end of the day, that's all I was, just another hick from Red Dog Road who didn't have the good sense to bathe and change his shorts on a regular basis. Jesus Christ, I thought, no wonder people didn't want to be around me.

Merle Smith was a freshman halfback who probably should have gone out for the golf team. He might have weighed a hundred pounds with his equipment. That day, while I was brooding over my conversation with Miss Singletary, the scout team offense ran a pitch to the left side and I hit Merle with a shoulder and forearm an instant before he took the pitch. The impact lifted him a foot off the ground and separated his chinstrap from his helmet. He flailed through the air like a man falling backwards over a cliff, his arms whirling in tiny circles. I scooped up the ball and ran ten yards until the coach blew the whistle. When I turned around, Merle was limping to the sideline, tears in his eyes and gasping for air. The defensive players smacked my shoulder pads for the hit, but I knew it had been unnecessary.

While the scout team huddled, Coach Battershell walked across the line of scrimmage, hooked my face mask with an index finger, pulled my face close to his, and asked, in a calm tone barely above a whisper, "You having a bad day, Jimmy Lee?"

"No, sir."

"You sure?"

"I'm all right."

"Maybe you've got a burr up your ass about something, but don't take it out on a little guy like Merle Smith. Got it?"

I lower my eyes and nodded. "Yes, sir."

I was deliberately slow to strip off my practice uniform and get into the shower. My pants were crusty with salt and stained with grass and soil. The white, numberless jersey was heavy with sweat. For the first time I noticed how badly they reeked. They went into a cloth duffel bag with my socks, T-shirt, and underwear. The shower was clearing out when I entered. I took a corner shower, turned the water up as hot as I could stand it, and let it pour down over me.

There was a cake of pink soap in the holder near the shower handles. I held it like a scrub brush and raked it through my bristled hair until suds ran down my forehead and into my ears and dripped on my shoulders. At first, I thought she was being helpful, but as I stood in the shower her attitude seemed so demeaning. I lathered up my chest and arms, scrubbed hard on my pits and rolled the soap over my package until my pubes were full of bubbles. They probably had a big laugh about it in the teachers' lounge. It was just like the Valentine I had sent Rebecca McGonagle or the morning erection that Lindsey Morgan found so humorous. Everyone was having a laugh at Jimmy Lee's expense.

Of course, I knew Miss Singletary would never do anything like that. I was more angry at my own ignorance than at her, but at seventeen, it is sometimes difficult to accept responsibility for your own missteps.

I washed each leg from the ankle up, rubbing the soap against the grain of my leg hair. I ran the bar over my face, then stood under the pounding water and watched the white lather snake toward the brass drain. I repeated the process, and when the lather had rinsed from my eyes, I could see Coach Battershell standing in the opening to the shower. "Don't wash the skin off," he said.

"I won't."

"Stop by my office before you leave."

"Why?"

His brows arched, surprised at the answer. "Because I said so." He left before I could respond. After drying off, I stuffed the towel into the duffel bag and pulled my blue jeans over damp skin. The underwear had gone in the duffel bag, so I covered myself with one hand and carefully zipped up my jeans with the other. The locker room had cleared out by the time I walked into Coach Battershell's office. His feet were crossed at the ankles and resting on the corner of his desk when I rapped twice and walked in. He didn't look up from the playbook he was flipping through, but pointed at a chair with his pencil. "Have a seat, Jimmy Lee." Without looking up he added, "Shut the door." I pulled it closed behind me, dropped the duffel bag, and eased down on the plastic chair, waiting for his eyes to leave the playbook. "Rough day at school?" he asked.

"Not particularly."

His brows arched as he finally lifted his eyes. "It looked to me like you were taking out some frustration on the freshman. Want to talk about it?"

"Not really."

He nodded, his eyes focused on the eraser end of the pencil he was tapping on the desk. "Are you upset with Miss Singletary?"

"Why would I be upset with Miss Singletary?"

"Don't play coy with me, Jimmy Lee." I folded my arms and looked away. "Do you think that conversation the two of you had was easy for her?"

"How'd you know about it?"

"She talked to me about it first. She was nervous about approaching you and wanted to know how I thought you would take it."

"What did you say?"

"The first thing I told her was that she had more guts than I did. I also told her you'd take it like a man. Of course, given your display of temper at practice, now I'm not so sure."

"It's football. I thought we were supposed to hit."

He ignored my comment. "Let me ask you a question, Jimmy Lee, and I want you to really think about it. When was the last time you had someone, anyone, climb out on a limb for you the way Miss Singletary has with this essay contest?"

"You did."

He shook his head. "No, I didn't. I'm just your football coach. I like you and I care about you, Jimmy Lee, but I haven't had to risk anything by putting you in a game. Anyone who watches can see you're a hell of a football player. I don't need to convince people of that. They'd think I was an idiot if I didn't play you. But as far as I can see, there's only one person in the whole school who believes you wrote that essay and believes it enough that she's willing to back you up."

"I never asked her to do that."

"Really? Do you think you could be any more ungrateful?" His tone turned harsh, as when a player missed an assignment on a critical play. "She wants you to succeed and she doesn't want you to embarrass yourself. There's not another teacher in this school who would have had that conversation with you. She's got your back and all you can do is whine about it?"

"The only reason I entered that stupid essay contest was to show Miss Singletary that I could write. I wanted to show her that she didn't need to worry about passing me out of junior English. Before that writing contest, everyone looked at me and told me how good I was at football. Now all anyone is talking about is me being a cheater. I wish I hadn't even tried at that essay contest. What do I need it for, anyway? You said maybe I could get a scholarship to play football."

"Your life in football is finite. Do you understand what that means?" I didn't, and shook my head. "There's an end to playing football. Sometimes it ends after high school. If you're fortunate it ends after college. If you're very, very fortunate, it ends after the pros. But it ends for everybody, and the number of years you get to play are pretty insignificant in relation to your entire life. When the day comes that you can't play football anymore, what are you going to do?" I looked blankly at him. "It's not a rhetorical question. What are you going to do?"

"I don't know. I haven't thought that much about it."

"You better start. Miss Singletary says you have talent. Use it, son." I looked away, feeling very much the scolded child. "And, as long as we're on this subject, I want to tell you something, but it doesn't leave the room. Understand?"

I shrugged. "Sure."

"You be damn careful how you act around Mrs. Johanessen."

"What do you mean?"

"Exactly what I said. Be careful. She's a snake, and she'll do anything she can to trip you up before that writing competition. She catches you doing anything that could be construed as improper or a violation of school rules, she'll try to get you suspended. Did you know that she had planned a celebration for Catherine the evening you upset the apple cart and won that contest?" I did not and shook my head. He couldn't hide a smirk. "She thought it was a lock and had invited a raft of family and friends, including a few teachers, to her house for a party. Then you trimmed her sails, so she'll be gunning for you, trying to find a way to get her kid into the county competition. She's got a strong ally in Principal Speer, so don't give her any ammunition."

"I won't."

Mrs. Johanessen was a dour woman who thought life had wronged her by planting her firmly in the middle of Ohio's Appalachian hills. She had moved to Vinton County from Cincinnati after her halitosic dentist husband bought Doc Verzella's practice in McArthur. She was openly disparaging of the locals and longed for the life of culture and entitlement that she believed had been her destiny when she married Ralph Johanessen in his third year of dental school. Stories abound at East Vinton High that Mrs. Johanessen had a wild side and had rebelled against her husband for dragging her to the hills by having a series of affairs, one of which was rumored to be with Principal Speer. Mrs. Johanessen rarely smiled, wore her hair in a bun so tight it seemed to stretch the corners of her eyes, and wore loose-fitting skirts in a vain attempt to hide her spreading rear end. From my perspective, it seemed almost beyond comprehension that someone could find her desirable.

Behind her back, Mrs. Johanessen was known as "the chess master," for the way she orchestrated Catherine's every move. There were those in Vinton County who said Mrs. Johanessen had a near maniacal obsession with her daughter and lived vicariously through her achievements. Those less kind said that her love for her daughter was conditional upon those achievements, and that she worked Catherine like an expert puppeteer.

When Catherine was in elementary school, Mrs. Johanessen carted her throughout the Midwest to compete in beauty pageants. During show-and-tell in those early years, Catherine was forever bringing in a sash for being the Pumpkin Festival Princess, or a tiara for being Little Miss Zucchini Festival, or a trophy proclaiming her Miss Tiny Tomato Queen. On the playground after one such demonstration, Kip Fillinger put one hand on his hip, one behind his head, and while shaking his butt said, "Look at me, I'm a beauty queen," and then made fart sounds with each wiggle of his rear.

Catherine burst into tears and ran inside. Of course, Mrs. Johanessen made a visit to the elementary school the next day, and Mrs. MacIntyre gave us a talk about not being cruel to our classmates on the playground, though she could barely do it with a straight face.

Mrs. Johanessen became the cheerleading advisor at the high school when Catherine was in junior high just so she could hold the position and ensure that her daughter spent four years cheering on the varsity. After carting Catherine off to Athens for two years of private tennis lessons from the Ohio University women's coach, Mrs. Johanessen organized a tennis tournament at the Vinton County Country Club, such as it was, with a nine-hole golf course, two tennis courts, and a swimming pool so small it was called the bird-bath. The tournament pitted Catherine against a half-dozen girls who barely knew which end of the racket to hold. She won the tournament three years in a row, for which her mother presented her with a trophy the size of a small car and had an article placed in the *Vinton County Messenger* that would have made you think she had won the U.S. Open.

Mrs. Johanessen worked diligently to raise a spoiled, entitled brat, and that's what she ended up with. Given her history, it was not beyond my comprehension to believe she might try to blindside me prior to the county essay competition.

Chapter Twelve

My shirt was a tad too small through the chest and it was cutting at my armpits. Mom had bought it at the Volunteers of America Thrift Store in Chillicothe the previous winter for my great-uncle Chester's funeral. It was a little thin at the elbows, but it was washed and pressed. The slacks were black and, I think, made of nylon. They came from the same thrift store and like the shirt, were a little snug. I had polished my belt and my only pair of black shoes. The scent of the antiperspirant was noticeable to me and I sensed that I had put on too much.

When I walked into Miss Singletary's classroom for my tutoring session, she looked up briefly, then back to the paper she was grading. "I'm sorry, sir, but I have a tutoring session this period and simply don't have time for a parent-teacher conference at this moment." She looked up again and feigned surprise. "Why, as I live and breathe, Jimmy Lee Hickam. I didn't recognize you all dressed up."

My lips quivered as I unsuccessfully tried to suppress a grin. "It's from the secondhand store in Chillicothe. I got it for my uncle's funeral."

"It looks nice," she said. She sounded sincere. She crossed her arms and smiled. "I'm proud of you, Jimmy Lee. This is a big step. Is that cologne I smell?"

"No, ma'am. Deodorant. I used too much."

"You'll get the hang of it."

"I've decided I want to get the new clothes you talked about yesterday."

"All right. I'll work on that."

"Good. Before we get started, I want to ask you something."

"Go ahead."

"I was talking to Coach Battershell last night and he said you told him I have a real talent for writing."

"I never told Coach Battershell that you had talent." The prickly heat of embarrassment crept up my neck. "A lot of kids in this school have talent, Jimmy Lee. I told Coach Battershell that you have a gift. There's a difference. I've been reading your essays for a week. They're excellent. You have a gift for visualizing a scene and recreating it on paper. There are a lot of good writers out there, but very few have the sensitivity to be able to completely pull a reader into their stories. You have that. A gifted painter doesn't need someone to explain perspective to him. He sees it in his mind's eye and the results come out the end of his brush. I told Coach Battershell that you have that kind of gift with words." She leaned closer to me. "It's the same message I've been trying to get you to understand. It's a gift. Use it."

For a long moment, I considered what she had said, chewing at my lip and avoiding her stare. "But what could I do with it?"

"The opportunities are endless, Jimmy Lee. You could write for a newspaper or a magazine. Have you been to the library? There are thousands of books on the shelves, many of them written by people a lot less talented than you."

"You think I could write books?"

"I think you can do anything you want, Jimmy Lee. You just have to use the gift that God gave you."

"How do I do that?"

Miss Singletary leaned back in her chair; she smiled and her green eyes danced. "Is it that difficult of a question to ask?"

"Ma'am?"

"Does going to college seem like such an unachievable goal that you can't even ask me the question?"

"College sure seems like a long way from Red Dog Road, yes, ma'am."

"Do you want to go to college?"

I shrugged. "Last year, when Coach Battershell said I might get a scholarship if I kept improving in football, I thought it was just talk. I never really thought I could go to college. I always figured college was for kids a lot smarter and, you know, better than me. Now, I'm wondering if maybe I could do it. But I've got no idea how to go about it. All I know about college is that it's for smart people and it's expensive."

"Don't sell yourself short, Jimmy Lee. There are a lot of people in this world who sell themselves short. They don't try to achieve their dreams because they're too paralyzed by the prospect of failure. You can do it and I'll help you, if you want."

At that moment, I remembered the words of my brother Edgel when he learned that Miss Singletary was my teacher. *You stay close to her. She's solid; she'll do right by you.* "I'd like that a lot, Miss Singletary."

"Good. Why don't we get started this Saturday? We could do your clothes shopping in Athens and take a visit to Ohio University."

"That would be great, but . . ."

"But . . . ?"

"What would people say if you took me out shopping for clothes?"

She smiled. "I've got it under control, Jimmy Lee." She tossed a blue notebook on my desk. Written across the top of the cover in perfect script was the statement, *Write an essay about the things you think about when you can't sleep.* "Now, get to work."

❖ ❖ ❖

There were two late plates on top of the stove—blue ceramic plates covered with aluminum foil. During football season, I ate most of my dinners cold—tepid at best. I peeled off the foil and found two pork chops, a mound of mashed potatoes covered with congealed gravy, and succotash, the green beans beginning to wilt. "Want me to throw that in a skillet and warm it up?" my mother asked, appearing from the living room with a wicker basket of dirty laundry.

"No, this is fine. Thanks. Where's Edgel?"

"He's off to Columbus with a truckload of parts for the Farnsworth boys. They said they've got enough work to keep him busy for a couple of weeks. That'll be good for him." She pulled a jug of milk from the refrigerator and poured me a glass, setting it and the jug in front of my plate, then snagged the loaf of Wonder Bread from the stainless steel bread box on the counter and dropped it on the table. "We're out of butter."

The other late plate was for my dad. I didn't bother to ask his whereabouts. I didn't really care as I preferred to eat my dinner in peace rather than listen to another of his drunken tirades. And if he wasn't home for dinner, it was a foregone conclusion that he was leaning against one of the bars between home and McArthur, running up his bar tab and railing against Mr. Morgan. Drunk and freshly unemployed, there was no morsel of gossip too insignificant about his former employer that it couldn't be repeated ad nauseam to anyone who would listen. I wondered how Dad was paying his bar bills now that he was unemployed, as I assumed all of my mother's money was going to keep the house running. He didn't seem overly concerned about finding work. Jobs were a scarce commodity in southeast Ohio, particularly if you were a drunk and a known troublemaker with the last name of Hickam. But as long as the barkeepers were giving him credit, I didn't anticipate that Dad would be launching his employment search anytime soon.

Before Mom scooped up the basket, I added my sweaty practice togs to the pile. Her mouth puckered and she headed to the basement. I ate in silence and was still hungry after cleaning up the last of the potatoes and gravy with a slice of bread. The old man's late plate looked tempting, but I instead went to the cupboard and retrieved a jar of peanut butter. I made myself a sandwich and poured another glass of milk. No sooner had I screwed the cap on the milk than my dad entered the kitchen from the front door and my mother from the basement. "Hungry?" she asked.

He grunted an affirmative and sat down without washing his hands. She put the plate in front of him and he promptly put an index finger in the mashed potatoes. "It's cold, goddammit. Heat it up," he said.

I could smell the beer on his breath from across the table. His head bobbed slightly, but his eyes were wide and alert. It had been a light night at the bar, I surmised. Mom scooped the dinner from the plate and placed it in a tin pie pan, which she covered with foil and slid into the oven. I tossed down my milk and put the glass in the sink, carrying the remainder of my peanut butter sandwich to my bedroom. "Thanks for dinner; it was good," I said. "I've got homework."

There was a stack of magazines in the living room on the shelf next to the staircase. At the bottom of the pile was the previous year's Sear's Christmas catalog—the Wish Book, as it was called. As I passed, I slipped it out of the pile and took it to my room. Using the catalog as a guide, I priced a sport coat, dress shirts, khaki and navy slacks, new shoes, a belt, socks, and underwear. If I was careful, I could buy a couple of additional collared shirts and still be under two hundred dollars.

This was a major step for me. I was tight with my money. Once I got a dollar in my hand, it would take a couple of Marines to pry it loose. I was not in love with money, but I thought it signified accomplishment and hard work. Having money that I had earned and could hold in my hand was as gratifying to me as wearing my letterman's jacket or having a gold medal for an essay contest draped over my neck. I looked at the money I made not for what I could buy, but more like a trophy. Since school had started, I had been earning about twenty dollars a weekend at the truck stop, bussing tables and washing dishes, and with my summer job money, had a grand total of four hundred and sixty-two dollars in my bank envelope. The thought of removing two hundred dollars from the envelope for clothes made me queasy because I knew how long it would take to replace it. Saving was now of particular importance as I wanted to put money away for college.

The very thought of Jimmy Lee Hickam attending college made me grin broadly. I wanted to get accepted somewhere so I could watch Lindsey Morgan's chin drop and hear her say, *"You're going to college?"* just so I could respond, "Well, of course I'm going to college. What did you think I was going to do with the rest of my life? Work in your dad's sawmill?"

I stopped grinning as soon as I got off the bed and entered my closet. Panic gripped my loins and exploded into my gut and chest, like a thousand frozen needles prickling my insides. The stack of magazines in the corner of my closet had been moved—not much, but noticeable to me. I slid the envelope from its hiding place and could tell by the weight that it was empty except for a few clinking coins. "Son of a bitch," I said. I unzipped the envelope to reveal the foregone results. Reaching back behind the stack of magazines, I swept them to the side, spilling them onto the floor. I wanted to vomit and cry. All the money I had in the world was gone.

Mom was washing dishes; Dad was finishing his dinner, staring straight ahead and making no attempt to look at me. "When's Edgel getting back?"

"Late," my mother said, not turning from the sink.

"How late?"

"I don't know. He said he'd be late. I didn't ask him . . ." She stopped in mid-sentence when she turned and saw the empty bank envelope in my hand.

"All my money's gone. All the money I earned this summer and on the weekends at the truck stop." Tears were welling in my eyes, a combination of frustration and hurt and disappointment. I dropped the envelope on the table. "My own brother."

Mom struggled to swallow, and then her eyes fell upon my dad, who chewed with his mouth open and washed a mouthful of mash down with a Rolling Rock. He looked up at her, rolled his tongue over his teeth, and said, "It's about time you started helping out around here."

"What's that supposed to mean?" I asked.

"You hard of hearin'? Just what I said. It's time for you to start helpin' out. No more free rides."

A burst of heat erupted in my chest. "You took it?"

He took another hit off his beer, sucked his teeth and said, "That's right. Times are tough. I ain't workin'."

"You couldn't ask me?"

"I don't have to ask, goddammit," he bellowed. "It's my house and we needed the money."

"For what? To pay your bar tabs? I need that money. It's mine."

He looked up at me, a thin grin creeping across his lips and said, "Too fuckin' bad."

Before I knew what I was doing, I snatched the front of my dad's shirt and pulled him out of the chair. I spun him as if he were a helpless running back, slamming him against the wall with such force that cupboard doors opened and a print of Jesus praying in the garden of Gethsemane fell from the wall, its plastic frame splitting when it hit the floor. I pinned him hard against the wall, tightened my grip, grinding my knuckles into his ribs. My breath came in short, staccato bursts. "I want my money. All of it."

His face was oddly calm. He smiled, hanging limp, his breath smelling of beer, cigarettes, and gravy. "Well, well, well," he said in a light, sing-song voice. "Looks like Mr. Touchdown finally grew himself a pair of balls."

"I want my money, Dad, and I'm not kidding."

"Sure you are." He smiled. I knew what was coming, but could not react fast enough. He brought his knee up into my groin with such force that bursts of white light flashed in front of my eyes and an electrical charge erupted in my testicles. All control I had over my limbs failed. In a single motion, like a marionette whose strings had been clipped, I crumpled to the floor. A searing pain raced from my groin through my stomach and chest and into my armpits and throat. I couldn't breathe and soon a thick, salty bile filled the back of my throat and I threw up on the kitchen linoleum. I wretched and sucked for air, feeling my face glow hot.

He snatched my nose between his index and middle finger, pulled me to my knees and said, "Not so tough now, are you? Next time, I'll make a woman out of you, and don't think I won't. If you weren't my blood, this is when I would put the boots to you until your own mama wouldn't recognize you."

I looked at him, tears rolling out of my eyes, and I felt oddly juvenile. I could not stop crying and pleading, the way an infant would carry on when the bully took his favorite toy. "I need that money."

My mother stood in the corner of the kitchen, arms crossed, tears streaming down both cheeks, staring at my father. He avoided her gaze and was, as usual, unrepentant. "You've been living here rent free for pert near eighteen years. I'll keep the money and we'll call it even."

"I need that money."

"You don't need it. You've been hoarding it up there for months."

If I had said I was going to use it to buy clothes he would have just laughed. But I knew the other reason would infuriate him. It would be an affront to his manhood and at that moment I was anxious to hurt him. "I was saving that money for college."

"Say what?"

"You heard me." I took a few deep breaths. "I'm going to college."

"Son, you ain't going to college. You're not college material."

"Yes I am." I sucked for air. "Miss Singletary says so. She said I have a gift. She said I could be a writer and she's going to help me get into college."

He laughed. "That's what Miss Singletary says, huh?"

"That's right. Coach Battershell says I can do it, too. They're going to help me get off Red Dog Road."

"There something wrong with living on Red Dog Road?" There was venom in his voice.

"Yeah, it's a place where your dad steals your money for booze, then knees you in the balls because you want it back."

He took a step toward me, but my mom cut him off at the edge of the kitchen table. "I guarantee you this, boy. A year from now, ten years from now, you'll still be living on this hillside somewhere."

"I want my money, you thief."

His lower jaw jutted out and he gave me a last hateful glance before he turned and left, slamming the door behind him. A moment later the car started and I listened to the sound of the engine disappearing in the night.

I crawled up the steps and fell into bed. My mom came to the room with a glass of water, aspirin, and a bag of ice. "Are you going to be okay?" she asked.

"I've never had anything hurt so bad in my life."

"Do you want to go to the emergency room?"

"No." The light was beginning to close in from the sides of my eyes. "Just turn off the light and let me get some rest."

I was roused by someone tapping on my shoulder. "Wake up, sunshine," said a voice that sounded like it was coming from another room. The tapping continued, harder, until my eyes opened. It was Edgel, sitting backward on the wooden chair he had pulled away from my desk. He was grinning and in need of a shave, a green and white FARNSWORTH SALVAGE ball cap sitting cockeyed on his head.

The sun was bright across my bed. "What time is it?" I asked

"Eleven o'clock."

"Oh my God, I'm late."

"Relax. I'll get you there by lunchtime. Missing half a day won't kill you. How do you feel?"

"Sore."

"I'll bet. Mom said the old man put the boots to you."

"No boots, just a knee. Ordinarily, he said the boots would have been next, but he spared me because I was his blood."

"Uh-huh. He was feeling in a particularly Christian mood, huh?"

"Apparently."

We both laughed, which caused further pain in my testicles. "He can be a son of a bitch. No doubt about it. How're your balls?"

I peeked under the sheets. "One looks like a plum. The other isn't too bad."

"Think you'll be able to play Friday?"

"I'll be all right. I'll take a couple of aspirin before the game."

"I talked to Mom before she left for work. She said you thought I was the one who ripped you off."

I shrugged, embarrassed that Edgel knew of my original suspicions. "Polio hadn't been over for a while and I didn't think Mom or Dad would take it."

"You didn't think the old man would take it? There ain't nothin' beneath that man. Trust me, I know that for a fact. Have you been asleep at the switch for the past seventeen years?"

"I guess."

"Don't worry about it. I was the most likely suspect. Mom said you were saving that money for college?"

"That, and Miss Singletary was going to take me to get some new clothes to wear to school and the writing competition."

Edgel reached into his front pocket, produced a neat wad of folded bills and tossed it on my chest. "There's two hundred and thirty dollars."

I picked up the cash and folded it into a neat pile. "Edgel, I appreciate it, I really do, but I can't take your money." I tried to hand it back to him.

He smiled. "I wouldn't give you my money. That's yours. I took it out of the old man's pants pocket. He's passed out and dead to the world."

"He'll kill you, Edgel."

"Nah. I didn't spend nine years in prison to come out and take a whippin' from him. I'll tell him I took it, straight up. He'll huff and puff, but that's all he'll do. Put it where he can't get his hands on it. Now, get your ass outa bed and I'll give you a ride to school."

Chapter Thirteen

There are some truisms about doggers and one is this: There is no slight or insult of pride too insignificant that it can't start a major incident. Obie Fithen shot his seventy-two-year-old twin brother to death in a dispute over which television show to watch. Angel Tate threw hot bacon grease on her sister Hazel because she had used Angel's hairbrush and didn't clean it afterward. To an outsider, these acts of retaliation would be considered egregious acts of violence. But to many doggers, the actions of Obie and Angel were justified.

Earlier in the summer, during one of our visits to the penitentiary to visit Edgel, when I had mentioned that Coach Battershell said I might be able to earn a college scholarship to play football, my dad had laughed at the thought. In his mind, it was distant and unlikely. Even if I was a good football player, that didn't mean I was smart enough to get into college. I was, after all, a Hickam.

However, the previous night, when I told him that Miss Singletary said I had a gift and she was going to help me get into college, it was a dagger to my dad's pride. Suddenly, the possibility that I would go to college wasn't so distant and he stood in fear of one of his sons succeeding in life where he had failed so miserably. I knew it would trouble him and that's exactly why I said it. I was emotionally hurt that he had stolen my money. I was physically hurt after he kneed me in the groin, and I wanted to hurt him back. The easiest way to inflict the most pain was to let him know that someone believed in me and wanted me to succeed.

This all came to the front of my mind as I walked into Miss Singletary's classroom for our tutoring session that afternoon. Before taking my seat, I stretched and looked out at the parking lot where I spotted Nick Hickam storming toward the school, arms pumping, his face darkened by a three-day growth of beard, hair combed to the side with his fingers, the cuffs of his untucked denim work shirt unbuttoned and flapping around his wrists.

"This could be a problem," I said.

"Pardon me?" Miss Singletary asked.

"Miss Singletary, I need a favor. I need you to hold this for me." I handed her the folded bills that Edgel had secured for me. "And, I need you to put it away, right now."

I suppose Miss Singletary was familiar enough with my family to understand that some events defied explanation, even having a dirt-poor dogger hand her a wad of cash that could choke a horse. And, bless her heart, she didn't hesitate or ask questions. She unzipped her purse, dropped the cash inside, and pushed it back under the desk with her toe.

No sooner had I taken my seat than my dad charged into the classroom and went directly for Miss Singletary, his index finger wagging in her face. "Lady, I got a bone to pick with you."

On my death bed, one of the images that I will see before I die is Amanda Singletary's green eyes lighting up like lasers while her face turned burning crimson. When she stood, her wheeled chair shot backward and spun across the classroom. With her jaw tightening, she leaned into my dad's face and said, "Excuse me, but just who do you think you are barging in here like that? In the future, when you wish to enter my classroom, you will first knock and request permission. And for the record, my name is not 'Lady,' it is Miss Singletary and you will address me as such. You also will get that finger out of my face or I will be happy to remove it for you. Furthermore, you will not use that acerbic tone when you speak to me as I am not the neighborhood mutt. This is my place of employment and I am a teacher and you will treat me with the respect accorded that position. If you are unable to conduct yourself in such a deferential manner, Mr. Hickam, then this conversation is over. Are we clear?"

A look of complete stupefaction consumed my dad's face. I'm not sure his poor, pickled brain was capable of comprehending the words as they flew out of Miss Singletary's mouth, and I was positive that he didn't know the meaning of a few of them. Sweet Jesus, I wanted to stand up and cheer, and I would have had I not been hindered by good sense and a swollen left testicle. Never in my life had I seen anyone back down Nick Hickam the way Miss Singletary did on that October afternoon.

For a long moment, my dad could not respond. He finally took a step back, began to raise his index finger, thought better of it, and planted both fists on his hips. "Okay, here's my beef: I'm tired of you putting crazy ideas in that boy's head."

She smiled, a little wickedly, I thought, as though anxious to hear my dad's reasoning. "Really? And what crazy ideas are those, Mr. Hickam?"

"You know darned well what I'm talkin' about. You've been tellin' him that he can go to college."

"Why, that's not crazy at all. Jimmy Lee is an extremely intelligent young man. He has the potential to go to college. I think it's only proper that someone is putting that idea in his head."

"All you're doing is setting him up for a big disappointment."

"Well, I must say that I find that an interesting outlook. Why do you say that?"

He was chewing on his lower lip and looked hard at me. "He just don't need it, that's all. Neither of my other two boys went to college."

"I'm not sure we want to be holding up Edgel and Virgil Hickam as role models for Jimmy Lee. Perhaps they could have gone to college, but they would have had to finish high school, first."

I choked back a chuckle.

"I'm telling you to leave it alone, *Miss Singletary*," he said in a condescending tone.

Miss Singletary crossed her arms; a broad grin consumed her face. She had the old man on the ropes and was enjoying it. "Let me ask you a question, Mr. Hickam. Do you know what a talented son you have? Not only is he the star of our football team, but he's a fine writer, one of the best I've ever had in my class. With a little support, he could go a long way—in college and in life."

"That's not your job to decide."

"Are you telling me not to educate your son or present him with the opportunities available to him? Is that what you're telling me, Mr. Hickam? Did you even read the essay? It was excellent. You should be proud. Instead, you're down here degrading me for trying to improve your son's future."

"All you're doing is filling his head with craziness."

"You have a wonderful son, Mr. Hickam. You should make an effort to get to know him." I ducked my head. "If you have nothing of substance to offer, Mr. Hickam, then Jimmy Lee and I have work to do. Good day."

The muscles in the side of his face rolled like ocean waves and the grinding sound of his clenching teeth came in terse, popping bursts. He looked toward me and said, "I'll talk to you later," then left, a defeated man.

After he was gone, she walked across the room and fetched her chair. The red began to fade from her face and recede down her neck. She took two deep breaths and another minute to compose herself. "I understand the financial concerns, but is there another reason why he doesn't want you to go to college?"

"He doesn't want me to be his better."

"Excuse me?"

"If I go to college, that means that I accomplished something that never even entered his radar space. It's an insult to his pride."

"That makes no sense at all. Parents are supposed to want better for their children."

I smiled. "Welcome to life on Red Dog Road, Miss Singletary."

"That's unbelievable." She handed me a blue notebook, shaking her head all along. "We're going to do this, Jimmy Lee." She pointed to the notebook and said, "In two sentences, tell me about your favorite tree. You have two minutes."

On the banks of Red Dog Creek, on a soggy piece of bottom land where the stream turns hard to the west, is an oak tree that grew tall long before the first white man walked across what is now Vinton County. One branch bends toward the ground, its bark worn smooth by the shoes of a thousand climbers, offering easy access to its interior, a place ideal for spying on the Nazis, hiding from pirates, or ascending the precipice of Kilimanjaro.

"Time," she said.

"Done," I answered.

She kept every blue notebook and had been flipping through them as I wrote. She gave me advice after each essay, telling me to write simply, and to be assertive. "In one paragraph, tell me about someone who has been a positive influence in your life. You have three minutes."

Coach Battershell extended me an invitation to play football. It was the first time in my life that someone outside of my family had taken an interest in me. He gave me an old pair of cleats—I didn't have the money to buy my own—so I could play. He would stay after practice and work extra with me. Coach Battershell not only gave me an opportunity to play football, but he gave me an opportunity to be accepted. His faith and concern for me has given me the confidence to excel on the field and in the classroom.

"Ready."

"Write three sentences on an event that you will someday want to tell your children about. You have three minutes."

Uncle Boots and Aunt Stephanie took me to Kennywood Park when I was nine. I had never been to an amusement park and was mesmerized by the squeals and screams and the smells of popcorn and cotton candy. Uncle Boots played a dart game and won a ceramic lamp in the shape of a hula girl, and I cried the first time we rode the roller coaster because I thought for sure that I was going to fall out.

"Okay. Done."

"In one paragraph, tell me about a place you've visited that people say is haunted."

The Headless Conductor haunts the Moonville tunnel. There are many ghosts haunting the tunnel, but sightings of the Headless Conductor are the most prevalent. For almost a hundred years people have seen the headless figure walking along the abandoned rail bed of the Marietta and Cincinnati Railroad, carrying his lantern and, supposedly, looking for his missing head.

"Grammar and spelling counts," she said. "Make sure you have a dictionary on the day of the competition. Watch your use of commas. Parenthetical phrases must be enclosed with commas. Did you read that copy of *The Elements of Style* that I gave you?"

"Most of it."

"Read all of it. Now, in two sentences or less, tell me why one of my students asked me to hide a wad of cash in my purse."

Chapter Fourteen

It was early on Saturday morning and the sky was a sea of dismal gray that stretched as far as I could see in every direction. There was a bite in the air and the wind whipped over the hilltop and cut hard across the front porch, whistling and tearing at the vinyl that had been tacked to our front windows as a makeshift barrier against the cold. It had finally stopped raining by the time I walked out on the front porch, eased the warped front door back into its place, and headed down the pockmarked drive, mud-slick from the rainstorm that began at noon Friday and didn't let up until just before dawn.

The rain had contributed to our first loss of the season to Brilliant Memorial the previous night on our home field, which the rain turned into a giant mud hole and icy water slopped over the tops of our shoes. Our defense played stellar, holding the Blue Devils to minus thirteen yards in total offense. But our offense couldn't get on track in the muck and a Brilliant Memorial defender intercepted a pass and returned it for a touchdown and the only score of the evening in a 6-0 defeat. The muck slowed down the pace of the game, which was fine with me, as I was still pretty tender in the groin. Fortunately, Brilliant Memorial was not in our conference and Coach Battershell, who didn't normally take losses with grace, said we had played a good game but the weather and the breaks just didn't go our way.

As I gingerly traversed the steep drive, searching for exposed rocks and gravel for footing and hoping to avoid a tumble, a white Pontiac Tempest drove past my drive and did a three-point turn in the road as I completed the last leg of the descent. I scraped the mud from my shoes on a patch of loose gravel along the berm of Red Dog Road before sliding into the backseat of Coach Battershell's Pontiac. Miss Singletary was grinning. "Good morning, Jimmy Lee."

"G'morning, Miss Singletary." I dipped my head, avoiding the familiar brown eyes that were staring at me in the rearview mirror, while trying to conceal my grin. "Morning, Coach."

"Good morning. How's the groin?"

Earlier in the week he had asked me at practice why I was so gimpy and I told him I pulled a groin muscle. "Okay. Good. It feels a lot better."

"Did you ice it when you got home last night?"

I had not. "Yes, sir. For twenty minutes. Just like you said."

"Are you lying to me?"

"Yes, sir. I forgot, actually, but it's feeling a lot better today, anyway. Really."

He closed his eyes for a moment and shook his head. "Jimmy Lee, it's not common knowledge that Miss Singletary and I are seeing each other and we would prefer to keep it that way, so it would be in everyone's best interests if you could just keep this to yourself."

"Yes, sir. I'm sure we can work something out."

His brows arched. "Work something out?"

"You know, I've been wanting to play a little fullback."

He laughed. " We'll see."

I couldn't stop grinning. "How about quarterback? I've always wanted to be the quarterback."

"I'd say now's a good time to quit pressing your luck."

"Yes, sir."

There had been rumors floating around the school for a year that Coach Battershell and Miss Singletary had been dating. "An item," they were often called in hushed tones. Someone—that nebulous "someone"—supposedly saw them together at a movie in Chillicothe and the news spread quickly around East Vinton High School. They maintained a professional appearance at school and you hardly ever saw them talking to each other. Still, it didn't surprise me that the rumors were true, though that morning it amused me greatly to see them together. There were no two people I admired more than Coach Battershell and Miss Singletary, and I thought they made a handsome couple.

The sun broke through the gray of October Ohio and began warming the valleys and dells of Vinton County. Boughs of oak and maple, soaked from the night's rain, hung over the edge of the asphalt back roads that snaked away from Red Dog Road. The ditches along the roads ran in brown torrents with tiny whitecaps lapping at the gravel berm. The saturated earth was dank after the rain, and the musty smell of decaying vegetation seeped into the wind as it sliced into the backseat from the passenger side window, which was rolled down a few inches. The air was wet and heavy from the rain, and the windshield wipers squeaked as they slapped away the morning mist.

Following my dad's visit to her classroom, Miss Singletary selected Saturday morning as our time to go clothes shopping. She had also decided that our sojourn would include a visit to the campus of Ohio University in Athens. It was, I knew, the initial step in the process. And in the world of James Leland Hickam, it was a giant step. I was simultaneously excited and terrified. For nearly eighteen years, I had been stuck in the rut that was Red Dog Road. No one had ever talked to me about going to college, or being a doctor, or a football player, or a writer. It wasn't my parents' fault; it was beyond their poor abilities to imagine such successes, too. Prior to winning the essay competition, my loftiest goal was to simply complete high school, something no Hickam male had ever managed. Afterward, maybe I could get a good job at a steel mill in Steubenville or at the glassworks in Wheeling or the shoe factory in Portsmouth. That seemed achievable—a good factory job and a house far from the dust and stench of Red Dog Road was all I wanted.

Until Miss Singletary had talked to me about my hygiene, I didn't know enough to use deodorant. Now she and Coach Battershell were taking me to visit a college campus. It seemed like too giant a leap. I was standing at the open door of the plane, my parachute strapped on, rip cord in hand, but I wasn't jumping. I knew that someone was going to have to put a foot on my ass and push me out of the plane.

We drove up Route 50 toward Athens and pulled into a Bob Evans Restaurant. "I need some of my money," I told Miss Singletary.

"I think I can spring for breakfast," Coach Battershell said.

We slipped into a corner booth. They ordered coffees. "Can I have chocolate milk?" I asked Miss Singletary.

"You're nearly grown up, Jimmy Lee. You can have whatever you want."

"Chocolate milk," I told the waitress.

They both took their napkins, unfolded them, and set them on their laps. I did the same and watched as they arranged their utensils, following their lead. It was just another reminder of how much I didn't know. The waitress set our drinks on the table and took our orders. I asked for scrambled eggs and sausage links.

"Have you ever seen a college campus, Jimmy Lee?" Miss Singletary asked.

"We took an eighth-grade field trip to Rio Grande and I've been to Athens before. I've seen Ohio University, but I've never been there to look around."

"Are you excited?"

I shrugged. "Kinda. A little nervous."

"What's there to be nervous about?"

"Going to college probably wasn't such a big step for you, Miss Singletary. Your folks were both teachers and they went to college. I'll bet going to college wasn't even a question for you. Probably the day you were born it was a given that you'd go to college and you knew what to expect. My dad, Edgel, Virgil—none of them even finished high school. It seems like another world to me and I don't know if I'm ready. I don't want to fail."

Coach Battershell said, "Jimmy Lee, everybody fails. Everybody! That's life. Do you want to know the secret to success?"

"Sure."

"It's really no big secret. In life, at one point or another, everybody takes a punch right in the nose. It hurts, it bleeds, and it's embarrassing. When that happens, some people walk over to the bench, sit down, and watch the rest of their life from the sidelines. They're too afraid to get back in the game. They want to play, you understand, but they won't because they want to avoid another punch in the nose. That's why you see a lot of really smart, talented people sitting on the sidelines. But a successful person just wipes the blood off and gets back in the game, even though he knows that eventually he's going to get punched in the nose again. The difference is, he thinks the punch in the nose is worth the possibility of success. You can't win if you aren't in the game."

"I hardly fit in at high school. If it weren't for football, I'd just be another dogger heading for the sawmill or the Farnsworths' junkyard or prison. How am I going to fit in at college? At least at East Vinton, there are other doggers. When I get to college, I'm going to look like the biggest hick on campus."

Coach Battershell stopped stirring his coffee and set the spoon on the side of the saucer. "You need to understand something, Jimmy Lee. Once you go to college, you start with a clean slate." He put his hand on the table and made a wiping motion. "Nobody knows who your family is or that your brother was in prison, or anything else. You'll be judged totally on what kind of a man you are. Once you get out of Vinton County, everything's even."

I smiled because I didn't believe him. "That doesn't seem possible, Coach."

"I'm telling you, if that's what you're worried about, then you're worrying over nothing."

"Yeah, but you never had that problem. You were always the star."

They looked at each other for a moment, neither revealing anything with their facial expressions. "You don't know that."

"I've heard the stories. You were the star quarterback for the O.U. Bobcats. You set all those records. You were all-conference and the team's MVP. The guys on the team say your picture is everywhere in the football offices."

"That's true, but it doesn't mean it came easy."

"It sure looks like it did."

He sipped his coffee and rolled the cup between his palms for several seconds. "Did you ever hear of a guy named Rex Battershell?"

"No."

The conversation halted while the waitress set our breakfasts on the table. After she had warmed up their coffees and left, Coach said, "Rex 'The Rocket' Battershell was an All-American quarterback at Pitt. They called him 'The Rocket' because he could throw a football eighty yards in the air. He also was my dad. He played a couple of years in the pros with Washington and then went to law school. He was an assistant U.S. attorney for a while and then ran for sheriff of Summit County and won every election in a landslide because everyone wanted to vote for 'The Rocket.' He was big, strong, handsome, great personality, a local boy who came back home to live after college and the pros. There wasn't a single person in the county who was better known than my dad. He was in the newspaper all the time—busting drug dealers, arresting murderers, visiting schools, taking turkeys to poor families at Thanksgiving. When I started playing football in high school, there was hardly ever a story in the paper that didn't say, 'Kyle Battershell, son of former Pitt All-American Rex "The Rocket" Battershell.' That's who I was—Rex Battershell's kid. No matter what I did or how well I did it, I couldn't get out from under his shadow."

I listened intently. When he paused to push a fork full of fried eggs and potatoes into his mouth, I said, "I'm not making the connection."

"That's because I haven't given it to you yet. I had a great senior year—first-team All-Ohio, Akron *Beacon-Journal* player of the year—and I accepted a scholarship to Ohio University. A bunch of schools offered me scholarships, including Pitt, and that's where my dad wanted me to go, but I was tired of living in his shadow. Everything was great until three days before my high school graduation when a federal grand jury indicted my dad on a host of felony counts of corruption in office—promoting prostitution, accepting kickbacks from gamblers and drug dealers, and money laundering. They had him dead to rights. The Feds had been watching him for years and had him on video taking kickbacks and payoffs. All of a sudden, the most popular man in the county gets exposed as the most corrupt. Here I am, ready to take on the world, make a name for myself, and every television news show is running video clips of my dad being led into the jail—his jail—with his hands cuffed behind his back. I hardly went out of the house that summer. I used to get in the car and drive for an hour until I found a vacant ball field or a park where people didn't know me so I could work out. All I could think about was how the guys on the team at O.U. were going to treat me when they found out my dad was the disgraced sheriff of Summit County."

"So what happened?"

"My dad swallowed his service revolver two weeks before I reported to camp."

I frowned.

"He committed suicide. Shot himself. I was devastated and didn't want to go to college, but my mom made me. She said everything a mom should say, that my life had to go on, that it wasn't my fault, that I needed to do what was best for me. But I couldn't get past it. I felt like I was reporting to football camp with a bull's-eye painted on my forehead. I got to Ohio University and not a single person on that team knew who I was, knew who my dad had been, or gave a rat's ass. There was another kid from Akron on the team and he never made the connection. Or, if he did, he didn't say anything. When someone asked me about my dad, I said he was dead and that always ended the conversation. In four years, I had one guy ask me how he died."

"What did you tell him?"

"I told him that he died of a cerebral hemorrhage. That's not the point. You're all concerned about your name being Hickam. That was a hurdle you had to overcome at East Vinton High School. In college, it's just going to be your last name. You'll be the only one to determine if people view it in a positive or a negative way."

We finished breakfast and headed to downtown Athens, a college town tucked deep into the Appalachian foothills. We parked on a side street three blocks from campus and walked to the Collegiate Corner men's store. The store was a shrine to Ohio University athletics. Football helmets, autographed basketballs, team photos, and baseball bats adorned the tops of the shelves. When we entered the store, you would have thought that Miss Singletary and I were walking in with a member of the royal family. There were a half-dozen men in the store and they immediately came walking up to Coach Battershell. "They love him down here," Miss Singletary whispered.

"No doubt."

When his well-wishers had backed away, Coach Battershell shook hands with a distinguished-looking man with salt-and-pepper hair, a crisp white shirt, and a cloth tape measure draped around his neck. "Hello, Kyle," the man said, holding out a long hand. "Is this our boy?"

"Jimmy Lee, I want you to meet a good friend of mine, Mr. Tom Lynch. Mr. Lynch, this is Jimmy Lee Hickam."

"Hickam, is it? Good to meet you, young man. Come on over here."

On a rack in the corner was a navy blazer, five dress shirts— three white and two pale blue—two pair of khaki and two pair of gray slacks, and five neckties, mostly reds and yellows and one green and navy. He handed me a shirt and a pair of the gray slacks. "Try these on for me and let's see how close we are in size."

I did. The shirt fit like it was made especially for me. Never in my life had anything felt as nice as those wool slacks. They needed to be hemmed and cinched in around the waist, but they were soft and comfortable. "What are these things?" I asked, pointing at the waves of material in the front of the slacks.

"Pleats," Mr. Lynch said. "Never had pleats before?"

"I never had anything that fit like this."

Mr. Lynch tugged and pulled and marked up the slacks with a piece of tailor's soap. We repeated the process with the other three pairs of pants. Then he fitted me with the navy blazer. I'm not a boastful person, but I will tell you that I never looked as good as I did with that navy blazer over a white shirt. As he was marking the back, I took a peek at the left sleeve and the hundred-thirty-five-dollar price tag. I looked over at Miss Singletary and silently mouthed, "I can't afford this."

Coach Battershell waved at the ground three times with his right hand, a tacit signal to relax and keep my mouth shut. Mr. Lynch pinched at the material in the back of the jacket and asked, "How does that feel?"

"Feels great."

He held up some ties, showing me how they would look with the jacket. "Do you know how to tie a necktie?"

"No sir. I've got a clip-on that I wear on game days."

"It's not hard." He put one around his neck and instructed me to mimic him. "Make sure the tip of the long end is hanging at your crotch," he said. "When it's tied it should just cover your belt buckle." It was easy.

I stood in the three-way mirror, with khaki slacks, white shirt, navy jacket, and a maroon-and-gold-striped tie. I could feel myself tearing up a little when I turned to Miss Singletary. "What do you think?"

"I think you're a handsome young man."

I smiled. "Don't say that in front of Coach Battershell. You know how he gets."

I changed back into my other clothes, which suddenly seemed woefully inadequate, and Mr. Lynch walked the new clothes to the seamstress in the back room. He came back out to the main desk and began adding numbers and talking to himself. "Let's see, one jacket, um-hum, four pair of slacks, hmmm, five shirts, pick yourself out an oxblood belt from the rack behind you, five ties, um-hum." I put the belt on the counter as he said, "How's a hundred and sixty-five dollars sound?"

Ridiculously low, I thought, but I said, "It sounds great." I counted out the money and placed it on the counter top.

"Thank you. It was a pleasure doing business with you, young man. Are you going to the game?"

"Absolutely," Coach Battershell said.

"Good. I'll get Alice working on them right now. Stop by after the game and you can take them with you."

As we walked away from the building and headed toward campus, I said, "He practically gave me those clothes."

"Someday, Jimmy Lee, you'll have a chance to do someone a good turn. When that opportunity presents itself, do it. It's called paying ahead."

The air was heavy with the smell of burning leaves—the first-burners, shagbark hickory, and buckeye. The hillside that surrounded the campus was still awash in gold and maroon and orange as the maples were only starting to drop their foliage. It was two hours until kickoff and Coach Battershell and Miss Singletary walked me around the campus and through a dormitory and a classroom building. "What do you think?" Coach asked.

"It's pretty big. How do you find your way around campus?"

"If you're on the football team, they give you a personal chauffeur to drive you around."

"Really?"

"No, not really." He grinned and arched his brows, a little disappointed, I think, that I fell for that.

"Who cuts all that grass?" I asked.

"Students on academic probation. It's part of the university's program to give them the incentive to do better."

I didn't bite that time. "How many times did you have to cut it?"

"Never. I was a four-point student . . . almost."

Miss Singletary groaned.

We were buying a hot dog and soda under the stands when the Ohio University band marched into the Peden Stadium. The drum section beat out a cadence that was like rolling thunder out of the hills, reverberating through the stadium. I had goose bumps from the top of my head to my ankles. We climbed the home stands and watched the game, an Ohio University loss to Bowling Green, but it was no less satisfying.

Afterward, Mr. Lynch was waiting at the store to hand me my clothes. He wished me good luck in the writing contest and we went to dinner at a restaurant outside of town that a hundred years earlier had been a warehouse on the Hocking Valley Canal. I ordered a steak and was the first to put the napkin in my lap.

Chapter Fifteen

The Vinton County chapter of the Alpha & Omega Literary Society would host its countywide essay competition on the third Saturday morning of November, the night after our last football game of the season. Although I was not privy to their conversations, I had the feeling that the scheduling of football and the essay competition was creating some angst between my football coach and my writing coach. My football coach, of course, wanted me focused solely on Friday's game with McArthur Central Catholic. We were both undefeated in the conference. A win would give East Vinton its first conference championship in decades and a chance to make the state playoffs.

My writing coach, however, was less concerned about McArthur Central Catholic than the Saturday morning competition, which began at 8 AM. She was drilling me hard during my study hall and sent time-consuming evening assignments home with me. This dissatisfied the football coach greatly as he wanted me spending my free time watching films of the McArthur Central Catholic Crusaders. As we were jogging out to the field on Wednesday, he said, "You need to be spending more time in the film room."

There was no one within earshot. "I know. Do you want to talk to Miss Singletary about it?"

One side of his mouth curled up and he said, "Not really."

On Monday morning of that week, my dad showered, shaved, and put on his only set of good clothes, the same ones he had always worn when we had visited Edgel in prison. As I was leaving to catch the bus for school, he was sitting at the kitchen table staring into a cup of black coffee, a cigarette burning in the crease of his yellowed fingers. He was twisting at the steel wristband of his watch the way he did when he was nervous. "Good luck," I said as I opened the back door.

He didn't look up, but nodded once and uttered a barely audible, "Thanks."

On that brisk November morning, Nick Hickam was swallowing his considerable pride and going back to the sawmill to apologize to Mr. Morgan and ask for his old job, or any job he would give him. He didn't care any longer. He was out of money, out of credit at the bars, and he simply had to work. I would imagine that this was about the most difficult and demeaning task of my dad's life, but he didn't have many options. Jobs were scarce in Vinton County, Ohio, and he was ill-qualified for anything beyond the mundane and dangerous confines of a sawmill. Virgil had called him a week earlier and told Dad that he could get him a job with the carnival, which was touring in Florida and Texas during the winter. I always figured that the prospect of working alongside Virgil at the carnival was what motivated Dad to go talk to Mr. Morgan.

I didn't like my dad, though I wanted to. In every failed relationship, each party usually carries part of the blame. But the only thing I did wrong was want to go to college. We didn't have much of a relationship before that pronouncement, but that sealed it. My dad was a bitter man who hated his lot in life, but was unwilling to do anything about it, and he took out his frustration and anger on his sons and wife.

That afternoon at practice, while I was waiting my turn at a blocking drill, I looked up to see the Farnsworth brothers' red, flatbed Ford parked along the drainage ditch on the far side of the parking lot. A green Pontiac station wagon with a crushed front end was chained to the bed. Edgel was in the stands watching practice. About once a week, he would stop by to watch when he was passing by and saw us on the practice field. Edgel liked watching me on the field and hadn't missed a game since getting out of prison, even standing in the pouring rain at the Brilliant Memorial game, wearing nothing but a vinyl jacket and his grease-smudged Farnsworth ball cap.

It was surprising that Edgel had taken such an interest in me. During the years of visits to the prison, he seemed so indifferent to his family. He had wearily tried to appease my mother by answering her many questions, but was often verbally confrontational with the old man and barely civil to Virgil. I was treated as an afterthought—the little brother that he didn't know. Now he was acting more like my father than my father. At least he acted more interested. When he got home each night, he stopped by my room and asked about the writing assignments. He read them all, every once in a while stopping to ask me the meaning of a word. I was afraid it would embarrass him, but he liked it. After he read each paper, Edgel would shake his head and say, "I can't believe a brother of mine can write like this."

I enjoyed the visits. I was actually getting to know Edgel. For years, I had been led to believe he was inherently evil. Every time the old man got mad at me for even the slightest infraction, he would slap me upside the back of the head and say, "You're going to end up in Mansfield, just like your brother." He intimated that Edgel was the devil incarnate and for years I had no reason to believe otherwise. But now, I found that I really liked Edgel. He was soft-spoken and thoughtful. He liked to talk about school and football. He wanted to know why I didn't have a girlfriend. "I thought the captain of the football team always had a girlfriend," he said.

"I don't have time for girls."

"Boy, there's always time for girls." He winked. "You ain't funny, are ya?"

"No, Edgel, I ain't funny."

"Just askin'."

Edgel told me on several occasions that he never wanted to go back to prison, revealing bits and pieces about the brutality inside the walls. "It's no place to be, and that's all you need to know about prison."

He had been working steady for the Farnsworth twins almost since he got home, driving and fetching wrecks and parts and occasionally stripping out cars in the junkyard for customers. The twins paid him cash and it was keeping him busy, which was a good thing for Edgel. He needed to find something a little more stable than the junkyard, but it put money in his pocket and kept him occupied.

After practice, Edgel was waiting outside of the locker room, leaning against the driver's side door of the Ford and scraping the grease from under his fingernails with a pocketknife. "Wanna ride?" he asked. "I've got to swing past the junkyard and drop off the Pontiac." He hadn't seen me since my trip to Collegiate Corner. He pointed at me with the tip of his knife and said, "Them's some pretty fancy duds, little brother."

I was wearing a pair of khakis and a blue shirt. "This is what I spent my money on," I said.

"Looks good. Maybe you'll get ya a girl now."

I checked the passenger seat for grease, covered a smudge with one of my blue notebooks, and slid in. Luke Farnsworth met us in the junkyard with a forklift. Once he had the Pontiac a foot off the bed of the truck, he said, "T-t-take 'er a w-way, E-edgel," and Edgel pulled the truck forward.

"See you in the morning," Edgel said.

"N-n-night," Luke said.

We got into the Rocket 88 for the short ride back to Red Dog Road. Edgel had been tinkering with the car. It was still covered in primer and needed some serious work on the interior, but its engine sounded like it had just come off the showroom floor. Edgel Hickam was not without his shortcomings, but he was good with his hands and a wizard under the hood of a car.

Edgel pulled the Rocket onto the gravel pad in front of the shed. Once he had killed the engine, we could hear my dad scream, slurring his words, "Do you think it makes me happy, woman? Huh, is that what you think?"

Edgel looked at me and blew air from his mouth. "Good God, not again," he moaned.

Through the torn screen of the storm door we could see my parents in the living room. Mom was crying and holding both hands to her cheeks. Dad was struggling to pull on a jacket that had gotten hooked under an elbow. The television news was on, something about the president and Watergate. Both parents turned and looked when they heard the squeak of the opening storm door. When we were both inside and the door closed, Edgel asked, "What's wrong?"

Mom held out an open hand toward Dad, her lips clenched shut and jaw quivering as she tried to fight back tears. She had a streaked red spot on the side of her cheek, the evidence of a Hickam back-hand. Her eyes were red and her chest heaved. She looked exhausted and ready to collapse, and I assumed they had been at it for a while.

"I'll tell you what's wrong, that cocksucker Morgan, that's what's wrong," Dad yelled.

"He wouldn't give you your job back?" I asked.

Dad looked at me with a familiar look of disgust. "No, college boy, he didn't. I got in there and was ready to practically beg for my job back and he had me thrown off the property. He called the cops and said if I ever set foot on his property again, he'd have me arrested." He looked for a moment as if he would cry, then he raised an index finger and pointed it at my mother. "This is all your fault, bitch. You're the one who made me go down there. 'Ask for your old job back, Nick. Please. Mr. Morgan will give it to you; he's a nice man,'" my dad mocked my mother. "Well, you see what he gave me, didn't you? Jack shit, that's what."

After being rejected by Mr. Morgan, I assumed that the old man had gone straight to the Double Eagle Bar, drinking away whatever cash he had in his pocket, and then mooching drinks for the rest of the afternoon. Like an ember that smolders in a couch for hours before erupting in an intense fire that quickly consumes everything around it, the old man had done the slow burn at the Double Eagle so that his temper could be in full rage by the time he got home.

He walked to the foot of the stairs and reached for a suitcase three times before finally latching hold of the handle. "What's the suitcase for?" I asked.

"What do you usually use a suitcase for?" he sneered.

"A trip?"

"Nothing gets by you, does it, college boy? I'm out of here. I'm done. I've had enough of all of ya. Virgil said he's got good work for me down in Florida. I'm leavin'." He looked at my mother and said, "I'll have work and I won't have to listen to you bitchin' at me all hours of the day and night." He looked at me and said, "And I won't have to hear any more of this hocus-pocus about you goin' to college."

"Nick, I don't want you to leave. I don't . . ." Her words trailed off.

Anger was at the root of nearly every decision Nick Hickam ever made. Alcohol was his propellant, but anger was his engine. There was no reasoning with my dad when he had been drinking or when he had his mind made up, and both factors were currently at work. It was the third time to my recollection that he had left home. When I was in the sixth grade, he left for a month and shacked up with a divorcee in McArthur that he met at the Double Eagle and who apparently found beer breath and an eighth-grade education attractive. When I was in junior high, he left for a week. No one ever found out where he went that time. Edgel told me that he left home once or twice before I was born, but he always found his way back, broke and meaner than when he left.

He stomped down the front steps and threw his suitcase in the backseat. "Dad, don't you think you should at least wait until morning, maybe sober up a little?" Edgel asked.

Dad didn't answer. He gave Edgel a hateful look and climbed into the driver's side of his 1963 Plymouth Belvedere, a former police car he had bought at an auction. It still had red lights in the grill, rusted fenders, and the faint outline of a badge on the driver's door. He slammed the door shut and after a moment of fumbling with his keys, twisted hard on the ignition.

And it wouldn't start.

It whined and backfired twice, and then started the slow *woo, woo, woo, woo* as the battery exhausted itself. He pounded twice on the dashboard, cursed, and tried the ignition again. Nothing but *click, click, click.*

The dramatic departure of Nick Hickam was halted by the failure of yet another of his two-hundred dollar junkers. The three of us, even my tear-streaked mother, choked back grins as my dad climbed out of the car and began kicking the door. "You sonofa-bitch," he yelled with each of a half-dozen kicks.

"Give me a ride to Route 50," he yelled to Edgel. "I'll hitchhike, goddammit."

"You're going to hitchhike to Florida?" Edgel asked.

"You're goddammed right I am." He didn't wait to see if Edgel was agreeable. Rather, he grabbed his suitcase from the backseat of the Belvedere and threw it in the back of the Rocket, then got in on the passenger side, arms folded over his chest and looking straight ahead.

Edgel was resigned to his job. "I'll be back in a little bit," Edgel said as he started down the steps. "I'll try to talk some sense into him on the way over."

The last time Edgel saw my dad he was standing along the berm of Route 50, thumb out, walking backward toward Athens.

"Did he say if he'd call when he got there, or anything?" Mom asked over a dinner of pancakes and fried eggs.

"Mom, he didn't say one damn word the whole ride. When I stopped at the stop sign at White Road and Route 50, he got out, grabbed his bag, and started hitchhiking. He wouldn't even look at me. I watched him for a minute, then turned around and left. What the hell. He's like a damned mule; he wasn't going to listen to reason."

I didn't like the look on Edgel's face. It was suddenly dour and his eyes distant, not unlike the face I had seen so many times before in the prison visiting room.

"God damn that Mr. Morgan," he said, his nostrils flaring. "He'd been a good worker for twenty years. Why didn't that bastard just give him his job back, for Christ's sake?"

Chapter Sixteen

There was not much to cheer about in southern Ohio in the autumn of 1973. Along the Ohio River, the steel mills and electric generating plants, long the faithful consumers of Vinton County coal, were crumbling under pressure from the Environmental Protection Agency for cleaner smokestack emissions. The culprit of the pollution was the high-sulfur coal that was pulled from the mines in our area. The river industries began buying coal from Wyoming and other Western states, even South America, that met the new governmental standards.

As the demand for Vinton County coal dwindled, the mines began to close. The big mining companies—Hudson Mining, Sunday Creek Mineral & Coal, Gem of Egypt Mining, Big Muskie Mines—all closed operations. None of the communities that speckled the Appalachian foothills had ever prospered. They were poor towns that scratched out an existence like the miners who lived there, but once King Coal was gone, death came quickly. The coal mines were simply the first to fall in a long line of dominoes. The stores and bars and businesses that relied on the paychecks of the coal miners began to struggle. Some closed. Others changed hands a few times, but eventually they all met with a similar fate.

But that fall, the East Vinton Elks had given the folks in those destitute hollows and dales something to cheer about. It had been years since East Vinton's football team had recorded a winning season, and decades since its last conference championship. We went from conference doormat to conference contender in three years. In the tiny communities of Creola, New Plymouth, Wilkesville, and Zaleski, porches were decorated in navy and gray crepe paper. Go ELKS signs that the booster club had printed were taped to windows throughout the school district. The cheerleaders painted spirited words on car windows in the school parking lot with white shoe polish and passed out ribbons that read, CRUSH THE CRUSADERS.

The students at the Zaleski Elementary School made a six-foot-tall good-luck card that was signed by every student in the school. It was great fun to be pivotal to such excitement. When I walked down the hall, kids were patting me on the shoulder and telling me good luck. It was a far cry, I thought, from my freshman year when I was virtually invisible in the same hallway except for looks of derision.

No one was talking about the essay competition, except for Miss Singletary, of course, who was relentless with her drills. Actually, it was probably good for me. It gave me time to clear the McArthur Central Catholic Crusaders from my brain. "You know, Coach Battershell always lets up on us a little right before a game," I told her, hinting that I was prepared for the essay contest.

"That's nice, but I'm not Coach Battershell," she said, handing me another blue notebook to fill. "I'm Coach Singletary and we're going to work right up until kickoff."

Thursday night practices were called our "socks and jocks" workouts. We wore no pads other than helmets and ran through the plays a final time before the game. It was by far the easiest practice of the week. Afterward, the Athletic Mothers Club had a spaghetti dinner for us in the school cafeteria. "We're proud of you, no matter what happens tomorrow night," said Carroll Ullrich, the president of the club and mother of our split end and kicker.

She was being nice and expressing a sentiment that was close to the surface of every parent and fan. Outside of the players and coaches, no one thought we had much of a chance against Central Catholic. We were the upstarts, the team that put a nice season together once every two decades, and the Crusaders were a perennial state power. Most of our fans silently harbored the belief that we would be soundly defeated, but they would be proud of us nonetheless, as though trying to soften the blow of the inevitable loss.

After the spaghetti dinner, I got a ride home with Coach Battershell, who used the time to drill me on the McArthur Central Catholic running scheme. Mom was sitting in the living room in her nightclothes, a worn and faded terrycloth robe that held little of its original blue and a pair of open-toed slippers that had worn through under her heels. Her brown hair was still damp from the shower and clinging around her face, and she sat with her dime-store reading glasses on the end of her nose and a tabloid from the truck stop in her lap. She looked remarkably at peace, as though my dad's departure had relieved her of a terrible weight. I realized that there is a look of weariness worn by people who are always scared. It's not caused by fear, but by the anticipation of fear and the knowledge that it cannot be avoided. When my dad wasn't home, Mom could never totally relax because he was always out there, drunk and mean, angry at life, and ready to come home and take it out on his family. When he was home, the slightest misstep could send him into a fury.

"Did you hear from Dad?" I asked.

Mom shook her head and looked back down to the tabloid. "No. Maybe he'll call when he gets to wherever it is he's going."

"Where's Edgel?" The Rocket 88 had not been in its usual place.

"He's off working."

"This late?"

"He said something about having to make an overnight run for the Farnsworth boys—over to West Virginia, somewhere, to pick up some parts."

"It couldn't wait until tomorrow morning?"

She looked back up, blinking twice and staring at me over the top of her glasses. "I didn't ask him, Jimmy Lee. I'm glad he's got the work. I'm going to need a little extra help around here."

"Okay. I've got some homework. I'll see in you the morning."

"Good night, sweetheart," she said, already back to her reading.

I stopped at the bottom of the steps and turned back. "Mom, you know that tomorrow night is Senior Night? You and Dad were supposed to walk out on the field with me before the game. You think maybe Edgel will come with you instead?"

"I expect he'd be tickled to do it. I'll ask him in the morning."

I went on up the stairs and read two chapters of world history and made a half-hearted attempt to write the last assignments Miss Singletary had given me before the competition. As I wrote, my chin kept falling to my chest and my pencil ran off the page. Finally, I gave up, set the notebook atop my history book, and crawled into bed.

At a few minutes before 3 AM on Friday, the day of the big game, I was awakened from a hard sleep by my mother, who was standing at the foot of my bed, rolling her hands upon one another. "Get dressed and come downstairs," she said.

It took me a minute to get my bearings. "What's wrong?"

She was already heading out of the room. "Just come downstairs."

I pulled on a pair of jeans and an ELKS FOOTBALL T-shirt and followed her down the stairs. She was standing at the railing on the front porch, the radio that was usually on the counter in the kitchen was at her feet, the electric cord stretched through the torn screen door and plugged into an outlet in the living room. The placid look that had been on her face a few hours earlier was gone. Her eyes were red-rimmed and a damp tissue was balled up in her fist.

"What's wrong, Mom?"

She nodded to the southwest. I looked over a moonless sky, unsure of what I was looking for until I spotted an orange glow that reached over a distant hill line. It was not unlike the flicker of a television in a dark room with staccato bursts of light flashing off the cloudy sky. Mom dabbed at her eyes. I didn't understand. Somewhere, deep in the hills between the deserted mining town of Moonville and McArthur, an inferno raged. It took a baritone newscaster at WCHI in Chillicothe to make things clear.

Good morning, this is Chet West at WCHI, your southern Ohio news leader. And this is your three o'clock report. Firefighters from four area departments are fighting a raging fire at the Morgan Lumber Company outside of McArthur. The blaze was spotted shortly after 1 AM by Vinton County Sheriff's Deputy Dewey LaMarr, who was on patrol in the area. LaMarr told WCHI that flames were already shooting out of the roof of the building when he spotted the fire. We have Deputy LaMarr on the phone. Deputy, thanks for joining us . . .

Without looking at my mom, I asked, "Are you sure Edgel went out of town for the Farnsworths?"

"That's what he told me he was doing. He called me at the truck stop yesterday afternoon and said he had to make a run to West Virginia. That's all I know."

That was Vinton County Deputy Dewey LaMarr. Again, four area fire departments are fighting an inferno at the Morgan Lumber Company, which you heard Deputy LaMarr say is fully engulfed and destined to be a total loss.

Tears were now rolling down my mother's cheeks. She was biting the first knuckle of an index finger. "They'll put him in prison forever, Jimmy Lee. They won't fool with him this time. He'll never get out."

"Mom, you don't know that it was Edgel."

She looked at me as though she had conceived, birthed, and raised the most ignorant human being on earth. "Oh God, Jimmy Lee, he'll never breathe free air again after this." I hugged Mom and she sobbed a wet ring on my shoulder.

After a while, I released my grip and she dabbed at her eyes while the tears continued to flow. I went back inside, slipped on a pair of shoes and a jacket, and went back to the porch. "Where are the keys to the pickup?" I asked.

"Why do you want them?"

"I'm going to drive over to the Farnsworths' junkyard and see if Edgel's car is in the lot and the truck is gone."

"I'm going with you."

A few minutes later, Mom came out of the house wearing a nightgown extending below her beige raincoat, a pair of white, thick-soled shoes that she wore at the truck stop diner, and carrying her purse. "That's a good look, Mom."

She hit me in the arm, glad for the moment of humor. We got into the pickup truck and headed down the drive. It was only a little more than four miles to the Farnsworths' junkyard, but it was a fifteen-minute drive over Township Road 3 as it snaked over Ingham Hill. "It could be a fluke, Mom. It might not have been Edgel."

"That boy has a good heart, but a temper like a firecracker and the good sense that God gave a goose. I love him to death, but I swear he has never made a rational decision in his life."

"I think you've been listening to Dad for too long. I've gotten to know Edgel since he came home. He's not as bad as Dad always made him out to be. Edgel's got a lot of common sense. And he told me he doesn't ever want to go back to prison. He wouldn't risk that by doing something like this."

"They'll blame him, no matter what. I know they will."

No amount of consoling was going to calm her down. We drove past the old entrance to the Gem of Egypt Mining Company's No.

9 mine and down the grade to the Farnsworths' junkyard, which consumed a plateau of a strip-mined hilltop. I eased the pickup onto the rutted, gravel parking lot that surrounded a cinder block building with milkweed growing from the cracked foundation. A ten-foot chain-link fence with concertina wire extended from both sides of the building. I swung the pickup around so the high beams could scan the yard beyond the gates. Edgel's Rocket 88 was nowhere to be found, but sitting just inside the gate and alongside the south side of the building was the flat-bed Ford. My heart and lungs felt as though they would explode and I was suddenly chilled.

"What?" my mom asked. I didn't answer. "Jimmy Lee, what?"

Finally, I nodded toward the Ford. "That's the truck that Edgel drives when he makes pickups for the Farnsworths," I said. "The Rocket 88 isn't here, either. He always parks it right there in that open spot inside the gate."

"He lied to me?"

I shrugged. "I don't know, Mom, I don't know."

Chapter Seventeen

My mom sobbed and struggled to catch her breath all the way home from the junkyard. I was silent in my disappointment. By the time we got back to the house, the orange glow had intensified in the distance. The newscaster on WCHI said that Elk Township Fire Chief Deek Daniels had decided to allow the fire to burn itself out. There were no fire hydrants that far out in the township and the pumper trucks were virtually useless in fighting a fire of that magnitude. It was, after all, a large, wood-frame building that housed tons of lumber. There was nothing in the building that wasn't fuel.

Neither of us could go back to bed. We sat on the porch swing, hands shoved deep in our coat pockets, our breath turning to vapor, and watched the orange glow until it was drowned out by the sunrise, which in turn revealed a haze of white smoke that had rolled into the hillsides. At six thirty, just as I was preparing to get ready for school, I spotted a cloud of dust rising from where Red Dog Road intersects with County Road 12. The dust billowed in brown clouds that moved up the road. I watched the rising dust until the sources revealed themselves in the clearing below our property— three Vinton County Sheriff's cruisers. Two of the cars came up our drive; the third parked across our drive on Red Dog Road, blocking any escape route.

"Oh God, oh God, oh God," my mother cried.

"Mom, go on inside. I'll talk to them."

The two cars that ascended the drive did so in a slow, deliberate manner. They were doubtlessly scanning the property for my brother. When the lead car stopped in front of the house, Sheriff McCollough stepped out, hitching up his belt and scanning the tree line, his trademark toothpick wedged in the corner of his mouth. Two frowning deputies exited from the second car. The sheriff hadn't changed much since the day I had been hitting stones in the yard when he came looking for Edgel the last time. I knew this was about to be a repeat of that meeting. "G' morning," he said, touching the brim of his black, cowboy-style hat.

"Morning, Sheriff."

"Your brother hereabouts?"

"Which one?"

"Edgel."

I shook my head. "No, sir."

The sheriff removed his hat and squinted into the morning sun as he looked around the property, craning his neck as he checked out the old shed in the back. He slowly removed a handkerchief from his hip pocket and wiped out the sweatband of his hat before using it on a wide forehead, though I didn't see any sign of perspiration. "Where is he?" He put his hat back on and adjusted it low on his brow. "I need to talk to him."

"I don't know, Sheriff, and that's the God's truth. He said he had to work last night and I haven't seen him since."

"Working, huh? Where's he working?"

"Farnsworth Salvage."

"That's an odd time to be working for a junkyard, the middle of the night, wouldn't you say?"

I shrugged. "He delivers and picks up parts. He has lots of odd hours."

"Uh-huh. He's not in that house, is he, son?"

"No, sir."

"Mind if I come in and have a look around?"

"I don't think that would be such a good idea right now, Sheriff. My mom's in there and she's been pretty upset lately. She and my dad split up, and I think this would just upset her more."

"Where's your dad?"

"Florida. He went down there to work with Virgil at the carnival."

"I thought he was working at the sawmill."

"He was, but he lost that job." It was information I suspect he already knew.

He nodded. "You know, it would be pretty easy for me to get a search warrant for that house."

"You could, but it would be a waste of your time. I told you, Sheriff, he's not here."

The sheriff pulled a business card out of his wallet and walked it up the steps to me. "When you see Edgel, you tell him it's real important for him to get in touch with me immediately."

"Yes, sir, I will."

As he started back down the steps, he turned, the brim of his hat covering his face in shadow. "Aren't you a little curious about why we want to talk to him?"

"My dad got fired from Morgan's mill and it burned to the ground last night. Edgel did nine years for arson. It doesn't take Sherlock Holmes to figure out why you want to talk to him."

He winked and said, "Be sure to tell him to call."

"I will."

"You've got a big game tonight, don't ya?" he asked as he reached for his cruiser door.

"The biggest I've ever played in."

"Good luck with that."

"Thank you. I appreciate it."

I watched as the cruisers turned around in the dried foxtail, leaving treadmarks in the frost, and headed back down the drive. The three cruisers parked at the bottom of the hill as the sheriff and deputies talked, I assumed, about how to keep an eye on the place. As the officers conversed, the school bus rolled to a stop at the bottom of the drive. When the door opened, one of the deputies walked over and spoke to the bus driver for a full minute. When he stepped away, the bus continued down Red Dog Road to the turnaround. I planned to go to school late as I didn't want to run out on my mother and I was hoping for a chance to speak to Edgel.

According to our quarterback and offensive captain Roy Otto, Coach Battershell was apoplectic when the bus arrived at school without me. Word must have reached Miss Singletary about the same time and she went running to the gym. "Where is he?"

"I have no idea," said Coach Battershell.

They both looked at Roy, who shrugged. "I haven't seen him since we left the spaghetti dinner last night."

Coach Battershell sent Roy to the office to tell Principal Speer to get someone to cover his classes because he was driving out to our house. Roy said Miss Singletary ran out of the school behind the coach. They jumped into Coach's Pontiac and headed toward Red Dog Road.

I was able to pick up the story shortly after this point as a parade of cars climbed our rocky drive. It was eight thirty when Edgel's Rocket 88 turned off of Red Dog Road into our drive. Coach Battershell's Tempest was right behind him, followed by two Vinton County Sheriff's cars, which had been hidden in the brush near the entrance to the dump. The cruisers charged up the hill with red lights flashing and sirens echoing off the hills. Coach Battershell stopped his car when he saw the lights and the sheriff's cars bound hard over the rocky edge of the driveway—one to the left, the other to the right—bouncing through the rock and weeded hillside and navigating around the rusting remains of the two-hundred-dollar specials, finally catching up to the Rocket as it pulled up alongside the front porch. The sheriff's cars slid broadside in the dirt and gravel in front of the house, sending up plumes of dust as the deputies climbed out with pistols drawn, screaming at Edgel to get his hands where they could see them.

Edgel looked up at me. Though I couldn't hear him over the dying sirens and the screaming deputies, I read his lips. "What the fuck?"

"Shut up and keep those hands where I can see them," yelled one deputy with a brush cut and moon-shaped scar around his right eye. The three deputies surrounded the car, holding their revolvers with both hands and pointing them at Edgel's head.

Not being a total stranger to this routine, Edgel kept both hands on top of his steering wheel and did not move. One deputy opened the door while the other two barked at Edgel to get out of the car and on the ground. Edgel turned in the seat and dropped out of the car to his knees, hands interlocked behind his head. One of the deputies gave him a push and he went down hard on the side of his face. The same deputy holstered his revolver and handcuffed Edgel behind his back.

"We got a lot of questions for you," said the deputy with the moon scar.

"Am I under arrest?" Edgel asked.

"We'll be the ones asking the questions, Hickam." He spat out the name Hickam as though he had a mouthful of dog piss.

"I've got the right to know if I'm under arrest."

"Right now, you're being held on suspicion of arson."

Edgel raised his head, one side was covered with dust and flecks of red dog, and said to me, "Tell Mom to call Mr. Crawford and have him meet me at the jail."

Timothy Crawford had been Edgel's court-appointed attorney on the burglary charge years ago. Moon Scar leaned down close to Edgel's face and sneered, "Lawyering up already, Hickam? I'd say that's a sure sign of someone who knows his ass is in the soup."

"I know my rights, deputy, and I'm not saying another word until I speak with my attorney."

Moon Scar watched as the other two deputies each hooked him under an arm and lifted Edgel to his feet. He looked at me for a moment and his eyes held a desperation that I had never seen, even when he was in prison. As they lowered his head and shoved him into the back of one of the cruisers, Coach Battershell and Miss Singletary walked up to the porch. Inside, I could already hear Mom talking to the receptionist at the Athens law firm of Crawford and Oschendorf.

As the two cruisers headed back down the drive and toward the county jail in McArthur, Mom came running out of the house and down the steps. "Where are you going?" I asked.

"Down to the jail. My boy needs me. I'll call when I know something." Coach and Miss Singletary stood on the porch with me while Mom gunned the pickup, throwing pebbles against the bare lattice at the bottom of the porch.

"What's going on?" Miss Singletary finally asked.

"They just took Edgel in for suspicion of arson," I said.

"Oh no, for the fire at the sawmill?" she asked.

"I think that's a safe bet."

"Where was he last night?"

I shook my head. "I don't know. Hopefully, working." But in my mind I could visualize Edgel parked along a dirt road on the top of a hillside, sitting on the hood of the Rocket 88, his back resting against the windshield, sipping a bottle of Pabst Blue Ribbon and laughing as he looked down on the carnage he had created. "What are you guys doing here?"

"Looking for you," Coach Battershell said. "I know you probably have a lot on your mind right now besides football, but you can't play tonight if you're not in school today."

"I know. I'll be there. I'll get my stuff together and take the Rocket. Edgel's not going to need it today." I started toward the door, but the coach and Miss Singletary just stood on the top step. "What?"

"We'll just wait here and give you a ride," Coach said. "Hustle up."

Hardly anybody at school was talking about the fire. Weeks after my winning the essay contest was announced, students continued to debate the veracity of my victory. But when one of the biggest employers in Vinton County burned to the ground, barely a word was spoken. Mostly everyone was buzzed about that night's game with McArthur Central Catholic.

Three times that day, I went to the school office and called home, but no one answered. I listened to the noon news on the radio in Coach Battershell's office. They interviewed the fire chief and carried a couple of minutes about the fire. The reporter said a suspect had been taken into custody for questioning, but no arrests had been made and no other details were available.

After school, Mrs. Ullrich of the athletic mothers was at the entrance of the locker room passing out bulbous, white mums to senior football players and cheerleaders. "What's this for?" I asked.

"Pin it to your mom's coat for the senior night introductions," she said. "It goes on the left."

I had completely forgotten that it was senior night, and I was certain that my mom hadn't given it a thought since seeing her oldest son hauled away in the back of the sheriff's cruiser. I stood to the side and waited for Mrs. Ullrich to hand out all of her mums. "Mrs. Ullrich, don't announce me tonight."

"What? Why?"

"I don't have anyone here. My dad's in Florida and Mom's busy. She can't be here."

"Jimmy Lee, that's too bad. Are you sure you don't want to walk by yourself? I hate to see you miss senior night."

I forced a smile and set the mum in the cardboard tray she was holding. "Thanks, Mrs. Ullrich, but I'd rather miss it than walk by myself."

The booster club fed us a pre-game meal of pancakes and sausage at four o'clock in the school cafeteria. I mostly picked at the food, unable to force anything into a stomach that was knotted high in my chest. Afterward, we stretched out on the wrestling mats in the gymnasium and relaxed, taking turns going to the training room to get our ankles taped. Gary Rittenhouse, our standout defensive end, had driven over to the little general store in Zaleski to pick up a copy of the *Vinton County Messenger*. Every Friday in the fall, the sports editor for the *Messenger* ran a photo of himself in a turban, gazing wild-eyed into a crystal ball, and predicted the outcomes of that night's high school football games. We had great fun reading his predictions and they served as minor inspiration as he predicted we would lose nearly every week. This week was no exception.

The East Vinton Elks have been the area's surprise team of the year, contending for a Black Diamond Conference championship and posting their first eight-win season since the Eisenhower Administration. Unfortunately for the men in navy and silver, the fun ends tonight. The undefeated McArthur Central Catholic Crusaders have won six consecutive conference championships and have no intentions of losing to the upstarts from the eastern side of the county. With bruising fullback Reno DiGaudio leading the way, the Crusaders roll, 35-6.

"Ouch," Rittenhouse said. "He doesn't even think it will be close."

"We'll invite him out here for a nice crow dinner after we beat their asses tonight," I said.

"I like your attitude, boss." He pushed himself off the mat. "I'm going to get taped." As he passed me, he dropped the paper on my chest.

I read the other predictions and casually flipped through the paper. When I folded and tucked the sports section away, I was face-to-face with a front-page banner headline:

Morgan Lumber Burns to Ground

And the subhead:

Convicted Arsonist Edgel Hickam
Jailed by Sheriff for Questioning

The Morgan Lumber Company, one of Vinton County's largest employers, burned to the ground this morning in a blaze so intense that area firefighters had little choice but to allow the fire to burn itself out.

The fire was reported by a Vinton County Sheriff's deputy shortly after 1 AM. Soon after, the orange glow of the inferno could be seen for miles away as the fire was fed by the tons of timber stacked inside the wood-frame mill.

By noon, the building had collapsed into the subbasement and was largely contained within the 100-year-old stone and brick foundation.

Meanwhile, a local man with a previous conviction for arson was picked up by sheriff's deputies this morning and is being held in the Vinton County Jail for questioning. Sheriff Malcolm McCollough identified the man as Edgel R. Hickam, 29, of 10107 Red Dog Road in Knox Township.

Hickam was convicted of a single count of burglary and arson in 1966 and sentenced to 12 years in prison. McCollough said Hickam was a suspect in several other burglary-arsons.

He was recently paroled from the state reformatory in Mansfield.

"Mr. Hickam has been less than cooperative," Sheriff McCollough said. "He must understand that given his criminal history, he needs to work with us if he hopes to clear his name."

McCollough said a relative of Hickam worked at Morgan Lumber until recently being fired. A source close to the investigation said the relative was Hickam's father, Nicholas.

Calls to the Hickam residence were not answered.

The story was accompanied by two black-and-white photos—
a six-column photo of firefighters standing around the building's
smoldering remains and a mug shot of Edgel from his first arrest.

The story went on in painful detail for many more paragraphs,
but I had read all I could stomach. I dropped the sports section on
the mat, balled up the rest of the paper, and threw it in the trash on
my way to get my ankles taped.

Unfortunately, I wasn't the only one in Vinton County who had
seen the story.

At six thirty, Roy Otto and I led our team to the field for warm-
ups. A half-dozen guys from McArthur Central Catholic were
standing inside the gate next to the cinder track that led from our
locker room to the field. When they saw me coming, each pulled a
cigarette lighter from their pocket and began flicking it on and off.
"Hey, Hickam, how's your brother—ol' Sparky?" one asked. Flick,
flick, flick. "Smokey says, 'Only you can prevent lumber mill fires,'"
said another. Flick, flick, flick. "How about a little fire, scarecrow?"
said a third. Flick, flick, flick. My face was burning with anger, and I
ran harder to get to the field.

Elk Stadium was in a low area behind East Vinton High School,
built on the floodplains of Raccoon Creek. It was a modest stadium
with wooden bleachers and dim lights that befit the quality of
teams that East Vinton had produced over the years. On this night,
however, the atmosphere was electric. The stands on both sides of
the stadium were full and crowds stood three deep all around the
field. It was the largest crowd that I had ever played before. For
the first time since three o'clock that morning, Edgel, the burning
sawmill, and my distraught mother left my thoughts. Adrenaline
surged through my chest and I screamed, yelling until my face was
crimson and my head began to ache at my temples. It was game
time, and I was ready.

There wasn't much for Coach Battershell to say in the locker room before the game. We all knew how important this game was to us, our school, and the denizens of East Vinton County. We were playing for respect. "The future of this program rests on your shoulders," he said calmly. "East Vinton has been a doormat in this league since before you were born. You have a chance to bring respect to this program and secure its future." When he finished his talk, he said, "Seniors, go meet your parents." The other seniors got up and started filing out. "Jimmy Lee . . ."

"I'm staying in here," I said, keeping my head down.

"Jimmy Lee . . ." His voice grew more stern. I looked up; he pointed to the door. "Now."

I didn't need one more thing to add to the humiliation of the day, but I wasn't going to argue with the coach, and I did as I was told. I stepped in at the end of the line, following the clacking of steel cleats on the tile floor, and walked out the locker room door. When I did, I saw Miss Singletary standing at the bottom of the stairs wearing a brown suede coat, to the breast of which was pinned a white mum with a VE made of blue pipe cleaners adhered to the top. Tears started to fill my eyes. "I want you to know that I wouldn't poke holes in my good suede coat for just anyone," she said. I quickly brushed away the tears that were rolling down my cheeks. "Give me your arm." I did, and she escorted me to the end zone.

The captains were introduced last. Mr. Evans said, "And senior captain, number thirty-eight, Jimmy Lee Hickam, escorted by Miss Amanda Singletary." She walked tall and proud beside me, squeezing the inside of my arm.

Over the past few months, Miss Singletary had gone out of her way to help me in more ways than I can remember, including putting her teaching reputation on the line, but I was never more grateful to her than on senior night. It was, I thought, one thing to help me hone my writing skills and explain to me about the importance of personal hygiene, but that night, in front of the entire East Vinton community, she bravely stood up and walked with me, Nick Hickam's youngest son.

Football is an emotional game and my body was bursting with emotions on that evening. I was sad for Edgel, angry at my father for leaving and my mother for not showing up, and embarrassed at being born into a family that was looked upon like dog shit on the bottom of a dress boot. While my mind was on the game, this cornucopia of emotions was about to burst out of my chest when I led the Elks onto the field for the kickoff.

Since the day I had first showed up at practice in black dress socks and misfit shoulder pads that left blood blisters under my arms, Coach Battershell preached to me the importance of the first hit of the game. He said that delivering a bone-jarring hit on the first play would set the tempo for the entire game. I was not a particularly religious boy, but that night I asked God to please put the ball in the hands of McArthur Central Catholic fullback Reno DiGaudio on the first play from scrimmage.

Reno DiGaudio was about five foot ten and looked to be about the same width. He was built like a refrigerator with arms and led the county in rushing and scoring since it was virtually impossible for just one person to tackle him. He was a cocky bastard and, essentially, the entire McArthur Central Catholic offense. Stop Reno DiGaudio, I told myself, and you stop the Crusaders. I didn't think he had been hit hard all year. That's why I wanted the ball in his hands. I wanted a chance to light him up early.

On that first Friday in November, the Big Man upstairs decided to spiff me one.

McArthur Central Catholic's first play from scrimmage was a fullback dive off right tackle—their bread-and-butter play. The hole opened and DiGaudio came through it, head down, knees pumping.

I anticipated the play and filled that hole with a vengeance. My last thought before our collision was how sorry I was that Edgel wasn't in the stands to see this hit. I got low and shot up under DiGaudio's helmet and never stopped pumping my feet. The top of my helmet hit his face mask with a loud pop and his head jerked up as I drove him back, driving my shoulder into his chest as we fell.

The East Vinton faithful, I think, were cheering wildly. But I'm not sure because I kept my focus on DiGaudio. I watched him wince and groan as the wind rushed from his lungs. I stared at him until he looked back. I wanted him to know who had hit him and who was going to hit him every time he touched the ball for the rest of the game. After the Crusaders completed a pass for six yards, they ran another fullback dive, this time to the left. Again, I met DiGaudio in the hole and drove him down with a booming helmet-to-helmet collision.

It was the last time he ran the ball hard all night. He started dancing, looking for places to run instead of creating holes with his strength. He was no longer running for yardage. Rather, he was running away from me, and with each play, the confidence of our defense grew. The offense fed off the success of our defense and the outcome of the game was never in doubt.

We defeated the McArthur Central Catholic Crusaders 24-0. They only earned two first downs all night. When the game was over, the East Vinton fans rushed the field. I looked for Reno DiGaudio to shake his hand, but he skulked away to the locker room, head down. That was fine. I was being mobbed by our fans. We had brought such joy to the little communities of East Vinton County. For one night, they had something to cheer about. Principal Speer walked by and patted me once on the shoulder and said, "Nice job, Jimmy Lee," but would not look me in the eye. They were the first words he had spoken to me since the day he summoned me to his office to question me about the essay.

The celebrations would go on well into the night, and I so wanted to be part of them, but I hadn't even gotten off the field when I was met by my senior night escort. Miss Singletary gave me a hug and kissed me on my sweaty cheek. "I'm very proud of you, Jimmy Lee. You played a great game," she said. "But you have another big game in the morning."

"I know, but you've got to let me enjoy this a little."

She smiled. "Absolutely. Enjoy it for an hour, and then I want you to go home and get your rest. I'll pick you up at seven-thirty."

When I got home that night, Mom was at the kitchen table eating leftover meatloaf and mashed potatoes and drinking a bottle of Rolling Rock that my dad had somehow missed in the refrigerator. Her face was swollen and her eyes were still rimmed in red. "How was your game?" she asked.

"Good. We won. We're conference champs—first time in about twenty years."

"That's nice."

I set my gym bag of sweaty clothes on the floor and made myself a cold meatloaf sandwich and poured a glass of milk. "When'd you get home?" I asked.

"Late this afternoon sometime. The whole day's been a blur. I stayed around the jail to talk to Mr. Crawford after he talked to Edgel."

"Did they charge Edgel with setting fire to the mill?"

She shook her head. "They don't have anything on him."

"Yet," I said and she glared hard at me. "So, you got home this afternoon?"

"About five o'clock or so, I suppose."

"Mom, it was senior night, you know? You were supposed to be there to escort me out on the field before the game."

She didn't look up, but sighed and said, "I've been awfully upset, Jimmy Lee. I just forgot."

"You know, Mom, you've got other sons besides Edgel." The look she gave me was too familiar. It was the one she wore after being slapped by my dad, and I immediately regretted allowing the words to exit my mouth. "I'm sorry. I shouldn't have said that. I just would have liked to have had one of my parents there, that's all. So, what did Mr. Crawford say?"

"He says Edgel claims he didn't do it."

"Uh-huh. Well, that would be my story, too."

She looked past me, her eyes distant and sad, and said, "You're a good boy, Jimmy Lee." She refocused on me and smiled. "But the rest of the men in this family have just worn me out. Your dad, your brothers, they were just so much work, always in trouble, drinking, fighting, and carrying on. You've never given me problems or cause to fret, Jimmy Lee, and I appreciate that, and I'm sorry that you never got the attention you deserved. Them other ones just filled up my dance card."

"I know, Mom. You've always worked hard and did your best."

"That doesn't make it right to ignore you."

I got up and put my dish and empty glass in the sink. "I've got to get to bed, Mom. I've got the essay contest over in McArthur in the morning."

She blinked twice and looked at me with puzzlement. "What essay contest is that?"

I kissed her on the forehead. "G' night, Mom. I love you."

Chapter Eighteen

I was feeling particularly dapper in my navy blazer, white shirt, red-and-gray-striped tie, and khaki slacks. After making the purchases, I ironed the shirt and placed all four items of clothing in the back of my closet and saved them for this day. The previous Saturday I had taken the pickup truck to Athens and bought a pair of oxblood loafers, which at that moment were too tight over the arch of my foot and I was wishing that I had broken them in before wearing them to the writing competition. "I think I'll take these shoes off once the competition begins," I said. "They're too tight."

"That bitch," Miss Singletary said.

"Excuse me?"

It was eight forty on Saturday morning. We had just pulled into the parking lot of McArthur Roosevelt High School. The vein in Miss Singletary's neck bulged like a weak spot in a garden hose and pulsated with the staccato beat of her heart. Her hands clenched the steering wheel, her knuckles turned the color of pearls, and red blotches suddenly peppered her neck. "Oh, that bitch," she repeated.

In all the time I had spent with Miss Singletary, never once had I heard her utter a curse word. I failed to see the object of her venom and sat quietly while she put the car in park and turned to me, her cheeks drawn so tight they looked like a drum skin stretched over her jaw. "You're starting to scare me a little, Miss Singletary," I said.

"Look who's here," she said.

I leaned forward in my seat and spotted the source of the outburst. Walking across the lot was the other East Vinton English teacher, Mrs. Johanessen, and her daughter, Catherine. "I can't believe she would stoop to this," Miss Singletary said as she bolted from the car and planted herself between the Johanessens and the front door of the school. "Well, what a surprise," Miss Singletary said in a sweet, sing-song tone. "Mrs. Johanessen, what brings you two here? Did you come to support Jimmy Lee?" Her tone was civil, but the words slipped out between clenched teeth and there was no disguising her anger.

Mrs. Johanessen swallowed, one of those hard, nervous gulps that looked like she was trying to force down a tennis ball. "Um, no, well, I certainly hope Jimmy Lee does well. But we're here because Catherine is participating in the county competition."

"How can that possibly be since she didn't win the East Vinton competition?"

"The Alpha & Omega Literary Society awarded her an at-large bid."

"An at-large bid, you say? Why, I've never heard of such a thing, which is odd because I'm the contest coordinator at the high school. Why wasn't I informed of this?"

Without answering, Mrs. Johanessen put her hand on the shoulder of her daughter, who had been staring at the sidewalk the entire time, and guided her around Miss Singletary and into the school. Miss Singletary was so angry she was shaking. "The nerve and unmitigated gall of that woman," she spewed. "This is so unfair to you, Jimmy Lee. I am so sorry. She lobbied the Alpha & Omega Literary Society to get Catherine in here, and that doddering Ernestine Wadell caved to her."

"Can she do that?"

"It's their contest, Jimmy Lee. I imagine they can do whatever they want. I can go in there right now and protest if you want."

I waved at air. "Who cares," I said. "I already beat Catherine once; I'll do it again. I'll just pretend like she's Reno DiGaudio. I'll give her a forearm under the chin and take her down." I winked. "In a purely figurative sense, of course."

Miss Singletary smiled. "Why don't you give her mother a forearm under the chin—in the purely literal sense?"

We assembled in the gymnasium, where nine desks had been placed in a large semicircle—one for each of the eight winners from each high school in the county and one for the newly created at-large berth. My name was hanging from a placard on a desk at the far end of the semicircle. Ernestine Wadell of the Alpha & Omega Literary Society stood at a table in the middle of the semicircle. She gave me an obligatory smile and said, "Please take your seat so we can get started on time."

Miss Singletary gave my elbow a single squeeze and said, "You're ready. Go get 'em."

As I walked to my desk, two pens and a dictionary in my left hand, I looked back at her, grinned, and made two lifting motions with my right forearm. It made her smile.

On each desk was a blue notebook. At 9 AM, Mrs. Wadell welcomed everyone and wished us good luck. "You will have two hours to write your essay and it is not to exceed five hundred words. It must begin with the words, 'My hero is . . .' You may begin."

It took me most of the two hours to compose my essay. Catherine and a girl at the other end of the semicircle continued to work on their essays as I stood and stretched. In the bleachers, Miss Singletary and Mrs. Johanessen were sitting a full section apart and doing their best not to look at each other. When I stood, Miss Singletary began packing away the stack of papers she had been grading.

I thanked Mrs. Wadell for sponsoring the competition and handed her my essay. "I appreciate the opportunity to compete," I said.

"You're so very welcome," she said, slipping my blue notebook into a manila envelope with those of the students who finished before me. She handed me a sealed envelope with my name written in a shaky script. I slipped a finger under the flap and tore open the top as we walked out of the school. It was an invitation to the awards luncheon in two weeks.

"It's for me and two guests. Do you think Coach Battershell will let me take you to the luncheon?"

"He has absolutely no say in the matter," she said, smiling. "Your mother will want to go, too, won't she?"

"We'll see."

When we were heading out of the parking lot, it was starting to spit snow, heavy, wet flakes coming in hard from the west. Miss Singletary finally asked in an excited tone, "So, how do you think you did?"

"Pretty good, I think."

"Who was your hero?"

"Coach Battershell."

"Oh, that's so nice. He'll appreciate that."

"Please don't tell him."

"Why? He'll be flattered."

"Please don't. I don't want him to know. Don't tell him."

"Okay, I won't."

"Promise?"

She crossed her heart with her index finger. "Are you going to the dance tonight?"

I shrugged. "I don't know. I might."

"Might? It's a victory dance for the football team; you're the defensive captain. You have to be there."

"Things are pretty crazy at home right now. I have to see what's going on with Mom and Edgel."

Chapter Nineteen

The sheriff had nothing on Edgel.

In the two days after he was incarcerated, deputies were able to verify Edgel's alibi. He gave deputies a terse account of his whereabouts the night before and the morning of the fire. The day before the fire, he had left about mid-afternoon and driven to a salvage yard outside of Grafton, West Virginia, for the Farnsworth brothers to pick up two stacks of hubcaps, a box of taillights, and the grill from a 1964 Thunderbird. Along the way, he swung by a body shop in Gallipolis, Ohio, to drop off the front bumper for a 1965 Volkswagen Beetle. Because it was a light load, Edgel just took the Rocket 88 instead of the flatbed. He got gas at Warren's Pennzoil in Athens and had a receipt, as the Farnsworths said they would cover his expenses. He ate at a fast-food restaurant along the way and had a receipt for two burgers, fries, and a small coffee. When he got to Grafton, Edgel stopped at a pay phone and called the owner of the salvage yard at home. The man drove out and met Edgel at the salvage yard. Edgel paid him in cash for the parts and got a handwritten receipt. It was after nine o'clock by then, and Edgel went to a truck stop for dinner. He had forgotten to get a receipt, but remembered that the woman who waited on him had dark hair, a hair-sprouting mole on her chin, and a withered leg on which the sole of one shoe was several inches thick to compensate for the defect. He thought it was her left leg, but couldn't be positive. Because it was so late and the Rocket had been running hot, Edgel got a hotel room at the Mountaineer Motor Lodge, not far from the truck stop. The room was $15.99 and he had the receipt. The owner couldn't remember the exact time Edgel checked out the next morning, but recalled that it was early. He guessed around 7 AM. He stopped for gas near Parkersburg and got a receipt.

Deputies had spent the two days covering the territory between Vinton County and Grafton. Much to their great disappointment, Edgel Hickam was nowhere near Vinton County when the fire began at the Morgan Lumber Company.

My mother showed up at the high school on Monday afternoon just before the start of eighth period—the last of the day. The student office assistant pulled me out of algebra and Mom was waiting in the lobby outside the office, still in her waitress uniform. She had been crying again and I anticipated the worst. "They're letting Edgel out of jail," she whispered. "Can you go over to McArthur with me to pick him up?"

Air rushed from my lungs and I felt light-headed. I signed out and drove Mom over to the jail. All along the way, she sniffled and said, "Praise Jesus, praise Jesus, praise Jesus." When we walked in, the deputy at the front desk lifted his chubby face only long enough to recognize us as Hickams and used the eraser end of his pencil to point to some chrome and vinyl chairs in the corner of the room. "You can wait over there. He'll be out in a bit," the deputy said.

It was thirty minutes before Edgel came out, looking tired and in need of a shave of his spotty beard. He was wearing the same clothes he had been arrested in and a brown stain from the muddy drive streaked across his thighs. Mom was bawling as she ran up and threw her arms around him. He hugged her and patted her back until she pulled away. "You whipped them Micks, huh?" were his first words to me.

"Whipped 'em bad. Coach Battershell said I could take the game film and the projector home so you could see it."

He nodded. "I'd like that. How'd it go with your writin' contest?"

I shrugged. "Good, I think. I was happy with what I wrote. We'll see. How're you doing?"

"Let's get the hell out of here," he said. As we walked to the pickup truck, he continued, "Them lousy bastards have known for two days that I didn't set that fire. When I got back Friday morning, I gave the Farnsworths all my receipts and they paid me back out of petty cash. Mr. Crawford had them receipts Friday afternoon and he showed them to Sheriff McCollough, but that wasn't good enough. He had his deputies crawling all over creation trying to figure a way to bust my ass, anyways. He was pissed when he knew it wasn't me. Now he'll have to go out and figure out who really did it."

I climbed behind the wheel of the pickup, Mom slid to the middle, and Edgel rode shotgun. "Maybe nobody did it," I offered. "Maybe it was just an accident—bad wiring or something."

"I don't care what it was, so long as my boy is out of jail and not involved," Mom said. "I just want you back home, that's all."

When we got to the house, Mom stepped outside the truck and said, "I'm going to the store and pick up some things. I'm going to fix us another celebration dinner."

"Mom, you don't have to cook a celebration dinner every time I get out of jail. It's not something I really want to celebrate."

I kept the pickup idling. She kissed Edgel on the cheek and ran around to the driver's side, dropped the truck in gear, and headed back down the drive. We watched until she made the turn out of the drive on to Red Dog Road. "Has the old man called?" Edgel asked.

"Nope. We haven't heard a word."

"Do you have the keys to the 88?"

"They're in the kitchen."

"How about snaggin' 'em? I want to drive over and see Mr. Morgan."

I had taken a step toward the house when his words registered. "Mr. Morgan? Why in God's name do you want to see him?"

"Because I want to look him square in the eye and tell him that I didn't burn down his damn sawmill."

"Edgel, the sheriff knows that. He'll tell Mr. Morgan. There's no need for you to do that."

"Do I need to go get those keys or are you going to get them for me?"

I had learned years earlier not to argue with a Hickam male. I fetched the keys from the brass hook under the cupboard. When I handed them to him, I said, "I still think it's a bad idea."

"I know. That's why I didn't ask you for your opinion." He grinned, fired up a smoke from the dashboard lighter and then fired up the Rocket 88. A minute later, we turned off Red Dog Road and were roaring toward the burned-out hull of the lumber mill.

A house trailer had been pulled onto the mud and slag lot. It sat at an angle near the northeast corner of the mill's blackened foundation. A garden hose ran from an outside faucet to the underside of the trailer. A sedan and a pickup truck were nosed up to the side of the trailer.

Edgel parked the Rocket 88 alongside the sedan, and I followed him up a set of pre-cast concrete steps and through an aluminum front door. Mr. Morgan's secretary, Nettie McCoy, was sitting at a desk just inside the door, a space heater at her feet glowing the same shade of orange as her makeup. The smile on her round face disappeared the minute she recognized Edgel. He looked just like a younger version of my dad. "Can I help you?"

"Yes, ma'am, I'd like to speak to Mr. Morgan, please. My name is Edgel Hickam."

She forced a smile, like a child pretending to enjoy an amusement park ride that was actually terrifying her. "I will see if Mr. Morgan is available."

Before she could push herself away from the desk, Cliff Morgan appeared from a room in the back of the trailer. He had his hands in his pockets and was wearing blue jeans and bedroom slippers. He was about five seven, had a belly that stretched his flannel shirt but looked like it could stop a bullet, and a pair of horn-rimmed glasses sitting on the top of a tuft of fading blond hair. He looked at Edgel for a long moment, withdrew his hands to his hips, and nodded a tacit hello. This was a no-nonsense man, I thought. No wonder someone as unpredictable as my dad couldn't get along with him. He stared at Edgel without offering entrée to a cordial conversation.

"Mr. Morgan, I'm Edgel Hickam."

"I know who you are."

"Then you know that I just spent three days in jail because Sheriff McCollough thought I was the one who torched your mill."

"Is there a reason for this visit, Mr. Hickam?"

"Yes, sir, there is. I wanted the opportunity to look you in the eye and tell you straight up that I did not burn down your sawmill."

He folded his arms. "That's a different story than what the sheriff told me. The last time I spoke to him he said it was just a matter of time before you were charged and placed under arrest."

"You call him again and ask him. He'll tell you they were able to verify that I was out of town from late afternoon the day before the fire until about eight o'clock the next morning. I was making a parts run for the Farnsworth brothers in West Virginia, and I've got receipts and witnesses that put me a long way from Vinton County when that fire started. I know you and my dad had some differences and given my record, people had good reason to suspect me. But I didn't do it. You can believe whatever you want, but I wanted to tell you that to your face."

Mr. Morgan looked at him for a minute, then at me. "You played a helluva game Friday night."

"Thank you."

"I used to play for East Vinton, you know?"

"No, sir, I didn't know that."

He nodded and said, "I played on the first conference championship team at East Vinton—1947. Unfortunately, we haven't had many in between those two." He looked back at Edgel. "You say you're working for the Farnsworths. Is that full time?"

"No, sir, just whenever they need a run."

"Are you looking for something steady?"

"Sure am."

"Okay, wait here a minute." He went to the office in the back of the trailer and returned with a pair of muddy work boots. "Mrs. McCoy gets perturbed when I wear these muddy shoes in the trailer." He laced up the work boots on a rubber mat just inside the door and pulled on a canvas work jacket as he pushed the door open. "Come on out here a minute."

We walked along a packed gravel road that circled around the north wall of the foundation. On the back side of the foundation was an opening that before the fire had been the service entrance to the basement. Fallen timbers crisscrossed throughout the basement and ash was ten feet deep. It was dank and smelled of smoke and ash. "I want to rebuild on this spot, so I need this cleared out and hauled to the landfill. Have you ever worked a front-end loader?"

"No, but I'm a pretty quick learner," Edgel said.

"How about a dump truck? Ever driven one?"

"I drive the Farnsworths' flatbed. I imagine it's about the same."

"You interested in the job?"

"Absolutely."

"Good. It pays three fifty an hour. You have to be here eight hours a day, but I'll pay time-and-a-half for overtime and you can work as many hours a day as you want. I need to get this cleaned out as soon as possible. You can do most of the basement with the front-end loader, but a lot of it will still have to be done by hand. There's a subbasement in the south end of the building. That's where the investigators from the state fire marshal's office say the fire started. The only entrance is a regular door and that will all have to be cleaned out with a shovel and wheelbarrow. Do a good job getting this cleaned out and we'll talk about a permanent job at the mill. No promises, but we'll talk."

"That's fair."

"It's a big job."

"I know."

"You start at seven in the morning. Don't be late. I'll give you a lesson on the front-end loader and you're on your own. You came down here to be straight with me, so I'll be straight with you. If you turn out to be a pain in the ass like your dad, you won't last long. I won't tolerate it."

"I understand."

"Good. I gave that man a good job and he pissed and moaned from the day he walked in here until the day he walked out."

"You're not telling me anything I don't already know, Mr. Morgan."

As we walked back around the side of the building, I asked, "Mr. Morgan, you said the fire started in the subbasement. How do they know that?"

"The propane tanks that heat the place in the winter and run some of the gear are in the basement in that end of the building. The main line running from the tanks was pulled apart at a union fitting. Whether it was an accident or done deliberately, who knows? But after the fire marshal's investigators said that was the cause, Sheriff McCollough got all excited because he said one of the houses you set on fire had the gas line disconnected in the basement to help it along."

"I was only convicted of one arson fire, Mr. Morgan."

There was an edge to his voice and I tried to keep the conversation rolling. "But you said the fire started in the subbasement."

"Propane is heavier than air and it all settled in the subbasement. It filled up with propane and sparked somehow. It blew straight up into the mill, hotter than hell. The gas kept feeding it. There was no way to save it."

Chapter Twenty

On November 26, a bright Monday morning and a day shy of two months since my dad left home, Mom served us a breakfast of sausage gravy, fried eggs, and toast. When the food was on the table she announced that after work that day she intended to drive to the county courthouse in McArthur and file for divorce from my dad. He had failed to call a single time or send her money. She considered that abandonment and she wasn't going to tolerate it.

I shrugged and said, "Okay."

Edgel said, "I don't blame you."

That night, Mom served us a dinner of chicken fried steak, mashed potatoes, and green beans. She confirmed that she had, indeed, filed for divorce. She then stated that the following morning she was leaving for Columbus for two weeks to attend a commercial driving school to obtain her license to drive tractor-trailers. Edgel and I looked at each other with furrowed brows.

When she finished truck-driving school, she said, she planned to leave Vinton County with a one-eyed truck driver—whose CB radio handle was Cyclops—named John Phillips, of Worcester, Massachusetts. Phillips was a regular at the truck stop and had, years earlier, professed his love for our mother. Once the divorce from Nick Hickam was finalized, she and John Phillips were going to be married and then drive his rig around the country. "He said we are going to be partners, in trucking and life," she said.

"What about us?" I asked. "Where are we going to live?"

"You can stay right here. The house is paid off. "

"But it's your house," I said.

"My name's on the title, but I'm not interested in spending another minute here. It's just where I lived with your father. It's not full of anything but his bad breath, cheap furniture, and enough horrible memories for one lifetime. You're both adults now and you don't need me. You'll figure it out. Now, I've got to get upstairs and pack. Be a couple of dears and clean up the kitchen for me."

My brother and I looked at each other as if our mother had suddenly announced she was running away to be, well, a truck driver. "Is she kidding?" I asked.

"She didn't sound like she was kidding."

"I'm not kidding," she yelled from halfway up the stairs.

In the sea of irrational behavior that was the Hickam family, my mother had been a beacon of sanity. I had never known her to act like a Hickam until that minute.

Edgel and I followed her up the stairs to her bedroom, where she had a suitcase open on the bed. "Mom, you can't be serious," Edgel said.

"I'm very serious. I've lived nearly thirty years with a man who screamed and yelled and slapped me around, and I'm not living that way the rest of my life. I'm getting out of Vinton County with a man who cares for me."

"But who is this guy?" I asked. "Where did you meet him?"

"He's a truck driver and I work in a truck stop. I surely hope you can figure it out from there, because that's all the detail I'm going to give. He's taking me to Columbus in the morning and paying for my school. He'll be back to pick me up on Friday and take me back next Monday."

"But, what do you know about this guy?" Edgel asked.

"I know enough. He says he loves me and I believe him."

I sat down on the bed next to Edgel. "So, I'm not going to have either parent around for the rest of my senior year?"

"Maybe your father will come back, but that ain't my concern. I'll be back for your graduation. I'm very proud of you, Jimmy Lee, but I have an opportunity here for a better life and I'm taking it. That may sound selfish to you and if it does, I'm sorry. But I may never get a better offer, so I'm going. Now, you boys shoo out of my room while I pack."

The next morning, Edgel and I drove Mom to the truck stop. There was an idling white Peterbilt behind the diner. When we pulled up, a thick-set man with dark glasses and a red ball cap with a creased bill jumped down from the cab and had both of Mom's suitcases stowed in his sleeper compartment before we all could get out of the pickup.

"Johnny, these here are my boys, Edgel and Jimmy Lee."

"Howdy," he said, shaking my hand without conviction.

Before we could try to strike up a conversation, Mom kissed us each on the cheek and walked to the passenger side door, her purse swinging on her arm. John Phillips climbed into the cab without uttering another word. The brakes hissed, the diesel roared, and black soot belched into the air. Tiny pieces of gravel shot out from under the tires as the rig eased onto the asphalt and headed toward Columbus.

"Did all this just happen?" Edgel asked. "Did our mom just leave home to become a truck driver?"

We watched until the truck had cleared the tree line and the last of the diesel exhaust dissipated in the brisk morning air. "Now what?" I asked.

Edgel climbed into the driver's side of the pickup. "You need to get to school and I need to get to work."

Chapter Twenty-One

The Alpha & Omega Literary Society luncheon was held the first Saturday of December at the Elks Lodge in McArthur. Edgel went as my guest. His interest in my welfare continued to surprise me. When I had first casually mentioned the luncheon, his eyes lit up and he asked, "Can I go?"

"Absolutely. They gave me three tickets."

So on the day of the luncheon, I sat at a circular table with Edgel, Miss Singletary, Coach Battershell, who had to pay for his own ticket, and a pimply faced kid from Adena Heights High School and his parents. Mrs. Johanessen and Catherine sat at a table with Mrs. Wadell and several overly made-up ladies from the Alpha & Omega Literary Society. Edgel was excited to be there with me and had bought a new white shirt and black slacks for the event.

"Nervous?" Miss Singletary asked as we were eating our entrées of roasted chicken breasts and asparagus.

"Not at all," I said. "There's nothing to be nervous about now. The votes are in. Are you nervous?"

"Extremely. I just want you to place—anywhere top three and I'll be happy. I'll take that plaque in to Principal Speer and nail it to his forehead and make him wear it for a week." I choked back a smile.

Mrs. Wadell walked to the lectern while we were still eating our dessert and began a ten-minute dissertation on the history of the Alpha & Omega Literary Society. Edgel asked the waitress for a second piece of cake. In reality, I was nervous. I wanted badly to win, not for myself, but to validate Miss Singletary's efforts. That, and I figured that if I beat Catherine Johanessen a second time, her mother would carry that agony to her grave.

Mrs. Wadell introduced all the high school winners and told the audience a little bit about them. When she got to me, she said that I was, "an accomplished football person."

"Our third-place winner is Beatrice Montgomery of Northwestern High School," Mrs. Wadell said. "Beatrice's hero is John F. Kennedy and she wrote a beautiful essay about our slain president." Beatrice read her essay, which I thought was very thin, as though she had been struggling to come up with a legitimate subject.

"Our second-place winner lists Ohio's own, John Glenn, as her hero. She is from East Vinton High School and was our at-large entrant, Catherine Johanessen."

Mrs. Johanessen jumped out of her seat, clapping wildly with flat hands in front of her face. I saw her look our way to see if we were clapping.

"That's shameless pandering," Miss Singletary whispered.

Catherine read her essay with great passion. It was a good essay, but I thought it lacked heart. Of course, that might be a biased view since I was also secretly hoping that she would trip on her way to the lectern.

"Our first-place winner wrote a fine essay. In fact, he stretched the rules a little in that he didn't write about his hero, but rather, his heroine." I could hear the air rush from Miss Singletary's lungs. I looked to her and she forced a smile, as though fighting back tears, and patted my hand. She put a hand in front of her mouth and whispered in the ear of Coach Battershell. She was, I imagine, telling the coach that I had written about him and that's how she knew I had been eliminated. It made me smile.

"You out of the runnin'?" Edgel asked.

"It is a marvelous essay and I must say that I am very impressed with this young man's abilities," Mrs. Wadell continued. "It gives me great pleasure to announce the winner of the 1973 Alpha & Omega Literary Society's county essay competition and a one thousand dollar scholarship is James Lee Hickam of East Vinton High School."

Miss Singletary sucked air and covered her mouth with both hands. Edgel was beating on my shoulder. Coach Battershell just nodded and winked. As I stood, I looked over at the Johanessens to see if they were clapping. They weren't; it made the victory even sweeter.

Mrs. Wadell handed me another gold medal, a plaque, and my blue notebook. I set the plaque on a table near the lectern and opened the notebook to the first page. Unlike reading the first essay, which had caught me off guard, I was prepared for this one. I read in a clear, confident voice.

My hero is a heroine.

Imagine living a life of constant derision. Imagine that your surname carried such negative connotations that you were constantly looked at with suspicion, your environment so fraught with despair that self-pity and anger consumed your being, and your actions, no matter how stalwart, could never override the reputation created by those who bore your name before you.

Now, imagine that after seventeen years, at a time when the two accomplishments in your life are perilously close to being taken away, that someone steps up to defend you.

My heroine is Miss Amanda Singletary, an English teacher at East Vinton High School. Twice in the past year, Miss Singletary came to my rescue. When I was in danger of failing junior English, she believed in my commitment to improve. When others found reason to call me a cheat, she believed that I was honest. She placed her reputation on the line and stood by me when others dismissed me as unworthy.

Sometimes, we perceive heroes and heroines to be those who are bigger than life—Washington, Lincoln, and Joan of Arc. Other times, we confuse them with those who are simply icons of popular culture—Elvis, Mickey Mantle, or Marilyn Monroe. We forget that fame or popularity should not be a determining factor. Miss Singletary is a heroine because her deeds are performed without the expectation of reward or recognition. She acts with an acute sense of right and wrong, and does so without fear of criticism or repercussion.

I do not think her a heroine simply for what she has done for me this year, but for what she has done for my future. It is said that if you give a man a fish, you feed him for a day. If you teach a man to fish, you feed him for life. Miss Singletary has taught me how to fish.

She has taught me about such intangible qualities as character, honor, and determination. She has taught me that not only is it important to stand up for yourself, but that it is equally important to stand up for others, even when the cause is unpopular, and especially when sentiment weighs heavily against a just person.

When I was filled with self-doubt, she encouraged me. When I wanted to run, she closed the door. And when I complained about the unfairness of life, she jerked me up by the collar and refused me pity.

A year ago, my goals were simple. I hoped to graduate from high school and find a factory job. But Miss Singletary has taught me to never underestimate myself. She has taught me that there is no shame in failure and that the only disgrace is to never try. Miss Singletary has made my future more impossibly promising than I was capable of imagining just a few months ago. No single person has had a greater impact on my life, and I can think of no more essential criterion for a heroine.

The ladies of the Alpha & Omega Literary Society and my fellow competitors, save one, gave me a warm applause. Miss Singletary stood and met me in front of our table, a moist tissue in one hand and a tear rolling down one cheek, and hugged me hard, slipping her hand behind my head and pulling it close so she could whisper in my ear. "I am so proud of you," she said.

I handed her the plaque. "Try not to mess it up when you nail it to his forehead."

When I turned, Mrs. Johanessen was standing near the door, staring at me with that familiar look of a woman who hated her life. Or it may have been the look of a woman who simply hated me.

The morning after the luncheon, a photograph of the top three finishers ran on the front page of the Sunday morning *Vinton County Messenger*. The third-place finisher and I were smiling and proudly showing our plaques. Catherine stood stoop-shouldered and looking like someone was holding a turd under her nose. Apparently, she had been thrilled to win second place until the moment they announced my name as the first-place winner.

Edgel ran out early that morning and bought five copies of the paper and woke me up by waving the front page in my face. Edgel just kept looking at the photo, shaking his head and saying, "This is so great."

I had believed that winning the Alpha & Omega Literary Society's county essay competition would bring me redemption. I believed that every student at the high school had for months been debating the veracity of my first essay and whether or not I was truly the author. But, in fact, I learned that my perception of everyone else's interest in the drama that had unfolded after I won the East Vinton competition was mostly imaginary. It was important to Miss Singletary and me, and apparently the Johanessens, but beyond that, no one had given it much thought after a week or so. Being accused of cheating had been so personally embarrassing that I assumed everyone in the school was equally intrigued with my redemption. But, like the fire at the sawmill, kids are too wrapped up in their own lives to be concerned with anything else.

When I walked into school Monday morning, no one said a word about the contest or my photo appearing in the newspapers.

At lunch, Kip Fillinger saw me in the gymnasium and said, "Hey, I saw your picture in the paper for winning that contest. So, you really did write that other essay, huh?"

"Yeah, of course I wrote it."

"That's awesome, man, way to go."

Miss Singletary had the editor of the school paper—the *East Vinton Herd*—write a story about the county competition and how two East Vinton students had taken the top two places. While the drama of proving that I wasn't a cheater was mostly conceived in my mind, I did notice one dramatic change in my life. When the story appeared in the high school paper, I didn't receive looks of astonishment because of my last name. For that, I was most grateful.

Chapter Twenty-Two

The storm blew in from the west before daylight on Friday, December 14, 1973, pelting the side of our house with sleet the size of grapes. It arrived in waves, like swarms of angry bees attacking the house as it hit the corrugated steel roof over our porch. The wind continued to whip up our hill and rattle our windows as Edgel stood at the stove fixing French toast and bacon. He slid my plate across the table and said, "This is going to be a hell of a day to be shoveling ash."

Edgel had taken just two bites of his breakfast when the phone rang. He pushed his chair back and groaned as he lifted himself out of his seat and answered the phone before the third ring. "Hello." He looked at me and rolled his eyes. "Yeah, I'll accept the charges." He waited another moment and said, "How are you doing? . . . Uh-huh. . . . Rapid City, South Dakota, huh? What are you doing there? . . . That's great. . . . Uh-huh, glad you're enjoying yourself. Glad you could finally call and let us know that you're still alive. That's considerate. Oh, and in case you're interested, we're doing just fine, too. . . . I'm not being a smart-mouth, I just thought you'd like to know, that's all." While he spoke, I stuffed a half piece of French toast in my mouth, gnawing away and keeping my eyes focused on Edgel, as though I needed to watch him to hear. "We're doing great. Just fine.

You have fun. . . . Uh-huh, you know, this phone call is costing me money that I really don't have. No, I'm not being a smart-mouth. . . . Fine. . . . Okay, I'm hanging up now. You take care of yourself." He hung up and looked at me, shaking his head.

"Dad's in South Dakota?"

"I don't know about him, but your mother is. She and Cyclops just got into Rapid City with a tanker full of liquid fertilizer."

"Mom? Are you kidding? I thought you were talking to Dad. Why did you hang up on her like that?"

"I know you were tight with Mom, Jimmy Lee, but she's no gem, either."

"Cut her a little slack, Edgel. It wasn't an easy life with Dad."

"She had a tough run with the old man, there's no disputin' that, but she had no business running off in the middle of your senior year, especially when you're doin' as good as you are. She could have waited another couple of months. Hell, you ought to be upset, too. She left you in the care of an ex-convict, for God's sake." He grinned, pulling on his coat and ball cap. "I'll see you tonight."

I looked out at the sleet that continued to pepper the windows and build up in tiny mounds on the sill. "Maybe you should wait awhile until it lets up a bit."

"I'm an hourly employee, Jimmy Lee. No work, no paycheck. This is why you're going to college. You don't want to work like this the rest of your life."

"There's nothing wrong with honest labor."

Edgel squeezed the top snap of his coat and pulled the collar up around his ears. "Jimmy Lee, do you know what kind of man it takes to stand out in the snow and sleet and shovel wet ashes for twelve hours?"

"A tough man?"

He shook his head. "No, just a man without a lot of options."

❖ ❖ ❖

By the time I started down the drive to catch the bus, the sleet had been replaced by a wet snow with flakes so heavy that they fell like rain and slid down my collar and chilled my neck. I wore my work boots and carried my dress shoes in my gym bag, not wanting to ruin them in the slush and mud. Polio Baughman was already at the foot of the hill, bouncing from foot to foot and shivering in a thin, hooded sweatshirt that he was holding closed by wrapping his pocketed hands around each other. His tennis shoes were untied and the laces sucked mud water like a candle wick draws hot wax. "Damn, Polio, don't you have a coat?"

He sniffed twice, drawing in the runny discharge. "I don't need no coat. I'm not cold anyways."

"No, of course you're not. My teeth always chatter like that when I'm toasty warm. Did you get your government report done?"

I think he shook his head no, but he was shivering so bad it was hard to tell what was intentional and what was the result of his plummeting core temperature. "Hell, no. I'm not doing any more of that shit. I'm not going back to school after Christmas anyways. I enlisted in the army."

"What? You enlisted? When?"

"Day before yesterday. The recruiter says I'm first-rate infantry material. That's exactly what he said—'first-rate infantry material.' I report to basic training right after the first of the year."

"Infantry material? Anyone with a pulse is infantry material. Why didn't you wait until the end of the school year? You've almost got your diploma in the bag."

The bus was creeping toward us on the snow-covered Red Dog Road. "I'm going to flunk government and senior English, and you can't graduate without passing both classes. Besides, I'm sick of school."

"Yeah, but it's East Vinton, Polio. If you keep showing up between now and the end of the year they'll pass you."

He gave me a look that said he could barely stand the sight of me. "You still going to college?"

"I hope."

"Well, goody for you, college boy. You get off Red Dog Road your way and I'll get off my way."

He got on the bus and stared out the window in silence all the way to school. For years, Polio had viewed me simply as another dogger—a kindred spirit. Then I won the essay contest, and earlier that week I had been named first team All-Ohio in football, the first player from East Vinton to ever earn the honor. He knew that I was getting scholarship offers for football and I think it was a little more than he wanted to swallow.

The buses were late getting to school and the front hall was covered with water and the dirty slush that had fallen from shoes and boots. Students took calculated steps to avoid becoming a victim of the slick linoleum. When I turned the corner of the main hallway, Coach Battershell and Miss Singletary were standing near the principal's office. Miss Singletary held a crumpled tissue in her hand, her eyes swollen and red and rimmed with tears. When she saw me, she ducked her head and climbed the stairs. Coach Battershell simply pointed toward the ramp that led down to the gymnasium; I followed. I could only imagine that the school administration had found out that Miss Singletary and Coach Battershell were dating and in light of Miss Singletary's confrontation with Mrs. Johanessen and Principal Speer, were now making an issue of their relationship.

I couldn't have been more wrong. I had seen Coach Battershell angry on numerous occasions, but there was no fire in his eyes on this morning. Rather, it was a look of hurt and fear, the same look found in the eyes of family members who had just followed an ambulance to the emergency room.

"Mrs. Johanessen has accused Miss Singletary of having an improper relationship with a student," Coach Battershell said, closing the door to his office.

I frowned, pondering his words only for a fraction of a second before realizing the implication. "Me?" He nodded, and I felt my knees buckle as a burning began deep in my loins, not unlike a kick to the balls. "Coach, honest to Jesus, there's never been anything going on between us, I swear, I never . . ."

He stopped me with a raised palm and a sad chuckle. "I know that, Jimmy Lee. That's not an issue. It's the allegation that's the problem."

"It's not a problem. I'll just march into Mr. Speer's office and tell him it's a bunch of bullshit. Nothing improper ever happened and I'll tell him so."

"Unfortunately, that isn't going to matter, Jimmy Lee. Mrs. Johanessen has made the accusation and Principal Speer is obligated to take it to the school board next Monday. There will be an investigation; Miss Singletary will be suspended with pay until it's completed. They won't find any wrongdoing, but the hook will have been set. Once someone makes that kind of allegation, you can never escape it. Other teachers will know. The community will know. Do you realize how personally embarrassing this is to her? She won't be able to stay, and the specter of doubt will follow her wherever she goes. It could end her career as a teacher."

"Why would Mrs. Johanessen do something like that?"

"Apparently, when she was unsuccessful in stopping you from winning the county essay contest, she turned on Miss Singletary. Mrs. Johanessen said she witnessed Miss Singletary give you a hug that was very intimate, kiss you on the ear, and heard her say, 'I love you,' after you won the contest."

"She gave me a hug and said she was proud of me. You were sitting there, for cryin' out loud."

"My word against hers. Again, it doesn't matter if it's true. It just has to be kicked around long enough to ruin her career. It's like cat piss in your carpet. You can scrub all you want, but the stink never really goes away."

I couldn't recall ever feeling so helpless. I wanted to punch something. "So, what can I do?" I finally asked.

"Keep your mouth shut and stay away from Miss Singletary. She's going home today so she won't be in class. Word might get out. If anyone asks you about it, just tell them you don't know what they're talking about, and for God's sake, no matter what anyone says, don't punch them."

I sat through three classes, staring out the window as the snow continued to fall. Principal Speer sent his secretary, Mrs. Green, to monitor Miss Singletary's class and we were instructed to read quietly. They closed the school at noon. I rode the bus back home and then drove to the truck stop in the 1963 Plymouth Belvedere, the old cop car my dad had been unable to start the day he left Vinton County. After football season, I had begun working at the truck stop in the afternoons and one weekend day a week. I knew Mr. Monihan would want me there early to shovel the snow. The job paid a dollar-fifty an hour and a tub of beef stew or whatever extra food Mrs. Monihan had in the kitchen.

That day, I spent six hours in the refueling docks, shoveling the freshly fallen snow and lugging away the dirt-caked ice chunks that fell from beneath the wheel wells and undercarriages of the tractor-trailers. It was mindless work and I could not get Amanda Singletary or Gloria Johanessen out of my mind. Miss Singletary I wanted to comfort, but Mrs. Johanessen I desperately wanted to hurt. The more I concentrated on the situation, the faster and harder I shoveled, wishing the grip I had on the shovel was around Mrs. Johanessen's neck.

By 7 PM, I could no longer feel my toes and it was difficult to uncurl my fingers from around the handle of the shovel. I was tired and smelled of diesel fuel, which had mixed with the slush and soaked into my work boots and the cuffs of my jeans. The temperature was beginning to rise slightly and a light, misting rain was coming in from the west. When I came in to sign my time sheet, Mrs. Monihan had an aluminum tub of sauerkraut, kielbasa, and mashed potatoes ready to go. Four slices of bread and two pieces of pumpkin pie were wrapped in separate pieces of aluminum foil.

She carried the hot tub to the Belvedere and sat it on the passenger side floor. "Share it with your brother," she said, repeating her daily admonition to me.

"I always do."

"I know you do, sweetheart." As she held the side of the door, Mrs. Monihan shook her head and made a clicking sound with her cheeks. "I surely do feel sorry for you boys up there in that old house all by yourselves. Your mother worked here for fifteen years and I love her like a sister, but I just don't understand how she could just take off with you still in high school and your brother just getting back on his feet. Of course, if I was . . ." Her voice trailed off and she looked embarrassed that her thoughts had nearly escaped unchecked from her mouth.

"What's that, Mrs. Monihan? If you'd been married to Nick Hickam you would have left, too? It's okay. I know what he was like. I lived with him for nearly eighteen years, too."

She tried to force back a smile. "You're a good boy, Jimmy Lee."

I put the pan in the oven to keep it warm, then took a shower until I felt the water starting to cool and realized I had drained the hot water tank. It was after eight by the time I had dressed and was ready to eat. But there was still no sign of Edgel.

Ever since Mom left, Edgel Hickam had been working like a man possessed. He took the responsibility as the new head of the household very seriously. He saved his money, paid the bills on time, and spent no time in the bars, which was virtually unheard of for a

Hickam male of legal drinking age. Edgel was up for work each day at five forty-five. He made us breakfast and we ate together before he headed out the door at six forty, and I went down to meet the bus. Most nights, he didn't get home until after seven. I would start warming up dinner while he jumped in the shower and tried to wash away ash that had crept into every crevice of his body. Some nights, he would eat a quick dinner and make a late-night run for the Farnsworth brothers. I'm not sure when he slept.

It was difficult for me to believe this was the same man convicted of burglary and arson. He was not the devil incarnate my dad had led me to believe. He was a hard-working man who was concerned about the welfare of his little brother.

When Edgel hadn't shown up by nine, I started to worry, so I hopped in the Belvedere and drove down to the sawmill. As soon as I entered the property, I could see the three stands of floodlights shining on the open doorway that led to the subbasement. The dump truck was backed in near the opening and a wooden ramp made of rough-hewn oak planks led from the ground to the bed of the truck. The front-end loader wouldn't fit in the subbasement, and Edgel pushed wheelbarrows full of ash up that slippery ramp and into the truck bed.

I walked around the side of the building and was making my way down the dirt hillside as he was heading toward the ramp with a loaded wheelbarrow. "Hey," I said.

It startled him and he nearly upset the wheelbarrow when he jumped. "Jesus Christ, Jimmy Lee, you scared the shit out of me." He balanced the wheelbarrow and set it down. "What are you doing sneaking up on me like that?"

"Sorry. I didn't mean to. I was worried about you. It's almost nine thirty."

He swiped at his sweaty forehead with a forearm that looked like a piece of twisted rope. Edgel wasn't big in stature, but there was hardly an ounce of fat on him and he was tight and muscular. The blue veins bulging in his forearm looked like a road map. "This might surprise you, little brother, but I know perfectly well how to tell time. I'll be home in a little bit. I've got one more load to drop off."

"Need any help?"

"No, I'm good. You scoot on home. I'll see you in a little bit."

"I can shovel for a little bit. I don't mind."

"I've got it under control, Jimmy Lee. Now, get your ass out of here."

I smiled. "You're awful damn protective of those ashes."

He picked up the wheelbarrow and started toward the ramp. "That's because Mr. Morgan hired me to do the job, not you."

"You've been putting in a lot of hours, Edgel."

He again set the wheelbarrow on its supports and stared at me with a look of aggravation. For a moment, the facial expression reminded me of the old man. "I know how many hours I'm putting in. Overtime is time-and-a-half and we need the money. Besides, you heard Mr. Morgan. If I do a good job, I've got a chance to get on full-time, with health insurance, and those kinds of jobs don't grow on trees around here. Now, get home before I kick your ass."

"I've been waiting on you for two hours. I brought dinner home—sauerkraut, kielbasa, and mashed potatoes—and I've been trying to keep it warm."

"You're starting to sound like an old woman. You're not my wife, you know?"

"That's just one more thing I'll be thanking Jesus for later tonight."

He laughed out loud.

"Keep it warm," he said, straining to push the wheelbarrow up the ramp. "This is my last load. I'll be home in a half hour or so."

An hour later, I heard the dump truck grind up the drive in low gear and idle for a moment outside the porch. Edgel had taken to dropping off the last load at the dump and just bringing the truck home afterward. When he came through the door his eyes were sagging to half pupil. He peeled off his filthy ball cap, revealing a red indentation running the width of his forehead, and tossed it into the corner of the alcove just inside the door. His gloves followed the cap; he unlaced his soaked shoes and kicked them off on a worn mat just inside the door, washed his hands in the kitchen sink, and plopped down in a chair. The warm air of the house was taking its toll and I wasn't sure Edgel could stay awake long enough to eat, let alone listen to the events of the day.

"Edgel, I've got a problem."

"Mm-hum," he said, stabbing a piece of kielbasa and shoving it in his mouth, grinding it for a while before attempting to speak. "What kind of problem?"

"A big one."

The brows arched over his tired eyes. "Let's hear it." Edgel continued to eat, listening intently as I recounted my conversation with Coach Battershell. When I finished, he nodded and asked, "What are you going to do about it?"

I shrugged. "I don't know. What can I do? They're going to take it to the board of education on Monday. Once that happens, her reputation is in the trash can."

Edgel used the side of his fork to scrape his mashed potatoes into a pile. As he slid the last of the potatoes into his mouth and swallowed, he waved his fork in front of his face, waiting for his mouth and throat to clear. "If there was one thing I learned in prison that is beneficial on the outside, it's this: when there's a fight coming, don't wait for it to come to you. You take the fight to them. There were a bunch of Black Muslims in the pen who were always stirring up shit, particularly with the white guys who were not part of the Aryan Nation. There was one Black Muslim, a guy named Kimmo, a big son of a bitch, arms like tree trunks, who was always stirring shit. Word was out that he wanted a piece of me."

"Why?"

"Don't know, doesn't matter. Maybe no reason other than he didn't like my looks."

"What did you do?"

"I went after him. Walked up to him in the cafeteria and punched him in the face, then hit him over the head with my tray."

"Did he leave you alone after that?"

Edgel chuckled. "Not immediately. As soon as he regained his senses he grabbed me and about choked me to death before the guards pulled him off me. But he never screwed with me again. A few of his puke buddies fucked with me, and every time they did, I went right at 'em. You had to. If you didn't, it was a sign of weakness and they preyed on weakness. When you know a fight is coming, you've got to go on the attack."

"I understand what you're saying, Edgel, but how does this apply to me? I don't have anything to fight with."

Slowly, like an April sunrise climbing over the Vinton County hills, a smirk crinkled Edgel Hickam's lips. He rubbed the stubble of his chin and squeezed the skin together, grinning and nodding. "I think I can help you take care of this little problem."

Despite the fact that he was my brother, there was something a little unsettling about a convicted arsonist grinning and telling you that he can take care of the problem.

"I really don't want to see you go back to prison, Edgel."

"It won't take anything nearly that drastic, little brother."

Chapter Twenty-Three

Despite my concern about what Edgel might do in a situation where he felt duty-bound to defend my honor, I admit that there was also something comforting about going into battle with an ex-convict at my side.

I had always cowered before authority. Teachers intimidated me. They were educated, polished, and represented authority and status. I considered it my destiny to be submissive and obedient.

Edgel and Virgil were the polar opposite. They had little respect and absolutely no fear of authority. They viewed teachers and school administrators with disdain. Growing up on Red Dog Road had given them the belief that there was little more the outside world could do to hurt or punish them.

And they had grown up in the home of Nick Hickam. To believe my father was to believe that the ills of the Hickams were brought on by those with status and money. The successful, like Mr. Morgan at the sawmill, were trying to keep us down. It was never the fault of Nick Hickam or his penchant for alcohol and fighting and trouble that caused his problems. Rather, he was continually looking for someone to blame or take vengeance on for his lot in life.

I can't say why I didn't believe that our misery was the fault of other men. It's said that you either learn from or emulate the mistakes of your parents. Virgil followed and became a devout disciple of my father. I was fortunate to learn the harsh realities of such self-destructive behavior, and it appeared that Edgel was weaning himself away from the dogger's way of life.

At about 8:30 AM on Saturday, we pulled the Rocket 88 out of the shed and inched our way down the drive, being careful not to slide sideways in the rutted, snow-covered slope. When we were on the road toward McArthur, Edgel grinned and said, "What's the problem, big man? You look a little pale."

"I am a little pale," I acknowledged. "I hate this."

"Are you kidding me? You've got nothing to worry about. What'd we talk about? You take the fight to her. Don't sit back and wait. Besides, you're holding all the aces. All you've got to do is pull the trigger."

"How about we not use that term anymore?"

Edgel cracked his window and lit a cigarette. "I swear I never saw a Hickam like you. You're nervous as a cat."

The roads were mostly slush, a combination of rising temperatures and an overnight rain. We roared into McArthur from the north on Market Street, past Elk Cemetery, slowing as we entered the downtown. Christmas lights adorned the storefronts of red brick buildings; the city had hung plastic candy canes and Christmas trees from the streetlight poles. A man in an ill-fitting Santa Claus suit rang a bell for the Salvation Army outside of Williams Drug Store. The clock outside the Vinton County National Bank flashed eight fifty-two and thirty-six degrees. We turned right on South Street and made another right on Boundary Avenue. It was almost nine. The lights were on inside the story-and-a-half house that had been converted into a dental office. As we passed, I could see Catherine Johanessen standing at a filing cabinet behind the receptionist's desk at the office, where she worked for her dad on Saturday mornings.

"That's his car in the drive; Catherine's inside," I said.

"Looks like all systems are go," Edgel said.

"My guts are on fire."

"Buck up. Who started this?"

"She did."

"Damn straight, she did. Just remember, you're taking the fight to her."

I nodded and continued to stare out the side window.

The Johanessens lived two miles east of McArthur in a white, two-story colonial with green shutters tucked behind a pair of naked maples on Seneca Street in Indian Acres, a planned subdivision that encompassed the country club. When we passed Paddy's Drive-In, I thought I was going to hyperventilate. By the time we turned off Route 50 and drove between the granite boulders engraved with crossed tomahawks that bordered the entrance to Indian Acres, my gut was in a full roil, and I swallowed down the salty bile in the back of my throat. No pre-game jitters had ever twisted my intestines to this degree. As Edgel slowed in front of the Johanessens', I said, "Keep driving. Go around the block one more time. I'm not ready."

"You better be ready," Edgel said. "She's making it easy for you. You don't even need to knock on the door."

When I looked up, Mrs. Johanessen had just finished locking the front door and was walking toward her car in the driveway. "I can't. I need time to get ready. Drive away."

Edgel slammed the car into park, his skin squeezing his jaws, the look of a predator in his eyes, and said, "Get the fuck out of the car, you little pussy. Take the fight to her."

He made a move to shove me out the passenger side door, but I pulled on the handle and escaped ahead of his hand. I sprinted across the road, more in fear that he was chasing me than to confront Mrs. Johanessen. Regardless of the motivation, I quickly found myself face to face with her as she reached for the handle of the car. Her first expression was that of surprise, but it quickly changed to that of pity. It was an insincere attempt to make me think she actually felt sorry for me. In a soft voice she said, "What are you doing here, Jimmy Lee?"

I swallowed hard and held out my left hand, which contained the envelope. "I need you to read something, please, Mrs. Johanessen," I said, my voice cracking.

She slowly lifted her right hand, clasping the envelope without taking her eyes off mine. "Jimmy Lee, I appreciate the fact that you have a sincere concern and fondness for Miss Singletary, but you have to understand that I am acting in your own best interests. I know what I saw. You understand that this is in no way an indictment of you? Miss Singletary should know better than to become so close to a student." She held up the letter for my inspection. "Did she put you up to this?"

"No, ma'am. Miss Singletary doesn't know I'm here, and she had nothing to do with this. I just would surely appreciate it if you'd read the letter."

I felt like I had pulled the pin on a grenade and couldn't bring myself to throw it. Mrs. Johanessen thought I had come to beg. Doubtless, she believed the letter was a futile attempt on my part to convince her that there was nothing going on between Miss Singletary and me. She used her ignition key to rip off the top of the envelope and held the letter in her right hand as she read. In seconds, her left hand doubled into a fist, crushing the envelope that had contained the letter, and a wave of scarlet consumed her neck.

Mr. Rick Shoemaker
Vinton County Prosecutor
c/o Vinton County Court House
McArthur, Ohio

Dear Mr. Shoemaker:

You are certainly familiar with me, my criminal record, and the problems I have caused in the past. For years I have struggled with what I believe to be the root cause of the erratic and antisocial behavior I have exhibited for the past ten years.

When I was just sixteen years old, I was sexually assaulted by a teacher at East Vinton High School. Her name is Gloria Johanessen. On several occasions, at Mrs. Johanessen's insistence, we had sexual intercourse. These usually occurred in her car at various remote locations in Vinton County. Once, when my parents were out of town for a funeral, she parked her car in our backyard and forced me to have sexual relations, which unfortunately was witnessed by my youngest brother. Another time, we had relations at her house while her husband and daughter were on a father-daughter camping trip with her Sunday school class.

The trauma of these experiences has left me feeling victimized and ashamed. It is my sincere hope that another child never endures such pain. I have decided to come forward because I cannot in good conscience permit Mrs. Johanessen to continue to teach and be around young boys.

As there is no statute of limitations for the molestation of a juvenile, you have my word that you will have my full cooperation in the prosecution of Mrs. Gloria Johanessen. I am willing to take a polygraph test to prove the veracity of my allegations.

Because I do not want this ignored, I am sending copies of this letter to the *Vinton County Messenger,* the *Chillicothe Gazette,* and the *Columbus Dispatch.* Also, I am sending a copy to the principal of East Vinton High School, the superintendent of the East Vinton local school district, and each member of the board of education.

Thank you for your prompt attention to this matter. I look forward to hearing from you at your earliest convenience.

Sincerely yours,
Edgel Hickam

The scarlet wave continued up the neck of Gloria Johanessen until her burning cheeks and ears looked as though they might ignite in flames. She folded the letter neatly, tucked it back in the envelope, and attempted to hand it back to me. I made no attempt to take it. With her right eye squinting, as though she was eyeing my forehead through the scope of a high-powered rifle, Mrs. Johanessen said, "You wouldn't dare."

"No, ma'am, you're probably right. I don't have the guts. But Edgel out yonder . . ." I pointed to the Rocket 88, where Edgel sat behind the wheel. When he saw me point, Edgel smiled and held up a stack of envelopes that he had splayed like a hand of playing cards. "I've got no control over him, Mrs. Johanessen, and those letters are addressed and stamped. So I think it would be wise of you to recant your story, and quickly, because if the school board suspends Miss Singletary on Monday night, I guarantee those letters will go in the mail first thing on Tuesday morning."

"If that happens, I'll sue you for slander and defamation of character."

"That's fine, ma'am. You can sue us all you want. We don't have anything anyways. Just remember, you'd have to prove it isn't true, and I suspect that'll be difficult because Edgel's willing to take a lie detector test, and he can be pretty convincing on the witness stand; he's had lots of practice."

She forced a smile and an exaggerated laugh. "I won't be black-mailed. Go ahead and send the letters, no one will believe you anyway." Gloria Johanessen tried to fend off my threat with a wave of her hand, dismissing me as so much trash. But fear was locked in her eyes, and I could see a hint of tremble in her lips.

"First of all, that's not true. Lots of people will believe it. Even the ones who don't will be talking about it. It'll be in all the papers. Reporters will be knocking at your door at all hours, I suspect." I took a minute to allow the words to sink in, repeating the speech as Edgel and I had practiced. "Everyone will probably want to ask Dr. Johanessen about it down at his practice. I imagine all the kids at school will want to ask Catherine if it's true. Besides, as long as you live in Vinton County, you'll have to live with the stigma that you had sexual relations with a Hickam, and that'll be plenty rough for you, Mrs. Johanessen, 'cause you look at us like we aren't fit to breathe the same air as you. How are you going to teach and live around here with everyone talking about how you did it with Edgel Hickam?"

The fight was over. I had said my piece and won. Her fists clenched and the letter crumpled in her right hand. "Get off my property you little bastard, and don't ever set foot here again or I'll have you arrested for trespassing."

"Yes, ma'am. I'll leave. But don't mistake our resolve. This isn't a bluff. What you're trying to do to Miss Singletary is as low a stunt as I've ever seen, and I won't stand for it." I was feeling bolder by the second. "I remember seeing you in the car with Edgel that night. I was little, but I remember. I'll put my hand on a Bible and swear to Christ in heaven that it's true. Edgel will do the same."

"Get out," she screamed. "Get out." I turned and walked away as Edgel pulled the Rocket 88 up to meet me at the end of the drive. "You Hickams are all trash," she yelled.

I turned one last time to face her, now feeling the confidence swelling in my chest. "That may be, but where's that put you, Mrs. Johanessen?"

Chapter Twenty-Four

Two days before Christmas, I drove down to the sawmill to take a look at the subbasement to get some perspective of how much ash Edgel had hauled out of there. It was cavernous and for the first time I earned an appreciation for how much work Edgel had performed. He was hosing down the last of the walls of the subbasement when I arrived. "How'd you get that ash up the steps and into the wheelbarrow?" I asked.

"Buckets," he said.

"Mother of Christ, that's a lot of work."

He poked me once in the chest with a damp finger. "Remember what I said. It's what a man without a lot of options does." He winked.

The ice-covered gravel crunched under our shoes as we walked up to the trailer so Edgel could ask Mr. Morgan for a final inspection. "I don't need to see it, Edgel. You've been doing a fine job," Mr. Morgan said. He offered us both seats in his tiny office. "You still interested in working here at the mill?"

"Yes, sir."

After the fire, Mr. Morgan had built a temporary shelter and set up ripping saws to keep the men working. It was slow, labor-intensive work, but it kept everyone busy while the new plant was being constructed. New joists now spanned the foundation and the first framed walls were going up. "I have a spot open for a picker. Do you know what that is?"

"No, but I could probably figure it out pretty quick."

Mr. Morgan held up a yellow order slip. "We get these orders for lumber. I need someone to go through the stacks picking out the lumber and putting the orders together. There's a lot of heavy lifting and it's damn hard work."

"I'm not afraid of hard work," Edgel said.

"You don't seem to be. Good." He stood and shook Edgel's hand. "I've got a stack of orders that need filled. Be here at seven, the morning after Christmas."

Edgel never asked how much it paid, though he knew it would be more than he earned for shoveling ash and it would include health insurance. He had earned himself a steady job and I think for the first time since he had gotten out of prison, Edgel felt like his life was getting back on track.

We got up Christmas morning and exchanged gifts. I got Edgel a pocketknife with onyx and mother-of-pearl inlays and a pair of waterproof work boots. I bought them both at the general store that was attached to the truck stop, and Mrs. Monihan had sold them to me at her cost. Edgel gave me the two best gifts I had ever in my life received. The first was my football helmet mounted on a walnut base with brass plates running around the sides, each listing one of my accomplishments—First Team All-Ohio, District Defensive Player of the Year, Black Diamond Conference MVP, East Vinton MVP. The second gift was a walnut shadow box encasing a backdrop of black velvet displaying the two gold medals I had won for the essay contests.

"Where'd you get this?" I asked, holding up the shadow box.

"Made it. I asked Mr. Morgan if I could have a few pieces of scrap, then I took them over to the Farnsworths' shop and worked them down."

They were perfectly formed pieces of wood—sanded, buffed, and finished. I was astonished at my brother's abilities. "These are the best gifts I've ever gotten, Edgel. I'll keep these forever. Thanks."

There was a tear in his eye when he pushed himself off the couch and went to the kitchen to make coffee.

It was to be the best Christmas of my life. The Monday morning after I confronted Mrs. Johanessen, Miss Singletary was back in class, demanding as ever, teaching as though she had never missed a beat. At lunchtime, I went to Coach Battershell's office and learned that on Saturday evening, Miss Singletary had received a call from Principal Speer, who said Mrs. Johanessen had reconsidered her allegations. She apparently said it was possible that she misinterpreted what was simply the excitement of the moment after I won the essay contest and since it was such a serious charge and held such long-term ramifications for Miss Singletary that it was best that the allegations be dropped. "I don't get it," Coach Battershell said. "It couldn't have been something as simple as a change of heart."

"Why not?" I asked.

"Because she doesn't have one."

I shrugged. "Well, I'm just glad it's over."

"Miss Singletary is, too. As you might imagine she's not too happy with Mrs. Johanessen, but she wants to let it rest, at least until you've graduated."

"What then?"

"Knowing Miss Singletary, she'll probably punch her in the nose."

Miss Singletary invited Edgel and me to Christmas dinner at the home of her parents, Esther and Wilfred, with her older brothers, their wives and children, and Coach Battershell, for the most wonderful prime rib I had ever tasted. Right after the blessing, as we were still standing behind our dining room chairs, Miss Singletary said it was going to be a very special Christmas and she held up her left hand in front of her chest, fingers splayed, showing off the marquise cut diamond engagement ring that Coach Battershell had given her. There was much hugging and clapping and Esther cried until dessert.

"The secret's going to be out now," I said.

"I'm okay with that," Miss Singletary said.

"I have an announcement, too," I said. "We also have a reason to celebrate. Mr. Morgan offered Edgel a full-time job at the sawmill."

Everyone at the table clapped and cheered. Wilfred offered a toast to what he called "two wonderful events."

Chapter Twenty-Five

On Tuesday, March 19, 1974, a letter arrived from the office of T. Edward Millard, attorney-at-law. The letter stated that the divorce of Mildred Katherine Hickam from Nicholas Oscar Hickam would become final at 9 AM on Thursday, April 4. The letter stated that our mother requested our presence at the hearing.

I had spoken to my mother in mid-January and late February. The first time she called from a truck stop pay phone somewhere between Demopolis, Alabama, and Meridian, Mississippi; we spoke for three minutes until the operator cut us off. The second time, she called collect from Tulsa, Oklahoma, and we spoke for about ten minutes. She and Cyclops were happy and she had seen more in the past two months than she had in her previous forty-nine years. Never in my life had I heard such joy in her voice. Edgel was still grousing about her running off with Cyclops, but I found it difficult to be angry with her. Part of me believed she was entitled to the happiness. She asked if I had heard from Dad. I said no and she said good. That was the last time I spoke to her until we saw her in the courtroom on the morning of April 4.

The white Peterbilt tractor of Cyclops's rig was parked on East Main Street across from the county courthouse. Mom was standing in the main hallway of the courthouse and started smiling as soon as we walked inside. She was wearing black half-heels and a black and green patterned dress that hung loosely over a frame that had shed a good twenty pounds and ten years since we had last seen her. Her hair, cut and framed around her rouged face, was colored a light brown that hid the gray streaks that had made her look so old. Edgel and I shared a shocked look; it was the best either of us could ever remember her looking.

She wrapped an arm around each of our necks and squeezed. John "Cyclops" Phillips and another man emerged from the men's room. Cyclops was wearing a shiny, gray polyester suit with a matching eye patch. His belly strained the buttons of his black shirt and bent his silver, polyester necktie. An unwieldy, dishwater blond moustache rolled under his upper lip and was damp on the tips. He nodded and Edgel and I extended our hands. Cyclops introduced the other man as a trucker friend named Dirk something-or-other who smelled heavily of Old Spice, had a pompadour haircut, a silver and turquoise belt buckle the size of a business envelope, and a tarnished chain running from a belt loop to an oversized wallet in his hip pocket. "Do we need to be witness to the divorce, or something?" Edgel asked.

My mother shook her head. "That business is done. We did it in the judge's chambers a half-hour ago. But we have some other business we need to attend to. Come with me."

As we walked toward the judge's chambers, Dirk something-or-other headed toward the main door of the courthouse. We entered the judge's chambers where T. Edward Millard was sitting at a conference table with papers spread before him. T. Edward shook our hands and said, "So, you boys are going to be landowners, huh?"

"They don't know why they're here," my mother said, finally looking toward us. "I'm going to give you boys the house. I'm selling it to you, actually, for one dollar."

"Why?" I asked.

"Because I don't need it, and I don't want it. It's where you boys grew up, so you can do with it as you please."

T. Edward Millard pointed for us to sit in two chairs across from him. In rapid succession he began shoving papers across the table for us to sign. I had turned eighteen a week before Christmas, and these were the first documents I had signed as a legal adult. He explained each, though I understood little of what he was saying and I suppose Edgel was in the same boat. "All you need to understand is that the property located at 10107 Red Dog Road will be sold to Edgel Nicholas Hickam and James Leland Hickam for the sum of one dollar." When I pulled my wallet out of my hip pocket and fetched a dollar, T. Edward Millard smiled and said, "I don't really need your dollar." I was even more confused.

The Honorable Horace A. Able entered the room as T. Edward Millard was clearing the last of the papers from the conference table. The judge was a tall man with broad shoulders that had begun to stoop with age. In his day, I imagine he was an imposing figure. He was deeply religious and often quoted scripture before sentencing the convicted. He now walked with a bit of a shuffle and was in need of a haircut. Rolls of gray hair covered the back of his neck like an animal pelt and wild sprays of hair resembling a sea urchin grew out of his ears. It wasn't until he crossed his arms at the wrists that I spotted the Bible. "Counselor, are you done with your business so we can get this couple back on the road?" Judge Able asked.

It was at that moment that I realized that the transfer of the house was not the only piece of business that my mother was going to take care of on this day. Not thirty minutes after she had divorced my dad she was going to marry a man who had yet to utter a dozen words to me. Dirk something-or-other came walking back in the room and stood to the right of Cyclops. "I want you boys to stand with me," my mom said.

The ceremony took, at most, two minutes, and my new step-father jingled the change in his pocket and rocked heel-to-toe the entire time. I was struggling to digest the entire four-month scenario since my mother had announced that she was getting her commercial driver's license, when I heard Judge Able say, "Mr. Phillips, you may now kiss your bride."

Edgel and I hugged our mother and shook hands with our new stepfather. He said, "I'm looking forward to knowing you boys a lot gooder."

They hopped into the big rig, Mom waved, our new stepfather gave two long blasts on his air horn, and they pulled away from the curb, spewing exhaust into the morning air. As they did, Dirk something-or-other slapped me across the chest with a backhand and said, "Watch this. It's gonna be great." Dirk had tied a couple of dozen tin cans to the back of the rig with fishing line and attached a Just Married sign between the rear tires. He cackled and pointed as the Peterbilt headed up Main Street and turned north on Market Street, the clatter of the cans drowned out by the whine of the diesel engine. "Don't that just beat it?" Dirk something-or-other said as he turned and walked away, laughing to himself.

Edgel and I walked to the Rocket 88 in silence. Inside, we stared at each other in mutual disbelief. "He wants to get to know us a lot gooder," I said. Edgel smiled. "One of these days, the old man is going to come wandering home and we're going to have to explain to him that we own his house and that his wife divorced him so she could marry a one-eyed truck driver who they call Cyclops."

"Maybe he'll never come home," Edgel offered.

"Oh, he'll come home. He's always found his way back before. He's like some mangy dog that you can't get rid of."

Edgel put the car in gear and slid into the empty street. "If he comes home, I'll tell him."

Chapter Twenty-Six

Virgil called home on the last Sunday afternoon in April while Edgel was painting the living room and when I was working at the truck stop. Barker Brothers & Sons Amusements was going to be in Richmond, Kentucky, the following weekend setting up for a carnival and he wanted us to drive down for a visit. "Did he say how Dad was doing?" I asked.

"No, but that's Virgil. He doesn't give a whip about anyone but Virgil, and I didn't ask. He told me where he was going to be and I said we'd try to get there. I didn't want to start a conversation with him and have him ask, 'How's Mom?' That's a discussion best had face to face."

The Vinton County Relays were the next Saturday at McArthur Roosevelt High School. When I had finished my events—we won the 880 relay and finished second in the 440 relay—I pulled on my sweats and jumped into a Ford station wagon that Edgel had borrowed from Luke Farnsworth for the weekend. The Belvedere Dad had left behind had died and been hauled to the salvage yard. Neither the Rocket 88 nor the rattletrap pickup my mother had left behind was fit for such a trip.

We drove south to Route 32—the Appalachian Highway—and headed west toward Cincinnati. It was in the low seventies and we drove with the windows down, filling the car with the sweet smell of spring growth. We hit Interstate 75 in Cincinnati and were in Richmond in just over four hours. The carnival was being set up in the parking lot of the first strip mall we found west of the interstate. We parked alongside of a semitrailer that bore a faded painting of a clown's face and BARKER BROTHERS & SONS AMUSEMENTS on its side. We had barely exited the car when I heard Virgil say, "Hey, them's my brothers over there."

He came striding hard between the Tilt-A-Whirl and the skeleton of an octopus ride that had yet to be adorned with cars. A cigarette smoldered between the index and middle finger of his right hand and there was hardly a spot on him that wasn't covered in grease. His clothes looked like they hadn't been washed in weeks and Virgil wasn't far behind. Strands of unwashed, grease-stained hair hung nearly to his shoulders and the decay between his front teeth had expanded noticeably. He stuck the cigarette between his lips long enough to pump our hands and leave them covered with a film of grime. "You sons of bitches, it's good to see ya," Virgil said.

"Good to see you, too," Edgel said, flicking at Virgil's scraggly hair. "This is a different look for a redneck from Vinton County."

"The chicks love it long," Virgil said. I found it implausible that there was a woman breathing air who could find anything appealing about Virgil Hickam, but I kept my mouth shut. "Where's the old man and the old lady? They didn't come down with you?"

Edgel looked up at me but said nothing. "Isn't Dad with you?" I asked.

Virgil sent a stream of cigarette smoke out his nostrils. "Why in hell would he be with me?"

"He left home six or seven months ago and said he was going to hook up with you in Florida and work for the carnival. You mean you haven't seen him?"

"I ain't seen him or heard from him since we went to visit you in prison last summer." He looked at Edgel and sucked hard on his cigarette. "Why would he do a fool thing like that, anyway?"

"He lost his job at the sawmill," Edgel said. "I'm sure everything's going to be fine. He was hitchhiking south and probably got distracted along the way. You know how Dad is."

"Why didn't Mom come?"

Edgel looked at the trucks lined up along the side of the parking lot. "What time do you get off?" he asked Virgil.

"About five or six. We're running ahead of schedule."

"Jimmy Lee and I are going to go find us a hotel room. You want to come over to the room, clean up, and we'll go to dinner? There's been a lot going on at home. I'll fill you in over a steak dinner."

"Hell, yes. I could go for a steak," Virgil said, seeming to immediately forget that he had two parents missing in action.

"Do you have any clean clothes?"

"No, not really. I haven't had much time to do laundry."

"What size are those jeans?"

Virgil twisted his neck to read the leather tag on his beltless waist. "Thirty-two."

"We'll get checked in, get you some clean clothes, and be back here about six to pick you up. You can shower up at the hotel and we'll go get something to eat."

When we returned, Virgil was leaning against the tires of the semi-trailer, his legs crossed at the ankles, one cigarette between his fingers, another tucked behind his left ear. While we were at a discount store buying Virgil a pair of jeans, packages of T-shirts, underwear and socks, shampoo, and a hand soap that contained pumice, Edgel also bought a roll of brown wrapping paper, which he used to cover the backseat and floor of the station wagon. Virgil frowned when he opened the door and saw the protective paper. "Hell, I ain't that dirty," he said, flicking his still-burning butt over the roof.

"Virgil, you've got more grease on you than the engine of this car," Edgel said. "It's not my car and I don't want to take it back all goobered up. Now, get in."

He was in the shower for better than an hour and when he finished, it looked like the grease-smudged walls of the Farnsworths' garage. Virgil cleaned up pretty well except for the grease that remained embedded under his nails and in the creases of his fingers. There was a locally owned steak house—DeLorreto's—at the far end of the strip mall where they were setting up the carnival and we were seated at a booth near the kitchen.

Virgil cut into a New York strip that lapped over the edges of his plate on three sides. He used the knife to stab a wedge of meat and fat and jam it far into his mouth until his cheek looked like it was hosting a plug of tobacco. Staring hard at Edgel and me, Virgil said, "So, you're telling me that right then and there, right after she divorces the old man, she up and marries this one-eyed mothefucker, Cyclone?"

"Cyclops," I corrected.

"Whatever the fuck his name is," Virgil growled. "That's a crock of shit. What was she thinkin', and what the hell's the old man going to do when he finds out? I'll tell you what he's going to do; he's going to lose his shit, that's what." Doing more talking than chewing, he struggled to swallow his beef, and a trickle of pink juice escaped from the corner of his mouth and rolled under his chin. He swiped it with the back of his hand, "How come you ain't been looking for the old man, or at least called the cops?"

"And tell them what?" Edgel asked. "That our dad ran away from home? He's free, white, and twenty-one, Virgil, and he can do as he pleases. Besides, we didn't know he hadn't shown up in Florida until a couple of hours ago. He left in one of his goddamn huffs, wouldn't listen to any reason, and started hitchhiking. The last time

I saw him, he was standing on the side of Route 50 with his thumb out. You know what he's like. What were we supposed to do?"

Virgil grinned for the first time since Edgel began explaining the situation on Red Dog Road. "He's prob'ly holed up with some whore somewheres," Virgil said. "But I still think you got to fill out a police report when you get back."

"Maybe we could call Sheriff McCollough and see what he thinks, but Dad's a grown man and they don't usually take missing person reports unless they think there's been foul play," Edgel said. "Just because Nick Hickam got a wild hair up his ass and headed out for Florida might not be a good enough reason."

"I'll do it," I said. "I think you should stay as far away from the sheriff as possible."

"Good point."

We hadn't yet told Virgil about the sawmill fire and Edgel's incarceration for questioning. We also hadn't told him—and didn't plan to, either —that we were now the proud owners of the Hickam family estate. He would have thrown a royal fit in the middle of DeLorreto's steak house.

Edgel offered to get Virgil a room in the hotel for the night, but he insisted that he needed to be on the grounds of the midway that night because he was some type of low-level supervisor. Edgel and I assumed this had more to do with some type of party than it did any level of supervisory status. In formidable Hickam fashion, Virgil would no doubt drink himself stupid and crash under a semitrailer in his sleeping bag.

The next morning, we took coffee in Styrofoam cups and warm cinnamon rolls from a local bakery to the mall parking lot and spent another thirty minutes with Virgil before pointing the station wagon north, both of us relieved to be putting distance between ourselves and our brother.

Chapter Twenty-Seven

At lunchtime on Wednesday in the school auditorium, I signed a letter of intent to attend Ohio Methodist University on a football scholarship. It was about the biggest day of my life. When an athlete at East Vinton High School earned an athletic scholarship, which wasn't often, the athletic director hosted a formal signing ceremony so that the entire school could attend. Coach Battershell gave me a royal-blue ball cap with a white interlocking OM on the front to wear at the signing. Most of the school showed up, even Lindsey Morgan and Abigail Winsetter. Edgel sat in the front row of seats with a camera, having taken his lunch hour so that he could watch me sign. The cooks from the cafeteria rolled out a cake that was decorated with white icing and OHIO METHODIST written in blue, block letters. My teammates gave me a standing ovation.

I had been recruited by several bigger schools, including Ohio University and Marshall University. However, Coach Battershell really pushed me to go to Ohio Methodist. While he said I was one of the best players he had ever coached, I was a bit small for Division I. "Let's get you to a school where you can get on the field and have some fun," he said. Ohio Methodist was a Division II school and it had, according to Miss Singletary, an excellent journalism department, which made both of us happy. The scholarship would pay all but about two thousand dollars a year, which was still a huge amount for me. The admission counselors said they would arrange for me to get loans for the remainder.

When I walked through the back door after track practice that night, the phone was ringing; it was Virgil calling collect from a pay phone at the mall in Richmond, Kentucky. "Hey, I was just checking in," he said. "What did the sheriff say about Dad?"

"Uh, I haven't talked to him yet, Virgil."

"What the fuck are you waiting for? I thought you were going to do that when you got back on Sunday."

"Edgel said he wanted to wait a few more days. He said if we filed a missing person report that it would get in the newspapers and that would make Dad furious."

"Well, that's a crock of shit. Who cares what they put in the goddamn paper? Our dad's been missing for six months and you two fuck wads don't give a shit."

"Look Virg, I'm sorry if you don't like it, but that's what Edgel said to do. He's in charge. If you've got a bitch . . ."

The phone went dead. I set my books on the kitchen table just as I saw the dust kicking up under the tires of the Rocket 88 as it climbed up the drive toward the house. I walked out front to meet him, but he got out of the car and went right to the shed to retrieve his ladder and a one-gallon can of white paint. Over the past week, Edgel had been using every second of daylight to paint the front and back porches and the trim on the old house. The dried wood sucked up the first two coats of base, but once he got the primer to take, the white trim made an astonishing difference on the house. It still listed to one side, the asphalt shingles that covered the house were faded and thin, but it was by far the best looking house on Red Dog Road.

"Nice ceremony today," he said, hardly breaking stride as he headed toward the back porch with his painting supplies. "I'm right proud of you."

"Thanks for coming. I appreciate it."

"Glad to do it, little brother." He pried open the paint can with a screwdriver and stirred it with a broken piece of a yardstick. After a minute he looked up and asked, "Got something on your mind?"

"I just got off the phone with Virgil. He's madder than a hornet because I haven't reported Dad missing to the sheriff."

"Virgil's got a mouth and access to telephones. If he's all that concerned, he can file the report."

I picked up one of the little trim brushes and began working on the window casing opposite Edgel. I was starving, but not about to disrupt Edgel or his work on the house. After it was too dark to paint, we would scare up something to eat. Edgel dipped his brush and made a clean, neat run along the window casing. His talent for working with his hands continued to amaze me.

"I've been giving some thought to something and I want to bounce it off you," Edgel said, never taking his eyes off his work.

"Shoot."

"What would you think about selling the house?"

"Selling the house? Why? Where would we live?"

"You're going to be living at college most of the next four years. I don't need this big a place. If we could sell it, it would help you out for college."

I was touched that Edgel would sacrifice the house for my education. "What about you? You need a place to live."

"That's no biggie. We put your college money back, and then split what's left. I'll use my portion to get a trailer or as a down payment for a little place. People are moving out of Vinton County in droves looking for work. I ought to be able to pick up a place pretty reasonable. Mr. Morgan said he would talk to the bank and get me the loan. We'll put your half in the bank and you can have it when you're out of college."

I shook my head. "No, that's not fair. This place isn't worth that much, and I'd be getting too much of the money and . . ."

"This isn't a debate," he said, cutting me off. "I don't want you to have any reason not to finish college. I've got a good job. It'll work out fine."

"Did you think about the old man? It's going to be bad enough when he comes back and finds out he's divorced and Mom gave us the house. What happens when he comes back and finds someone else living here?"

Edgel continued to paint until he finished a corner piece of the window frame. After resting his brush across the can of paint, Edgel looked at me as if I were a complete puzzle, the last clue in a crossword that just would not come to mind. He looked away, his knuckles digging into his hips, and after a minute walked into the house without a word.

When he returned a minute later, he sat down on the top step of the porch and with an index finger motioned for me to sit next to him. Something was clasped in his fisted right hand. After I sat down, Edgel extended his right arm until I put an open hand under his. He loosened his fingers and a scorched, oval piece of steel dropped into my hands. It was black and brown, and parts of the burned metal had a rainbow sheen, like oil spread across the water. It was a watch, and its glass crystal had melted into its face, blurring the numbers. In spite of the damage, it was immediately recognizable to me. It was the remains of my dad's Twist-O-Flex wristwatch. I rolled it around in my hands for several seconds, examining the gnarled lump, unable to grasp its significance. "Where did you get it?"

"I found it under a couple tons of wet ash in the subbasement of the sawmill."

I thought about his words for a moment. "What was it doing down there?"

"Lying next to what was left of the old man."

It was a ridiculously obvious question, but still I asked, "Dad's dead?"

"Extremely."

"He burned up in that fire? What in God's name was he doing down there?"

Edgel scratched the back of his neck and squinted past me to the western hills.

"'What was he doing down there?'" Edgel said, repeating my question in a mocking tone. "If you can't figure that one out, maybe you're not college material, after all. The reason he never hooked up with Virgil was because he never left Vinton County. That whole tirade about heading to Florida was just a cover. I suspect he ducked into the woods for a couple of days, then broke into the sawmill to set it on fire to get back at Mr. Morgan." He looked at me until our eyes met and he had my full attention. "Jimmy Lee, our dad liked fire. He always liked fire."

"Always?"

Edgel nodded once. "Always. He thought that was the best way to get revenge."

"Or cover up a crime?"

"Or that."

"Like burglarizing a house?"

Edgel nodded again, the corners of his mouth curling in a sad grin. "Yeah, like burglarizing a house."

"It wasn't you that burglarized and torched those houses?"

"Nope."

"Not once?"

"Not ever." He rested his elbows on his knees and looked away, appearing to blink away tears. "He was hitting the homes of widows and divorced women, mostly. He figured out when they worked, or when they were at church, and hit 'em then. He didn't always burn them, but he would if he thought he needed to cover his tracks or if he wanted to get even for something. Mrs. Zurhorst, that old widow who lived down by the railroad tunnel, he robbed her place and burned it to the ground because her son gave Dad a beating down at the Double Eagle Bar one night. Ain't that something? He gets drunk and gets his ass beat, and he burns down some old lady's house to get even. That poor old woman lost everything and I don't think she lived another month after that."

"But how did you get blamed for them?"

"Dad bought that Rocket 88 off Rocky Johnson. The transmission was going bad and he threw a rod, and you knew Dad, he wouldn't spend ten minutes to fix something. He just dumped it out on the hillside with the rest of his junkers. I asked him if I could have it and he started laughing. 'If you can get it running, you can have it,' he told me. 'You won't get that thing running in a hundred years.' It took me all of two days and I had that thing purring like a kitten. Once I got the Rocket running, the old man couldn't stand it. He said it was still his car, and he started taking it out on his bar runs and using it when he was burglarizing houses. Some people had seen the Rocket parked near some of the houses that got hit, so the cops figured it was me. I was drunk one night and put the car in a ditch. The sheriff went through my car and found road flares, Sterno, and some jewelry from one of the burglaries." He held out his hands, palms up. "Game over."

"Dad never told them it was him?"

"Come on, little brother, you're not that naive. Of course he didn't. He and Mom came down to see me in jail one night and told me that if he came forward that both of us would end up in prison. That was it. Sorry, pal. Keep your mouth shut, do your time, and we'll see you later."

I looked down at the slab of steel, shook my head, and asked, "What kind of man does that to his son?"

"Nick Hickam, that's who."

"So, Mom knew you didn't do it, too?"

Edgel nodded.

I looked out over the property and watched as the sun seemed to balance itself atop Buckingham Ridge to the west. "What did you do with his body?"

"Remember that night you surprised me at the mill?"

"Sure."

"He was in the back of the truck, mixed in with the ashes. There wasn't much left; a skull and crumbled pieces of bone. What I found fit in the bottom of the wheelbarrow."

"What do you think happened?"

"The inspectors found the propane tanks upstairs had been opened. Mr. Morgan told us that the day we went down there. Propane is heavier than air and it sank into the subbasement. My bet is he opened those tanks figuring once he got the fire started down below that it would fuel the flames. But when he tried to fire it up, probably with one of those road flares, he was standing in a compartment up to his ass in propane. Like I said, there wasn't much left to bury. He blew himself to pieces."

I continued to stare out over the barren hillside, trying to digest everything that Edgel had just told me. "You lost nine years of your life because of him," I said. "Nine years, Edgel. Did he even say he was sorry?"

Edgel snorted out a laugh. "Dad? Say he was sorry? Come on, Jimmy Lee, what do you think? He never said he was sorry 'bout anything. He never said he'd make it up to me. After I went to prison, he ran the Rocket until it conked out again. The only thing he did for me was put it up on blocks in the shed and leave it alone."

The thought of Edgel sitting in prison for nine years, being portrayed as inherently evil and a pariah by my father, sickened me.

The sadness that I had felt when I realized my father was dead evaporated. Rather, I felt only anger and disgust for him and sadness for my brother, whom I had learned to love and respect. I also felt relief in knowing that I would never again stare into my father's sneering face and that justice—divine intervention, perhaps?—had been served. I fervently hoped that, even for just a fleeting second before he died, in the instant after he lit the flare, that Nick Hickam understood the magnitude of his own stupidity.

"Did you tell Mom?"

Edgel shook his head. "Nope."

"Are you going to?"

"I might tell her someday."

"She might be relieved to know that he'll never be around to bother her."

"Nick Hickam is the last thing on her mind, Jimmy Lee. She's divorced, remarried, happy, and got no reason to come back here. The fewer people who know, the better."

"Why don't you tell the sheriff?"

"Where would that get us?"

"It would eliminate any suspicion he might have that you did it."

"All it would do is put another black mark beside the name Hickam. No, Jimmy Lee, let's just let it rest. The old man's dead; Mr. Morgan got himself a new sawmill; I've got a good job; you're going to college. That's good enough for me."

He took the Twist-O-Flex out of my hands and pushed it back in his pocket.

"What are you going to do with the watch?"

Edgel pulled the blistered metal back out of his pocket and stared at it. "You want it?"

I shook my head. "Nope."

"Let's take a walk."

Edgel and I walked up the hillside past the spot where authorities had tackled and arrested our grandfather and cut through the wooded ridgeline to the ponds—old pits left behind by strip mining operations. Rumors had floated around Vinton County for years that the Youngstown and Steubenville mob used the ponds as a repository for bodies because the acidic waters supposedly ate away everything but a corpse's teeth. I doubt the stories were true, but they made for great local legend. At the edge of the first pond, Edgel bounced the twisted metal in his palm a few times, and then pitched it far into the middle of the water. We stood in silence for a few minutes, watching as the ripples moved away from the point of entry and dissipated long before they made shore.

"Good-bye, Nick Hickam," I said.

"Good riddance," Edgel said.

As we walked back to the house, I recalled an incident at the dinner table at least ten years earlier. "Edgel, I remember that night you gave mom that necklace that had been stolen from Mrs. Radebaugh, that woman who worked up at the truck stop. Do you remember that?"

Edgel smiled with just the corners of his mouth. "Oh yeah, I remember that." He looked at me and said, as though reading my mind, "So, if I didn't do the burglaries, how did I get the necklace?"

"Uh-huh."

"I was pissed at the old man because he kept using the Rocket to pull the burglaries. I told him to quit doing it in my car and he told me to kiss his ass. 'It's not your car,' he said. He gave me a backhand upside of my head and said no snot-nosed kid was going to tell him how to live his life. A couple of days later, he gets into the trunk of the Rocket, digs around under the spare tire and pulls out that necklace. He gives it to me and tells me to take it up to Columbus and pawn it. I said okay, then that night I gave it to Mom just to piss him off. I knew it would make him madder than hell."

"You and Dad got into a fistfight out in the yard after dinner."

"You thought he was giving me a beating because I stole the necklace from Mrs. Radebaugh, didn't you?"

"Of course."

"Stealin' didn't bother Dad, little brother . . . unless, of course, you were stealin' from him."

Chapter Twenty-Eight

I got up at 5 AM. The smell of coffee and bacon already filled the house on Red Dog Road. After pissing away my morning erection, I pulled on a T-shirt and staggered to the kitchen. Edgel was dressed, shaved, and looking sharp in a pair of khaki slacks, a blue Ohio Methodist University golf shirt, and one of my white busboy aprons from the truck stop. "You look good in that apron," I said, pulling out a chair. "What time did you get up?"

"It's a big day," he said. "You've got to get up and get rolling." He slid a plate of bacon, three fried eggs, and white toast across the table. "Eat up. We need to be on the road by six thirty, at the latest."

"You know I've got to run over . . ."

"I know. That's why you've got to eat and get your ass moving."

It was the last Sunday of August 1974, the day that I was to report to summer football camp at Ohio Methodist University. Edgel was taking me to camp and could not have been more excited or more nervous. All summer he had monitored my workouts and asked on numerous occasions, "Do you think you'll get to play as a freshman?" Each time he asked, I would point to a flexed bicep and nod. This always made him smile and he would yell, "Yeah, baby." Edgel wanted a part in my success and I was happy to share it with him. We were now the only family each of us had. Virgil had called back the week after Edgel had shown me Dad's watch and demanded that we file a police report. Edgel talked to him and said he didn't care where the old man was and if Virgil was so damn concerned, he could call the sheriff and report him missing. "You want to call? I'll give you the phone number." Virgil called Edgel a selfish prick and was spewing other vulgarities when Edgel hung up the phone. We had not heard from him since. Mom called occasionally, but had not been back in the area since the day she had divorced, remarried, and deeded us the house on Red Dog Road. When Edgel had finished painting the house, he had the Farnsworth boys haul away the rusting junkers that lined the drive and the improvement to the property was impressive. In late May, after the property was cleaned up, he put a House for Sale sign along County Road 12, with an arrow pointing up Red Dog Road. A second sign was staked at the bottom of our drive.

After breakfast, I showered and headed down the stairs. The keys to the Rocket 88 were on the brass hook by the back door. I snatched them on my way out. The rusty spring had yet to pull the screen door back against the jamb when Edgel yelled, "You be back here by six thirty. I don't want to be late."

"I'll be back in plenty of time."

Amanda Singletary lived about four miles from my house. I wanted to see her before I left for college. So, at a few minutes after six on this Sunday morning, I rapped three times on her aluminum storm door. Within a few seconds, I could hear someone stirring inside. The door cracked open and Miss Singletary squinted into the morning sun. "Jimmy Lee," she said, clutching a pink, quilted robe closed with one hand and pushing open the aluminum storm door with the other.

"Sorry to come over so early, Miss Singletary, but I'm leaving for college in about a half hour and I needed to talk to you."

She nodded and said, "Come in, come in." She pushed the door shut and pointed toward the kitchen. "Let's sit down in there." She buttoned her robe as we walked. "You're leaving for college already?"

"Today's the day we report to football camp. Two-a-day practices start in the morning."

"Goodness. In this heat?"

I shrugged. "If I can get through Coach Battershell's two-a-days, I can get through this."

She pulled a can of coffee from the pantry shelf. "Want some coffee?"

"No, ma'am. I've got to get back. Edgel's waiting on me and he's more nervous about this than I am. We've got to check in at the stadium at Ohio Methodist by nine o'clock. I just wanted to stop by and say good-bye and . . ." I choked up on my words. "You know, tell you thanks for everything you did for me last year. None of this would have happened if it wasn't for you."

"Oh, Jimmy Lee, I appreciate that so much, but I didn't do anything. This was all about you. You wrote the essays and you did it without my help. All I did was help get you the opportunity. You did the work."

"But if you hadn't been there, they probably wouldn't have let me even compete at the county competition. They would have found a way to take that award from me. You were the first person to ever stand up for me, and I'm very grateful."

"Well, I appreciate that, Jimmy Lee, but don't sell yourself short. This was a great lesson for you and for any kid in that school who chooses to believe in himself. You are the one with the talent. No one can take that away from you."

"I would have given up without your help."

"I don't believe that, Jimmy Lee. It's not in your nature to quit. Sometimes in life we just need a little nudge. You just needed . . ."

She frowned for a minute. "What's the first guy in the backfield called, the one without the football who runs through the line first?"

"The fullback."

"Yes, but you call him something else."

"The blocking back?"

"Yes, that's it. I was your blocking back, but you were the one who had to carry the ball and run through the hole. I appreciate you coming down here and thanking me, Jimmy Lee, I really do. It touches my heart. But you were the one who worked and those were your words and thoughts on that paper that won, not mine."

Miss Singletary promised to come to a game early in the season, and I left before the coffee pot had stopped percolating. Edgel was pacing the kitchen floor when I returned at six forty. "We're going to be late, dammit."

He was wearing a white cap with a blue bill that he had bought when he had taken me to Ohio Methodist for my freshman orientation. It was pulled down close to the ears and the bill was flat across the brow. I took the cap from his head, rounded the bill and tightened the plastic strap in the back. "You've got to learn how to wear your cap," I said.

"Get your suitcases and get in the car," Edgel said.

I snagged the suitcases and put them in the trunk of the idling Rocket 88. I was proud to have Edgel taking me to school. He rolled down the driveway, leaving billowing clouds of dust in our wake. The Rocket squealed onto County Road 12, heading into the morning sun and leaving the dust to settle over Red Dog Road.

Discussion Questions for *The Essay*

1. A young Jimmy Lee is a target for derision by his classmates. Despite all the anti-bullying campaigns, have things really changed that much in the United States? Are the poorest and most vulnerable still at risk?

2. Miss Singletary gives Jimmy Lee a second chance to keep him eligible for football. Do teachers have a moral obligation give a student like Jimmy Lee a chance to remain eligible for athletics when they fail in the classroom? Would Jimmy Lee have gotten the same consideration if he had not been an athlete? Should sports play such a prominent role in our schools?

3. Jimmy Lee discovers the joy of reading when he ventures into the attic, finds the old steamer trunk full of books, and begins reading the Hardy Boys book, *The Mystery of Cabin Island*. Can you remember a book that changed your life? Can you remember a specific book that reinvigorated your love for the written word?

4. Early in the book, Jimmy Lee does not care for his brother Edgel and says, "I believed that prison might be the ideal place for him." This changes the day Jimmy Lee comes home with the essay medal and Edgel tells him it's a ticket out of Vinton County. Discuss how this relationship grew and helped to transform both

Lee and Edgel. Were you surprised by Edgel's transforma-

ingletary takes extraordinary steps to help Jimmy Lee. d most teachers extend themselves to that degree, particu- y when a colleague is pushing to have him stripped of the prize? Did you have a Miss Singletary in your life?

What would have happened to Jimmy Lee if there had been no Amanda Singletary and Coach Battershell in his life?

7. How did you feel when you learned what happened to Jimmy Lee's secret stash of money? Where you surprised?

8. Jimmy Lee's mother is a sympathetic character early in the book. How do you feel about her as the novel progresses?

9. We all went to high school with a Jimmy Lee Hickam. What became of the star athletes from your high school? Why do so many former high school stars fail to grow beyond their glory days?

10. How do you envision Edgel's life after the novel ends? What does his future hold?